Just
ANOTHER DAY

BOOK 1

VIVIANA SANTOS

authorHOUSE®

AuthorHouse™ UK
1663 Liberty Drive
Bloomington, IN 47403 USA
www.authorhouse.co.uk
Phone: UK TFN: 0800 0148641 (Toll Free inside the UK)
       UK Local: (02) 0369 56322 (+44 20 3695 6322 from outside the UK)

Published by AuthorHouse   04/07/2022

ISBN: 978-1-6655-9743-2 (sc)
ISBN: 978-1-6655-9742-5 (hc)
ISBN: 978-1-6655-9741-8 (e)

Prologue

Just another day – another ordinary, robotic day. I feel like that's my thought most mornings lately. Get up, have my coffee, do some work around the house, get dressed, brush my teeth, cover my face with beauty, feed the cat, slide into my shoes, and go to work. That's my life.

After everything I've been through, all the pain, the crying, and disappointment, all I can think of is, *Why do I bother getting up, going to work, paying my dues? Why do I complain?* So many selfish thoughts I have when a child is dying somewhere in the world, and I keep thinking, *Why do I bother?*

Chapter 1

It has been two years the floor was pulled out from under my feet again. Is there something wrong with me? Does a guy only want to stay with me for a few years before he decides to cheat on me? What is it about me that makes them do that? Is it even me? It has to be – I mean, how could the same thing happen with two different guys, right? Although our life was quite lonely and sometimes boring, I'd thought we were happy – I actually thought this time I'd found my other half. I went back to being myself with him after the other idiot.

Do I just not recognize assholes anymore?

Now I share a flat with my best friend, Nat. Can't believe I have a friend. I know it seems sad, but it's true – these days, it's so hard to trust anyone enough to call them friend. Nat has been really good to me, taking me in. I really thought for a moment I was going to be sleeping on the street, but now I wonder what I'll do after she gets married. Don't get me wrong. I'm very happy for her. And she's happy, but it's another issue I have to solve.

We're having a bachelorette party in a few weeks. I'm so excited. Maybe it will do me some good to get out a bit. Can't keep going thinking of all that's wrong with the world. I mean, what am I going to do? I'm just me: nobody.

She knows I hate going shopping, especially for dresses. 'Why can't I go with my skinny jeans? I like them. Some guys like them. What's the problem?'

'I've told you I want all of us to look great, and it's my party, after all, so you do as I say.' You have to love Nat even when she tries to tell you off. You know it comes from a good place, but I still have issues with my body, even though I've lost a lot of weight since Adrien and I broke up. It's hard to keep it in check, but I've been a good girl.

'Honestly, V, I don't see why you're like that. You have a great body. You're beautiful, babe – own it!' Charlotte is one of Nat's oldest friends and also her maid of honour. I content myself being a bridesmaid – not really my thing being in the spotlight. Charlotte is very tall, which makes me feel even more like a dwarf. In contrast to Nat, her hair is so blond it's almost white. Her skin is very pale, but her beautiful blue eyes make her look like a model. Very intimidating, my group of friends, especially when you add Chloe to the mix.

'Hey, where are you?' I spit from my daydream face at Nat's voice.

'I'm right here, trying on the hundredth dress.'

'Sure, the fourth dress might make you say that. What were you thinking so hard about?' Nat has on her usual concerned look.

'Nothing special,' I say with a nonchalant shrug.

'I know you guys are still planning my hen party, and I already told you as long as it involves looking at naked guys I don't really care.'

I exchange a look with Charlotte. She grins at me, a very wide grin, to which I whisper, 'You haven't won yet.' She replies with a wink that says *yet*.

We've been in this stuffy boutique dress shop for what feels like hours, Charlotte helping by handing me dress after dress. In and out of dressing room I go.

'What are you guys on about?'

'Nothing you need to know,' I say.

'Yet.' I glare at Charlotte as she says this and feel that she will take the best of me, especially after Chloe hears her proposal for the hen party. I guess we'll see tomorrow.

It's nice to have some time off work. Although I can't afford to go anywhere for my holiday, it's nice to break the routine and feel my mortality a little less.

None of that tonight. Only party faces on. Next week is the hen party, and Nat was still insisting that we go out this weekend.

'I won't have much opportunity to do it once I'm married. Might as

2

well enjoy now.' A very serious look crosses her face, and I know there's no point in arguing anymore. At least tonight, I get to choose my own clothes.

'Is Chloe meeting us there?' I can hear the impatience in Charlotte's voice and see it in the way she doesn't look up from the couch to Nat for her answer.

'We're waiting for her.' That's all Nat says. We both know exactly how Charlotte feels about Chloe.

At least, two of us are patiently waiting in Nat's flat. Charlotte keeps tapping her foot while she sips on a premature drink that Nat been making for us. I feel giddy already and am actually excited to go out. It has been a while. My life is pretty much work and house, and even though Nat has tried to get me out of the house many times, I just can't find it in myself to go.

'What if I meet a guy?'

'Why would that be a bad thing?' She raises both her brows, though I can see the understanding in her eyes.

'Well, I'll spend my next five or ten years with him, and then the same shit happens again – that's what's bad about it.' I almost raise my voice. I know she understands, but I still get defensive when I'm told it's been long enough. Most nights, she doesn't try do get me out of the flat, or I flee to my room, but it makes me think sometimes: even though I'm not looking for a guy – far from it – I still wonder if I'll be alone the rest of my life, destined for disappointment.

As I predicted, Chloe goes crazy with Charlotte's proposal for the hen party – of course, she would. The idea is as crazy as she is.

'How can you not see how great of an idea it is?' She really is surprised, but I can't get it truthfully.

'You're saying that instead of planning a proper party for your friend, like she asked, you would rather spend time with some celebrity?' She still can't believe what I'm saying.

'What's wrong with that? It's a celebrity, come on. You might even find your crush there.'

Ignoring her comment, I carry on. 'OK, do you think he'll get naked?' My bluntness takes both of them by surprise.

'I don't think it will be that kind of a meet and greet!' Charlotte is laughing so hard she hardly finishes talking. I'm relieved as they forget Chloe's comment.

'Look, all I'm saying is that what Nat asked was to be in London and see some naked dancing guys. Do you think she'll be happy with just this?' I'm hoping this will convince them, but Chloe opens her mouth in disbelief.

A smirk plastered on her face, Charlotte says, 'I might have a solution for that.'

'Of course, you do,' I mutter.

She pretends she can't hear me. 'We will apply – I mean, we don't even know if we will win. It's such a long shot. We plan our normal naked-guys-filled night, and then we see.'

How can I argue with that? I mean, I know it's a long shot, but with my luck, I just know we'll win. I didn't even know celebrities did that – post on Instagram a night out with them and a group of friends. I get that a tenner isn't that much and they will donate to charity – that's the point of their party – but I still think it's weird.

'I think you're the only girl in the world that wouldn't apply to. How do you not care?' Charlotte says.

I shrug. 'It's just a guy.'

'A very hot guy.' I can see the smirk in Chloe's eyes.

Finally, I say, 'Fine, but you can't get drunk. You're crazy enough when you're sober.'

'Now where's the fun in that?'

'Promise.'

'You know me – you know I can't promise that, but I can try.' She does seem sincere, but I know it'll be a disaster.

'Yes!' Charlotte is over the moon but has no time to celebrate because Nat walks in from the loo.

'What have I missed?'

'Well' – filled with glee, Charlotte stands – 'I'm pleased to inform Your Highness that your party is settled.'

'How long was I in there?' Nat asks, looking in disbelief at all of us and gesturing for Charlotte to sit. 'You guys were trying to decide for weeks, and you make a plan in under ten minutes?'

'Well, let's just say that there were only some details to polish,' Chloe says, looking at me.

Nat leans in, saying, 'You caved, haven't you?'

I smile. 'Hard, but I made some demands.' I try not to lose face, but she knows me way too well, and she tilts her head and chuckles.

I take advantage of the fact that it's ladies night to get a few extra drinks in me. Maybe it will be good for my mind to just let go and have fun.

We form a circle, each of us with a drink in our hands, dancing and laughing. It feels good. Even Chloe isn't in the mood for guys tonight. When one of them tries to squeeze himself between us, it's like a routine: she turns first, and then we follow, leaving the guy alone going bonkers.

Finally, we settle on what we're wearing. I did tell her that buying two dresses was too much. But she said we needed options. In the end, I gave in and let Nat choose my dress without a care. Kind of woke up feeling like that, I guess. When she showed it to me, my immediate thought was *I can't possibly fit in that*, but it really was a beautiful dress and so sexy that it made me want to try it on.

When the two of them gasped looking at me when I left the changing rooms, all I said was, 'I know. I can't believe it fits.' I hadn't looked in the mirror, always thought I didn't look good in a dress. Even slutty hot Charlotte was looking at me like she was going to eat me.

'Why are you looking at me like that? I don't play for that team you know?' My whole face was turning magenta.

'Babe, the way you look right now, even I don't care if you're a girl.' She was smiling and still sweeping her eyes all over me.

'What are you—?' As I was talking, I turned to the mirror. I couldn't believe my eyes. I looked hot. But how? The dress hugged me in all the right places, but it wasn't too tight. It was a beautiful shade of purple, or violet, as I said, to go with my name.

Nat smiled.

'I can't wait for this weekend.'

Chapter 2

I know we're in over our heads, but how can I argue with three hyper-excited girls on their way to see hot famous guys? I decided I will at least try to have some fun out of it. I'm so immersed on my thoughts in the train that I don't even hear Charlotte scream. Only when Chloe gets up and joins her, jumping up and down and giggling like two little girls do I wake up to reality.

'What's going on?'

'We won!' The highest pitch I have ever heard filled my ears, and just then, I know what she was talking about.

'What did we win? A private dance from a naked guy?' Nat smirks and winks, getting up to look at Charlotte's phone.

'No, no, no, no! It's a surprise. You can't see this.'

Nat pouted but sat back down.

'What do we have to do now?' Chloe also tries to have a look at the phone, and Charlotte starts to explain.

'Well, it's tomorrow evening. We go here, show them the email and our names, and I guess we're in.' Both shriek and jump again.

'You guess we're in? How far is it from the hotel?' I can't help being concerned. It just seems so weird that it might actually not be true.

'You're going to regret that tone when you're surrounded by all of them.' Charlotte throws me the most condescending tone together with a finger

'Whoa, whoa, whoa, them? As in more than him?'

'Well, yeah, you thought he was the only one doing … this kind of thing?' It's hard to try and speak without giving too much away to Nat, but Charlotte tries her best.

'Are you guys saying that there will be only one naked guy at my bachelorette party? How can you do this to me?'

'What? I didn't do anything. Talk to your crazy maid of honour.' Nat looks at Charlotte with a set of raised eyebrows.

'You're going to love it, babe. I promise!'

'Okay, I trust you'.

A lost cause, I see. Maybe it won't be so bad spending an evening surrounded by celebrities. Like Charlotte said, many girls would give anything for this opportunity.

I lean back again on my seat and look out the train window. I see the city life in the lights that fill the sky. Even though there is still a lot of daylight, you can still see it. It's not like we haven't ever seen the city before. Nat and I used to live in London four years ago before we moved to the Midlands it's a calmer, cheaper life. But sometimes I can't help but think about moving back, like I miss the bustle of the city. Every time we come back, I remember how beautiful this city is, so full of life that at times I just want to get lost in it.

For the first time ever, I'm staying in a suite. It ended up being cheaper for us and it is a special occasion. Charlotte has good taste. I can't deny that. The room overlooks the Thames, and it's high enough that we can see Tower Bridge and the peak of London Eye. It's dreamy.

'Guys, this is amazing. Really pretty, thank you so much.' Nat's eyes well up, and we hug her.

'Anything for you, hon,' I tell her.

'But the weekend is just beginning.' Charlotte tightens the hug and smiles while she talks. 'There's a lot more to do and see.'

To my despair, she had arranged a few visits for the rest of the afternoon, which would be fine if it didn't include the London Eye tomorrow. I would rather go to London Dungeon, but the girls aren't too keen on getting scared this weekend. I just don't like to feel trapped, and being inside that cart for so long and so many feet above the ground does something to my claustrophobia. They keep teasing me for the heights, but it's not that. It's the fact that I know I can't get out of it. We visit museums and the Tate Modern before we go back to the hotel.

The next day, we stop by a pub on our way to the deadly ride to grab lunch and a few drinks. I love British pubs, maybe not the smell of same of them but the feel, the light and chandeliers, the food. Mm, I love the burgers. I really shouldn't, but it's not like I eat like this anymore, and it's a special occasion so that's what I'm ordering.

'I cannot believe my eyes. Violet Smith isn't ordering a salad.' Charlotte mocks me, and they all laugh. Worst to me is that we're so close to the bar that when I'm rolling my eyes at her, I see a guy sitting there, and he can clearly hear our conversation because he almost spits his drink to the bartender as he laughs as well. I'm so flushed that all I can say is 'Shut up.' While I glare at the guy. He seems familiar, but looking at his profile, I can't really place him.

Man, I had forgotten this taste, so much so that I let a moan escape my mouth as I eat it.

'It doesn't look like V will need any guys for this party. Just get her a room with that burger.' Charlotte still mocks me, but this time I don't let it slide.

'Babe, me and this burger anytime over any guy and I'm set.'

The guy laughs again, which makes me glace over at him once more. He's tall and lean, with broad shoulders, slightly curly hair, almost blond but not quite. A bit of a scruff covers his face just enough to make the half of him that I can see sexy. Still can't shake the feeling that I know him.

Chloe catches my eye and, smirking, says, 'See something you like?' I follow her gaze to the mysterious guy.

'Yes, I do, my favourite guy.'

The guy stiffens, and they all look at him, but before they have a chance to say anything, I continue. 'Jack Daniels, my best friend. I'm having a shot who's in?' They smile. The guy chuckles.

'Okay, I think that even for me it's too early for shots. What's up with you?' Chloe looks serious, like she's worried, all of them looking at me expecting some kind of profound explanation or even maybe a confession, trying my best to conceal my real feelings I press on.

'I think I just need liquid courage before London Eye.' They nod without mocking me, which surprises me. We each take a shot and pay the bill. Only then, I notice the guy is gone. Something delicious for my dreams later.

I feel butterflies ruffling my belly while we're in the queue for the ride. I feel like I need a distraction, something to keep my mind of the prison I'm about to put myself into. I look around and see an ice cream stand that will keep me busy for a while.

'You guys want some ice cream?'

'I don't think you can take it in there.' As Chloe says this, I turn my head around so fast that I almost get whiplash.

'Are you serious?'

She shrugs. I step out of the line and ask one of the security guards and come back to the girls.

'No problem, he says. So you guys want anything?'

Smiles spread and I take orders. It gets tricky to carry all four ice creams through the crowd. I almost trip, but I feel a hand steady me. Before I look up I make sure the ice creams are safe and balanced. By the time I straighten, he's releasing me and turning away, but I couldn't forget that profile. It's the guy from the bar, and I still can't see his face.

'Hey, you following me?' I shout, but he just keeps walking. It's an unnerving feeling, but I shake it off and take the ice creams to the girls before they melt.

'Okay, vanilla for the bride, strawberry for saucy Chloe, caramel for sweet Charlotte, and mint for me.' I have a smile from ear to ear as I distribute the deserts.

'No coffee available?' Chloe mocks me.

'I'm sorry. Did you just call me sweet?' Charlotte asks as her ice cream is halfway to her mouth.

'I have to butter you up in hopes you won't make me stay too long tomorrow.' I wiggle my eyebrows but not quite looking at her.

'You keep telling yourself that, babe.' She winks and I sulk. Worth the try at least. We're next in the cart. It's quite big, I know, but I can't help feeling helplessly trapped.

I've been here once before and was so teased that I really didn't look around, just waited for the time to pass so the doors would release me. I tried to focus on my ice cream, but Nat sat next to me.

'You're missing a great view, you know?' Nat looks at me with kind and expectant eyes.

'I know, honey, but I'm good here. Why don't you go and enjoy it? This is for you.' She smiles very softly.

'I have more opportunities to come here, but with you? Not sure. I know it's not the heights you're afraid of, so why don't you try and relax and enjoy?'

I can't help but think I'm being childish and selfish. She is right. Heights do not scare me, so with a newfound resolve I get up and lean on the rail by the window. She walks up next to me.

You can see everything from up here, from beyond Tower Bridge and way past Big Ben. There is no denying how beautiful it is when you see it, and just like that, the thirty minutes are up, and I don't rush to the doors as they open.

We decide to do a little gambling across the way. I turn to them.

'Guys, I know I'm a pain sometimes, and facing fears isn't really my thing, but that was awesome. So thank you.' They feel the sincerity in my voice, and they all smile, and to my surprise, Chloe is the one that speaks.

'You don't have to explain or thank us. I know what is like to be scared and powerless to fight it. Darkness isn't really my friend, but I don't let it lead my life.'

I'm taken aback by her words and sincerity as all other faces seem to be as I look around. Still no one says anything. We smile and keep walking.

It has been a while since I felt my heart so full, but my mind is independent and keeps thinking of all that is wrong with the world. Somehow Chloe's voice comes back to me. Even though she is scared, she doesn't let her fears lead her. I think I should be more like her.

After I found myself again with Adrien, I thought that was it. My life was complete. We were trying to get pregnant. Everything was on track for a perfect normal life, and I guess the ending part of it was as well. Sometimes I'm thankful that we didn't have kids. It would be so much harder that way. I'm not even sure I want kids, but it just seems normal. That's what's expected after so long together, and when you're a certain age that just seems natural. But I was always afraid that I would mess up, that I would ruin them and their lives. It's such an incredible responsibility that I constantly feel overwhelmed thinking about it.

We play for a couple of hours. I'm having a lot of fun but was never keen on wasting money, and the girls want to go and get ready for tonight anyway. Apparently, it takes hours to get ready, they say.

Back at the hotel, after we almost used up all the water in the hotel, we start getting dressed. I was never good at putting make-up on. I just apply the bare minimum and go my way. This time Chloe decides to take over everyone's look. I don't really mind. She's really good at it. Being a beautician helps.

'Please not too much, please,' I pled. Don't like to be too pasty like I've rolled over my pillow and put yesterday's face on.

'Will you just stay still and trust me? Look at Charlotte. Doesn't she look good?' She does look good, not so pale anymore, but she is undeniably beautiful, I try to relax and enjoy and let a breath out.

'Okay, go on.'

She smirks and does her work in silence, me, Nat, and then herself. I can't deny she did a great job, even though with make-up on, I look very natural and yet very pretty.

I know I was against this idea, but I can't help to be nervous and excited.

'Guys, this looks too much of a nice place to have naked guys. And it looks like it's a hotel. What's happening?' Nat's look is both concerned and confused. Charlotte clears her throat.

'I've told you that you'll love it, and you will.'

'Hum.' She still doesn't seem convinced.

It actually is a hotel, a very nice one. We don't ask Charlotte again and just follow her to the reception. The hotel is actually very beautiful, with beautiful chandeliers clinging to high ceilings, marble floors, and massive heavy wooden doors. It's very beautiful and warm and also very traditional. It doesn't look like we could have afforded a suite here.

There are a lot of people by the front desk, and I can't help but notice that most of them are girls. Wonder why.

I spot groups of them being directed somewhere downstairs, giggling and jumping with silliness and excitement. Usually in hotels you go upwards. Guess they must have a special place.

Our turn is up. Charlotte gives all the information that's requested from her. We're given a few passes and wristbands. Such a silly thing, but I actually notice that they're violet, and that little detail makes me smile.

As we're stepping down the stairs, I can already hear it, and Charlotte looks at me. 'Calm down. Just breathe. You'll be okay.' I seriously doubt that. I hate big commotions and screaming groups of girls, and I hadn't thought about it happening until now.

It looks like a ballroom. Although it's underground, it's tastefully lit and decorated. There are bar tables all over the place, a very long bar protected by a wall of various drinks on the left and a dance floor on the right. There are so many people I can't help but think they should have put some kind of limit.

'This is too much, Char. We won't even get five minutes with him.' I'm getting so flustered that even my neck is turning red.

'Babe, it's just people, and we know exactly where the exit is. We can leave anytime we want.' I can see Nat's expression. She doesn't want to leave, so I tell her I just need to go to the loo and freshen up my face. Even though she offers, I refuse company.

'Just keep your phone on you, please.'

'Will do, babe.' Before I walk I take a look around. Only at the opposite end of the long room, I see doors; everything else is wall. There's no way I can cut through the middle. I would never make it to the other side, so I decide to go around. There are no people dancing right now. Everyone has just arrived.

I turn right and get a quick move on. Still, I keep being shoved and pushed, makes me really want to push someone back. Why can't people just be civil? Thankfully, there's some kind of commotion close to the bar, and the crowd moves that way. I stop and take a deep breath. Only then I notice that the room walls are covered in beautiful landscape paintings, and in the middle of all that beauty at the very end of the room sits a table with several photos. I can't help but feel drawn to it. It isn't pictures of historical buildings or beautiful landscapes – it's people. As I approach, I feel the pit in my stomach tighten even more. It's like my nightmares are coming to life.

At the top of the photos, I read, '*Why We Do It.*' There are men, women, and children, all of them in dire need of help. From everywhere, Sudan, Yemen, Kenya, Zambia, Nigeria, everywhere, and I feel so overwhelmed that I start crying and run to the bathroom.

I pinch myself, but I'm not dreaming. This is real. How do I get myself in a situation I've been thinking so much about? Can't help but think what I can do. *What can I do? I'm only me, no one. What can I do for them?* I cry. A few seconds pass, and someone clears their throat. I didn't even hear the door opening.

'You can try.' Only then, I realize I wasn't thinking to myself. I was talking, and that wasn't the only surprise. The fact that voice belonged to a man was another.

'Am I in the man's room?'

I hear him chuckle. 'No.'

'So you're in the ladies'? Lost?'

'Not really.' I still don't say anything. I'm embarrassed enough already. 'I saw you over at the charities table. I couldn't help but stare. I'm sorry. Are you okay?'

'I'm fine, thank you.' I try to convey a dismissive tone, hoping he'll leave.

'I know how you feel. I've been there. It's very overwhelming, and if you let it, it will crush your soul.' He speaks slowly. His voice is low, soft, so kind it made my heart ache even more, so I cried.

I cried because of all that happened to me. I cried because I was being selfish, crying because I didn't think I could do anything to help when a child was probably starving right now.

There was a long moment of silence after I stopped crying. I cleared my throat and said, 'I'm sorry, and thank you for your honesty, really.' I had no intention of leaving my cubicle. I was too embarrassed but was surprised when his return was.

'Anytime.' And he left. I was stunned. Don't think I've ever witnessed such kindness.

Nat's name flashes on my screen. 'Where are you?'

14

'Just finished in the loo. Will be right out. And you guys?'

'Oh man. This is amazing. There're so many celebrities I'm dazed. You know we have already met Charlie? He is so nice and hot.' She stretches and shrieks the last word, and I try to wedge a word in, but she is on a ranting mission. 'And there are actresses and some singers. It's amazing. And, oh, it's Sean Penn! OMG!' So much screaming I had to get the phone away from my ear.

'Honey, calm down. I'll be right out.'

'Ah.' And with that I hang up, couldn't take it anymore, and now I have to go outside, after my meltdown with no idea who the guy that spoke to me was. How embarrassing.

After stepping out of the cubicle, I gaze at myself in the mirror, still look good. Chloe did a great job. I wash my hands, dab my face, take a very deep breath, and go outside.

The lights look dimmer now, and people are more spread through the room. I look around but can't spot anyone looking at me, but I do spot the girls by a table. They seem oblivious to my absence, can't really blame them, though. It actually looks like a lot of fun. Still I can't help but look back at the charity table. My feet move.

All those faces looking back at me, I try to remember the stranger's words, can't help but feel miniscule. I turn my back to the table. 'Breathe, breathe.' I turn again, grab a pamphlet, and walk away to the girls.

'Well, took you long enough.' Chloe is so giggly and flustered I can't help but think she might be a bit tipsy already.

'Sorry, guys, I really had to go. What I miss?'

'Well, you missed me.'

I don't giggle but stutter a little and seeing him so wide eyed with a smile from ear to ear, I'm sure he is also quite tipsy too.

'Mr Charlie Hunnam, it's a pleasure to meet you. Thank you for having us.'

'What?'

I get confused with that retort, have I offended him somehow? 'Sorry?'

'Come on. We're friends now. Call me Charlie.' Yeah, he's a goner. Still can't help but smile.

'Yes. Charlie.'

He laughs and moves to another table.

15

'Wow. This is amazing, guys. Thank you, thank you.' Nat starts crying we all hug her.

'So you don't need any naked guys then?'

How hard she laughs, it's so contagious that we all burst into laughter. We can't stop. We can't drink. Just grab our bellies, and I swear I thought I was going to pass out at one point. We calm, we laugh, we cry, and we giggle on our way to the bar.

'So what's the leaflet for?' Charlotte is still trying to keep her balance from laughing and looking sideways to me.

'Well, you know, it's about the charity.'

'Oh, so what? You're going to donate all your pennies?' She laughs and scoffs.

'If I had any, I would,' I replied and glared at her. I really had no reason to be this mad at her, but I couldn't help it. I turned my back at them and made my way to the charity table again. I was almost at the table when I felt a hand on my shoulder.

I turned and was going to totally lose it and fan girl. 'Wow. Scarlett Johansson. I can't believe it, I'm such a fan of yours.' I was going to hug her but thankfully stopped myself on the way. She smiled and hugged me. I could not believe it.

'Oh, um, that's nice of you,' the actress responds.

Releasing her to not make it awkward, I say, 'It's nice to meet you. I'm Violet.'

'Nice to meet you too. Were you getting to know our work with the charity?' She was looking at the pamphlet on my hand and glancing at the charity display.

'Hum, yes, I was trying to learn little more.' For some reason, I blushed. I couldn't stop it creeping up my face, and I look away, embarrassed. It's not like she was the one who'd seen my previous freak out, but I couldn't help it.

'What's wrong? You don't think it's a good idea?' She looked so serious that I responded very quickly, stuttering.

'N-n-no, th-that's … no, of course, it's … it's a good idea, obviously.'

'Yeah, you need to tell your face that. It doesn't look happy. More like, um, disappointed.'

'I guess I am disappointed.' I actually thought she was going to punch me at some point.

'Um, okay, why?'

I can't help but chuckle at the sight of her face. 'I'm disappointed that I can't do much about it, that I can't make a difference or even a ripple in the water for that matter.'

I feel bare. She can see my internal struggle and guides me to a bunch of sofas that sit before the dance floor. I hadn't noticed them on my way to the loo. We sit and stay in silence for a while. After my confession, I'm too embarrassed to look at her, so I glance at the girls. They're still having loads of fun, and I smile. When Nat meets my eyes, I widen my smile and wink at her. She winks back and wiggles her eyebrows while looking at Charlotte next to me.

'Friends of yours?' Scarlett pulls my attention back.

'Yes, they are, my best friends, actually.' I name all of them from our seats and give her a little on their personalities. I tell her about our party plans and the fact that I didn't want to come here. Why did I do that?

For some reason, she makes me so comfortable that I just talk. That reminds me of Nat's phone call when I was in the loo, and I shut up. She gives me an inquisitive look, and I say, 'Sorry, I didn't mean to blab, you just have some skills into making people talk.'

I laugh, hoping I hadn't made the situation worse, but she joins me in my laughter, slapping her hand on the arm of the couch.

'Please stop or you'll make me pee myself.' This time, I laugh harder. It's not that funny, none of it was, and yet we can't stop laughing. The girls join.

'What's so funny?' Chloe is smiling but just a little, wanting to understand what's going on.

'She is.' Scarlett points at me, not laughing but smiling.

Chloe only nods, but Nat and Charlotte speak at the same time. 'Yes, she is.'

'I'm not that funny. We're just bubbly, I guess.'

At that point, I realize I haven't had a drink yet, and Charlotte points it out. 'And how many bubbles have you had, huh?'

I stick my tongue out.

'Well, maybe I should get us some drinks no?' Scarlett is being very nice, maybe too nice.

'Scarlett, you don't have to do that.'

'Oh, I'm happy to. I need another drink anyway. You want to come and help me? You guys can guard these couches or we'll have to sit on the floor.' They all smile and nod.

Chloe nods rapidly and says, 'Of course,' way too loud, but I can't help but feel Scarlett just ditched my friends.

We take orders and move to the bar. I can't help but look at her sideways, and apparently, I have a suspicious look on my face because she catches it.

'Yes, Violet?'

'Huh? What? I didn't say anything.'

Chuckling, she says, 'No, but your face did. Your eyes agreed. You're so transparent.'

'Am I that obvious?'

'Yup.'

'I'm sorry. I'm not very good at lying, and I didn't mean to be rude.'

'You weren't rude. You're concerned. I understand that.'

I cock an eyebrow, she smiles, and I say very slowly, 'And what should I be concerned about?'

This time she really laughs, like really. Only I don't join. I just wait for her hysteria to stop.

'See? I said you were funny. You can relax now.'

I still don't. My shoulders go stiff. I don't know what's going on. She puts a hand on my shoulder, and I follow it with my eyes.

'Relax please. I mean well.'

'What *do* you mean?' I still don't get it

'I was asked to calm you down and get to know you. Sorry, I didn't want to ditch your friends. I just wanted to get you alone at the bar.' Yeah, that was definitely weird. I take a step back.

'Okay, what's happening? Who asked you that?' My eyes are wide, and I take another step back.

'Please, I really enjoyed talking to you and getting to know you. I mean it, you know?'

'What?'

18

'You're funny and easy to talk to, looks like you got some skills too.' She winks, and I give her a faint smile.

'What do you mean someone asked you to get to know me?' I can't just forget that piece of information. I mean how does she even know me? Or does she at all? She doesn't get to answer. The bartender comes to take our drink orders. She holds my arm as if to say, *I got this*, and puts in the request for all the drinks except mine. Guess she won't be waitressing anytime soon. I smile and raise my other hand. She grabs that one too.

'Okay, what are you doing? I really need to get a drink in me.' I sound a bit too desperate, but right now, I don't really care. The situation is already weird enough. Then I notice she isn't looking at me. Instead, she gazes at the space behind me.

Before I turn, she releases the hand I raised and someone slides a drink in it, saying, 'Jack Daniels for the lady.'

I can hear the smugness in his voice, and I also recognize it as the man from the bathroom. I'm glued to the floor. My feet don't move. I just stare at Scarlett. The bartender comes back with four drinks, and I see her balancing them on both hands, so I move to help her. She shakes her head, winks at me, and goes back to return the drinks to the girls. I follow her with my eyes, my mouth half open, still holding a drink in my hand, but I don't turn around.

'Okay, I know that was a very vulnerable moment, and I swear I didn't mean to pry. I just couldn't help it. It looked like you needed some comfort.'

I'm still looking forward, and I shiver. He's so close to me I can feel his breath down my neck. I don't know what it is, but all I want to do is step back and hope he embraces me.

'Are you ever going to look at me?' His voice is soft, sweet like caramel, melting against my skin. I shiver again but nod and turn around.

He's tall, lean, but fit, towers over me. He got cute curls and almost blond hair, and just then, it's like a switch flicks inside me.

'You're the guy from the bar.' I don't raise my voice but do point my finger at him. He raises both hands and gives me the most heart-melting smile possible.

'Guilty, but I promise I had no idea you would be here.'

'It was you at the London Eye as well.' I say this with a cocked eyebrow.

I know it was him, and by the embarrassed look on his face, I see that time he did follow me. 'Why did you follow me?' I don't know why, but I fold both arms across my chest as if I'm telling off a child. He chuckles and sits on the barstool, probably tired of looking down at me.

'I heard you guys talking about it and … I don't know. Got curious? You should be glad I did.'

'Oh?' I try to be sarcastic, but it comes out a little too flirty, still smiling he continues.

'Well, if I hadn't, your face would have been covered in ice cream.'

'Maybe then, you would have truly saved me.' He looks so confused that I throw my head back as I laugh. 'I would have had to go back to the hotel to change and skipped London Eye altogether, win-win.'

Raising a hand, he tells me, 'No offence, but from what I've heard at the pub, I don't think your friends would have let you do that.'

I don't say anything, I smile and still wonder why Tom Hiddleston is talking to me.

He has the kindest eyes I've seen. Ask me his eye colour, I will tell you kind. I realize I'm staring and look back at the girls. Not seeing any of them, I get up on the barstool to try and find them through all the heads, and I spot from the corner of my eye that he's looking up at me.

'What are you doing?'

'Trying to find my friends.' I'm looking from one side to the other of the stuffed room

'Bored with me already I see.' His tone is both flirty and very sarcastic, I look down so fast that I lose my balance and fall forward. 'Seriously? You need to be more careful or hire me as your personal guard at least.' His strong arms hold me above my chest just under my arms. If I make a false move, I might give him more than just the pride of being my saviour. Actually, I don't really know what to do. My knees are still on the stool. He moves to face me and lifts me up. I guess he's stronger than he looks.

Neither of us says a word. We just stand there, my hands on his, face to face. Again I get myself into embarrassing situations. Why am I so clumsy?

Someone screams his name next to me, and that finally breaks our eye connection. Being polite, he releases my hands and turns to the group of shrieking girls for introductions. I take the opportunity to get away from him and go back to the girls. I spotted them while I was getting down from the stool, they're all dancing, including Scarlett. I guess it's time I had some fun as well, enough with depression.

I'm almost there. They all see me, and we all smile. The dance floor is sticky from spilled drinks, and I think, *Violet, don't be clumsy. You cannot fall here.* Scarlett is gesturing to me, but it's not a join-us gesture, more like a turn around one. Just then, I feel a hand pulling my arm, turning me around.

'Not even a goodbye, huh?' He doesn't drop my arm. Instead he puts his other hand on my waist and pulls me to him.

'What are you doing?' I don't think I've ever been so calm before. If it was any other guy doing the same at some pub, I would have slapped him already or maybe kicked him. Yeah, I'm more of a kicker.

'I'm dancing, obviously.' He has such a gallant tone on his voice that all I can do is smile, shake my head, and look up at him. He calls for my hand, waving his to me. My heart stomps, and I hope he doesn't notice. I place my hand on his and the other on his shoulder, or almost his shoulder. He's really tall compared to me. He gives me a cocked smile, pulls me closer, and starts swaying. We float around the room for a few minutes, and I find myself giggling.

'You should know this isn't safe.'

'What do you mean?' He doesn't stop moving. I give him a flat smile.

'I'm not a dancer, and clumsy as I am, I'll probably end up on top of your feet.'

This time he stops, looks down at our feet, and says, 'Maybe we should get that out of the way then.'

What does he mean? Should we dance on our knees? What? While I have this discussion in my head, he grabs me by the waist and balances me so I end up with my feet on top of his. I almost fall back, but he grabs my arms and puts them tight around his neck while he wraps his around my waist very, very tightly. I'm sure my face is all red, but I can't stop laughing. He tilts his head sideways.

'See? No more danger.' He's so close, smells so good. I have to focus.

'No, only the danger of you not being able to walk tomorrow.' He doesn't laugh. I have to tell Scarlett that apparently I'm not that funny. Instead he looks down at me, the most intense gaze I've ever seen, and shrugs.

'I'm not going anywhere tomorrow.' It's hypnotizing that look, drawing.

'Why did you follow me?' I had to ask. I've been wanting to ask again for a while now, and the first time I asked, his answer wasn't very serious.

'I don't think I've ever met anyone like you. I felt drawn, curious.'

'You haven't met me. You don't know me.' My voice comes out very assertive, and I can't help but shake my head. I can tell he's surprised when he stops moving. I hop off his feet. He grabs my hand and pulls me somewhere towards an enormous wooden door. I don't stop him.

Why don't I stop him? Why do I let this man that I don't know take me under his spell so easily?

You would think all the famous people here would be dressed in the best couture and nice suits. Tom is in dark jeans and a long-sleeved, light-blue sweatshirt that makes his eyes an oceanic kind of blue. Man, he's bloody hot. Don't get drawn.

After the door, we climb some stairs. At some point, I wish he had taken the elevator. We take a right turn, go through a corridor, and come up to more doors. These are stained glass and are guarded by a man. Hotel security, I guess, but that doesn't seem important because all Tom does is nod to the guard, and he opens the door. At first, I thought it was Tom's room, and I was relieved to find out it wasn't. That would have been awkward.

It's a little room with a bar. A nice girl waves at us as we enter. On the opposite way, a double door stretches open, giving me the most amazing view from a balcony to the Thames. I'm still panting from climbing so many stairs that as I gasp at the sight of the Big Ben, I choke a bit, trying to swallow. He pats my back but still doesn't say anything. I smile at him and move to the balcony, but he doesn't follow.

My gaze is on that view, and I inhale sharply. The smell of algae from the river fills my lungs, and I close my eyes. I tilt my head to the sky, and for a moment, I forget my issues, worries, dreams, dramas. A touch of his hand brings me back to reality, and I open my eyes.

He stands there looking at me, a drink in each hand and a pant-dropping smile. *Man, he's gorgeous. I have to be careful.*

I lift an eyebrow, looking at the drinks and back at him. 'Are you trying to get me drunk?' My smile betrays my intention of being serious and his brightens.

'Maybe.' And he winks at me. 'I don't know what else you like, so I got you the same.' He hands me the drinks and turns at the view, leaning on the edge of the balcony.

'Tom?' I lean next to him. He exhales for what it seems like an eternity. I don't push, just wait. We both contemplate the view for a long time. Finally, he breaks the silence.

'Why did you cry so much in the bathroom?'

I wasn't expecting that. I honestly hoped he wouldn't mention it. I turn to the view again, clearly embarrassed.

He slides his hand down the side of my jaw to my chin and gently turns my head to him. 'I'm just trying to get to know you.' He doesn't smile. He doesn't change his expression. He just looks at me, waiting for an answer with his hand still on my chin.

I inhale and exhale, very slowly.

'What exactly did you hear in the bathroom?' I was hoping he would say nothing, but I know that isn't true. He releases my chin and slides both hands in his pockets.

'You don't have to be so embarrassed. It's normal you feel that way, so powerless.'

'Normal? Really?' I can't help but scoff.

'Of course, you care. That's why it's so hard for you. You feel like you can't do much, but you can, you know? Like I said, you can try.' His eyes are very soft, and he caresses my cheek as he talks.

'What can I do, Tom?' My eyes water. 'I'm no one. I have no money. How am I going to help?' I cover my face with both my hands, and he hugs me.

We stand there in the brisk breeze for a while, me sobbing against his comforting chest and him holding me tight. He kisses the top of my head when I stop crying, and I step back, looking at the puddle I've made of his shirt.

'Sorry.' He doesn't let me go even though I try. 'Your shirt.' As he looks down at his shirt, loosening his grip and me, I take a full step back. He shakes his head.

'You know this is just water, right?' I can't help smiling at him. 'You're okay?'

I turn to the water. I'm far from okay.

'Yeah.' After a moment of silence, I say, 'It's very pretty here.'

'Yes, it is.' His retort is so quick that when I look at him, I see that his gaze is on me not the view. He closes the distance between us, and at that moment my phone rings. A breath escapes my lungs.

'Hey, Nat.' I answer the phone, looking at Tom.

'Where are you? We've looked everywhere. Are you okay?'

'Nat, calm down. I'm fine.'

'Okay, so where are you?' This time she shouts, and Tom can clearly hear it. I have no reaction time. He takes the phone from my hand so fast I can't keep up with what's happening.

'Hello, Nat, this is Tom. I just wanted to let you know that Violet is fine and safe. You can trust me.'

I giggle a little. That was sweet, but I know Nat. She won't leave it at that.

'Well, Tom, I don't know you and have no reason to trust you, and Violet doesn't either, so if you please could return my friend to me, I would be very grateful. Or I can always get all of the security of the place looking for her.'

His face goes blank and serious, and I get so worried that I take the phone back. 'Nat, I'm fine, what did you tell him?'

'Why?'

'Well, he just went a bit pale, that's all.' I don't take my eyes off him. I'm actually concerned he might pass out or something.

'I just warned him if he doesn't return my friend, I'll basically call the National Guard on him.'

'Seriously? Did you have to do that?' He looks quickly at me.

'Do what? She didn't call the police, did she? I didn't kidnap her.' I put a hand on his chest, still wet from my tears. He takes a breather and calms down.

'It's okay. Don't worry.' I keep eye contact with him. At least, I'm glad I'm not the only one who freaks out, although I don't know what he freaked out about.

'Nat, I have to go. If I'm not with you by the time you guys are going back to the hotel, I'll meet you there.' All I hear is 'But—' before I hang up.

He goes inside and falls on the sofa that sits in the middle of the room and lets his head fall back. He looks drained. What the hell did Nat told him? I sit next to him, but not too close.

'Are you okay?'

He chuckles and nods.

'What did she tell you to scare you so much?'

'I looked scared?'

I laugh a little. 'I actually thought I was going to see a hole with your shape on that door.' He laughs hard, and I join him. Yeah, I'm funny.

'Your friend loves you and cares for you, you know?

'Yes, and I do for her as well.'

'She really did threaten me. I can't believe it. You know when I told her you were with me, and she could trust me?' I nod for him to carry on. 'Well, she said she doesn't. She doesn't know me, and neither do you. That got me thinking …'

It doesn't seem is quite finished, so I wait, looking at him. I can't take my eyes away. He looks so vulnerable.

He turns to me and lifts his hand to brush away a lock of hair that fell in front of my face. I keep my eyes on his. Such a strong gaze, how does he have such power over me? He tucks my hair behind my ear, and I can feel myself blush. I try to look down, anywhere his gaze isn't, but he grabs my chin and turns my head to him. I can't look away anymore. I so want to kiss him. My eyes keep glancing at his lips. Not full, thin, but they look so soft I wonder how they taste. I see he's quickly closing the distance between our lips. My phone vibrates in my pocket, and I jolt, moving away from him.

'Babe, I hope you're okay. We're still going to be here for a while. Apparently, we were one of the few selected groups to stay, but most people left. Scarlett says she misses you, and so do we. We should be together tonight, but I'm happy for you and hope you're having fun. Be safe. Char.'

A tear starts rolling down my cheek, and Tom wipes it away, reminding me how selfish I'm being, again.

'What's wrong?'

'I'm sorry I have to go.'

'What do you mean? Why? Is everything okay?'

'Yes, yes, everything is fine. Don't worry. I just realized I have to get

back to my party. It's supposed to be a special night, and I have to be there.'
I get up as I talk, and he grabs my arm.

'Tom, please, I have to go.'

He smiles, stands, grabs my hand and says. 'I know.'

Déjà vu runs through me. We walk out of the room, see the guard, take a left down a corridor, travel down some stairs, and come back to the ballroom. Already inside, he stops, still doesn't let my hand go, takes a quick scan of the room, and starts moving again. I see we're going towards the girls and try to let his hand go, but he just tightens his grip.

The girls are in a circle at the dance floor. They stop moving when they catch sight of us. Tom pulls me forward, plants each of his hands on my shoulders, and pushes me towards Nat, saying, 'Here, she's safe and sound. Please do not call the National Guard.'

'Hey, what am I, some package?' They all burst laughing.

Still with his hands on my shoulders, he leans so close to my ear that I feel his lips brushing it as he talks. 'A very precious package.'

I shiver as I feel the cold space left by his body and turn around. He's already halfway down the room, and I turn back to the girls. It's a flood, of arms, voices and smirking looks.

'Guys, I can't breathe.'

'What happened with you guys?' Chloe is so excited that she can't stop hoping from one foot to the other.

'Nothing happened. We just went to a balcony to watch the view and talk.'

'Right talk.' Charlotte wiggles her brows.

'Yes, talk, nothing else. Nat, can I talk to you?'

'Oh, so it's like that, huh?' This comes from Scarlett, clearly drunk. 'You only share with one friend now?'

'Who let her drink so much?' I can only imagine how much she has drank in such little time to be in that state already

'She's a force of nature. It's hard to tell her no.' Nat puts an arm around her, and I suspect she's trying to steady her, so I hold the other side of Scarlett and guide her to the sofas with us.

'How about some rest, darling?' I'm sounding so condescending

'No. You can't make me.' She shouts to the air, her eyes half closed.

'Of course not, darling. I just need your company.' Charlotte and Chloe stay on the dance floor. They know we need a moment.

I can feel Nat is upset. I just hope not too much. After we sit Scarlett down, she waits for me to talk. I oblige.

'I'm sorry I left. I don't know what came over me. I couldn't get out of his gaze. It was weird.' she looks me in the eyes for the first time since I walked back into the room.

'V, I'm happy you connected with someone, really. I know how hard it is for you to trust someone again.' I nod for her to continue. 'I just was expecting to be your first priority today, I guess.' She looks down, a little embarrassed.

'I know. I'm sorry.' There's not much more I can say.

'Just talk to me, please.'

'Babe, I said I was sorry. I really don't know what else to say.'

She opens her eyes wide. 'Ah, I don't care about that anymore. You're forgiven. Now tell me about him.'

I laugh, throwing my head back. Chloe and Charlotte join us.

'So, what's up with the hottie?' Chloes curiosity nudges my shoulder

'Yeah, he's yummy. What's up with you guys?' Charlotte misses no chance into being nosy as always

All eyes are on me, and I start getting nervous.

'Nothing happened I told you. We just talked.'

With a hiccup, Scarlett says, 'Tom, is a gentleman. He wouldn't take advantage of a girl. He's mesmerized by you. He called me yesterday after he saw you at the pub, so I told him to go after you.'

'Why? He didn't even know me, and honestly, neither did you.' I let it escape a little more honest and harsh than I intended, but it was true. How can someone get that strong of a connection without even knowing them? I couldn't understand that. Scarlett continues, and I get the feeling she isn't as drunk as I thought.

'I know Tom, have known him for about ten years now, and he's always so guarded. When he told me about you, I could feel the connection in his voice. Look, it's not something I can really explain, and – trust me – no one is trying to trick you or anything.'

I swallow hard, stunned by her words, not really knowing what to say.

Nat looks at me and says softly, 'I think you should give him a chance. Just forget the past and move forward.'

I didn't feel hopeful or a warm fuzzy feeling in my chest. I felt pissed. How could she say that after everything I had been through? She knew every little detail of my past and just like that told me to forget it? I turned my back and went to the bar. I don't see Tom again.

I had to get my head straight. He was just a guy, and if I gave a chance, it would just end up the same way, especially with him.

'What can I get you?'

'Vodka, please.' I didn't know what I wanted, and JD reminded me of him now.

'How do you want that?'

'Surprise me.' I keep my eyes on my hands, fumbling with the bracelet that I was given at the start of the party. Violet, the colour of my wristband is violet. After a few mysterious drinks, that's all I see, and I ask the bartender for another.

'Sorry, we're closing.' I part my eyes from the sight of my wrist to look at him for the first time.

'Have you run out of drinks?'

He chuckles and says no.

'So please get me another.'

My pitch shrieks a little, and my tone goes up a decibel. Not enough to turn head, but the barman says, 'Look, I think you had enough maybe you should you should go back to your friends and take a break, huh?'

I know in my gut that he's being caring, but I get up from the barstool glare at him and yell, 'I hate you.' God knows I wasn't talking to him.

All heads turn, and the girls come to me.

'You're okay, hon?' Nat rubs a hand softly on my back

I don't answer. My fury might give the wrong retort.

'I think we should take her back to the hotel.' Charlotte's tone is concerned

'And I thought I was going to be the one to get wasted.' Chloe keeps her eyes on me, surprised.

'Maybe you guys should stay here.' They all look back at Scarlett like she's crazy.

'She can't stay here, Scarlett. I won't let her drink more, and she

28

can't dance obviously.' Nat scoffs and starts to drag me with Chloe's and Charlotte's help.

'I don't mean here at the party. I mean this hotel.'

'Thank you, but we can't afford that, and we already paid for ours.'

Seeing a decision in her eyes and voice, Scarlett doesn't insist.

'Please, just let me help you at least with a driver. I won't need him as I'm staying here, and you don't have to cram in a cab.'

They exchange a look and nod. 'Thank you, Scarlett.' She grabs her phone and sends a text. Before long, I find myself stepping onto the street and feel a slap of cold wind against my face.

'Listen, Nat, I'm sorry if I overstepped. I was just trying to help.'

'It's okay, Scarlett. I know. I didn't mean to be bitchy, but I think she's had enough for a day.'

'Yeah, I know. I didn't know someone could care so much.'

'Well, she does.'

'I can see that.' Scarlett smiles, and the driver arrives. They all get in, and before Nat steps in, Scarlett ask if she could get in touch with us. 'It really was a pleasure to meet you all. I had a lot of fun.'

Nat can't help but smile, gives her number and waves goodbye.

It was supposed to be a great night, meeting celebrities, making friends, having so much needed fun. If I had woken up in my own room, I would be certain that yesterday had been a dream. Instead of meeting famous people, I spent most evening feeling sorry for myself. What a selfish prick I was. And going around with Tom, swooning over him. So pathetic. What was I thinking? Last thing I remember was shouting at the very nice bartender. Jeez, what a night, and all I have to remember it by is a purple wristband and a pounding head. I'm actually happy I woke up before anyone else. Not hard, it's only six in the morning. Which means I've slept a misery of four hours.

I knew Chloe and Charlotte wouldn't let me leave last night, and after meeting Tom, I didn't get a chance to slip away, so I tiptoe to the bathroom, and the mirror tells me just how bad I look. After cleansing my face, I wait until I'm out in the hall to put my trainers on. Finally, on my way to where I wanted to be last night.

I walk along the Thames. A cold breeze brushes my face, and I feel the morning mist in the air. The first rays of light start to pierce the night sky, and I inhale sharply breathing in the river. Maybe it would have been better to come last night, but it was still very nice. Thankfully, there's a little cart-kiosk to stop me from yawning, I feel the need for caffeine. After I get my lovely black coffee, I stop and lean on the stone ledge, looking at the river. That brings me back to last night at the balcony gazing at the same view. The sky was so clear we could count all the stars surrounding the moon. *Why the hell did I go with him? What is it that he had that made me so drawn to him?* Thankfully, we're leaving today, getting back to our lives, our normal robotic lives and never see him again.

So I take a last shot of my cup and turn to throw it in the bin next to me. *Why, God? Why do you do this to me?* Standing there in all his gorgeousness is Tom looking down at me with kind eyes and a smirk. I look up at the sky. 'Really?'

It's not like I never wanted to see him again. I mean, it was him, kind, gorgeous, and for some reason, I couldn't help but feel drawn to him. But this isn't a good thing. I have to be practical and realistic.

'You can pinch me if you like.' Such a warm smile he holds that I can't help to smile back. I curse to myself, and I actually think of pinching both of us.

'What are you doing here?' My tone, like my expression, is quite serious. If he's still following me, it's not funny anymore. Then again how could he if he didn't know where our hotel was?

'I just felt like going for a nice walk, couldn't sleep.' He shrugs and continues. 'Little did I know that my walk would be so nice!' he winks at me stretching the 'soooo.' I need to keep my head straight, be serious, no flirting!

'Yeah. I couldn't sleep more either.' I start walking as I talk. I have to do something. I can't just stand here looking at his penetrating gaze. He follows, hands in his pockets. We walk side by side and in silence for a long time. By the time we reach the Tate Modern, all of the night light has disappeared, and I look at my phone to check the time. It's nearly nine, and I have a text from Nat.

'Hey, hon, where are you? Are you okay? Xoxo.'

I start texting her back, no need to let them worry, and anyway, I intended to go back soon, I'm getting hungry. I walk and text her back: *'Hi, hon, I woke up early, was so restless couldn't sleep anymore.'* I suddenly stopped texting. Tom was behind me and had grabbed my shoulders. When I lift my head, I see why. Almost drove myself into a lamppost. 'oh.'

'I think you should finish that in a stationary position, no?'

He teases me, but he's not wrong, so I smile. 'Thank you.' I sit on the bench that is near and carry on texting. He doesn't sit. Instead, he paces. He's making me so nervous.

'So I went for a walk by the river. Everything is fine. Don't worry. I should be back in an hour or so, but I'll let you know, love you.'

I put my phone down and look up at him. He has stopped pacing and is now looking at me.

'What are the odd of this happening?'

'What?' I try to seem distracted as if I wasn't thinking the same thing, and I get the feeling he sees right through me.

He smiles softly and sits next to me. 'We, seeing each other again, and today, here.'

I'm not really sure what to say. For a while, we just stare at the impressive building.

'I really didn't think I would see you again, honestly.' I broke the silence first with a sigh but still wasn't sure what else I should say. I didn't want to lose myself in him again.

He chuckles. 'Neither did I.' This time he looks at me, dead in the eyes, and I can't look away. 'But I'm happy we were both wrong.' He speaks slowly, softly, not breaking eye contact, and I blush and turn my gaze away. I decide it's better if I keep moving. We're getting dangerously close. I hear him sigh and get up and follow me again.

I feel my heart thump in my chest, and for a second, I'm afraid he'll hear it, so I stop.

'I think I should be going back.' His expression is confused, almost hurt. I can't see why. It's not like I owe him anything, still I don't move. What am I waiting for?

'Can't we just walk a little while longer, please?'

Please, he says. Please. I could tell him we can keep walking together while I go back to my hotel. Yeah, I could and really should do that. Instead, I start walking in the opposite direction. Why? What does this man do to me? Clearly, I can't trust my judgement right now.

31

'When are you guys leaving?' I don't look up at him, but I can see from the corner of my eye his head is turned to me.

'Late this afternoon.' I answer without thinking, I was never good at lying but right after I blurt my answer, I realize I shouldn't have.

'So you don't actually have to leave now then?'

'Actually, I do. I've already missed breakfast with the girls. I don't want to miss lunch too.' This time I do look at him, he looks hopeful, but I don't want him to assume that I would immediately do whatever he wants, even though, deep down, that's what I probably would do.

He hums and stops, turns to me, and stretches his long right arm. I can't help but smile to myself and think, *are we going to dance?* I keep looking between his hand and his eyes.

Finally, he says, 'Give me your phone, please.'

Well, can't say he isn't polite, but his tone is very assertive. I reach for my phone.

'Do you need to make a call?'

'No.'

'So what do you need my phone to?' I can't help to cock a brow, and I stop halfway to meet his hand

'I lied. I do need to make a call.' Somehow, I don't believe him, but I hand him the phone anyway. 'You know it would work so much better if it wasn't locked.' He laughs and turns the screen at me, right in front of my face.

'What in the world are you doing?'

'It doesn't unlock with your face? That's what everybody does.'

I give him the most sarcastic laugh I can muster. 'Well, I'm not like everyone else.' I tilt my head as I wink at him, touch my thumb on the side of the phone, and the screen comes to life. 'No snooping.'

'I didn't even think of that.' His smugness makes me want to slap his arm, but I stop myself stepping back to give him privacy.

I'm still within earshot when he says, 'Hello, Nat, it's Tom.'

I turn so fast that I trip and fall on my face.

'Wait,' he says to the phone. 'Are you okay?'

'I'm fine. Why are you calling Nat?' I was definitely not fine. I could taste the blood in my mouth. 'Well?'

'Nat, I'll call you back in a sec.' I hear her protesting in the background, but he hangs up and pockets my phone.

'You're so clumsy. You should be more careful with yourself, you know?' He's not just worried he's telling me off, the nerve.

'What … why …' I can't form words. Snap out of it, V. I try to free myself from his hold, but since he helped me up, he hasn't let go. 'Can you please let go of my arm? I'm clearly fine.'

I look sideways at his hand clenching my arm and then at him. Before he lets go, he grabs my waist with his other hand. He sweeps some stray hairs from my face, reaches to his pocket, and pulls out a handkerchief.

I do nothing, only gaze at him and at all the very slow movements he makes.

He reaches for my lip to wipe it, and I wince back at the touch.

'I'm sorry. You're okay?'

I nod, still looking at him.

'I'm good. Thanks.' I grab the handkerchief of his hand to wipe my lip myself and try to scoot away from him. He's not having any of that. Taking advantage of his second hand free, it joins the other at my waist.

'Is it okay?' I brush my finger over my lip and feel it hot and tender. It hurts but not too much, and I'm relieved that there's no blood on my finger when I look at it.

'It's perfect.' He hushes softly and very close to me. My eyes still inspect my finger when he speaks and I just freeze looking down at it. It seemed like I was moving in slow motion when I looked up at him. He holds such an intense haze at me that I hadn't realized I stopped breathing until I chocked trying to get a puff in. He still doesn't let go, just chuckles.

'I don't know what it is about you that fascinates me so much, but I can't stop thinking about you.'

We are so close that I start getting uncomfortable. He can't say something like that so close to a girl. Can't kiss him. My eyes are on his lips. Can't kiss him.

'Why did you call Nat?' That does it. He lets go of me.

'Shit.' He fishes my phone from his pocket. 'Unlock please.'

I smile and obey.

He calls Nat back and puts it on speaker.

'Hey, sorry about that.'

'What's going on? Is Violet okay?'

'Yes, yes, she's fine now.'

'What do you mean *now*, Tom?'

'Well, you know how clumsy she is.'

'Yes.' She says for him to carry on.

'Well, when I called you, she didn't know and tripped and fell.'

'Of course, she did. Is she okay?' She laughs as she asks, and I interject.

'I'm fine, thank you, and I'm not that clumsy.' I feel miniscule now.

There's a silence from both of them before they burst laughing. Now I'm offended. Tom doesn't know me that well.

I cross my arms over my chest and tap my foot. 'Are you guys finished?'

'I'm sorry, honey, but that was very funny.'

'Yes, it was.'

'Nat, who's that? Am I on speaker phone?'

'It's Scarlett. I came to have breakfast with you guys, and you were missing. It's been a drama here.' They all giggle.

'You guys had some special mimosas already?' I can't help but ask. They do sound drunk.

'No. Only coffee.'

'Sure.'

Now Tom speaks. 'Hey Scarlett.'

'Hey, Tom.' She sings more than she speaks, and I raise an eyebrow at him. No, V, you're not jealous.

He continues. 'I see you made some new friends, good for you.'

'Yeah, they're really great, but we're missing one. You need to stop stealing her.'

'I'm sorry, but this time wasn't my fault.' His eyes are on me. 'It was fate.' I can't keep my smile away.

'Why did you call, Tom?' Nat's tone is serious, and everyone is very quiet, waiting for his response. Even I'm curious. How can I not be? He intrigues me so much.

'Listen, I know this was your weekend, and I kind of ruined it yesterday.'

'Kind of?' She interrupts.

'Okay, I totally ruined it.'

'I wouldn't go that far.' She's taunting him, and it's very funny. He lets out an exasperated breath.

'Anyway, I wanted to ask, as you have her always to yourself, if I could spend today with her. I promise I'll bring her back by the time you guys have to leave.' I don't let her answer.

'Hum, excuse me. You should ask me, no? She's not my mother.' It's not my intention to be mean to him or her, but I just felt like someone was trying to decide my fate without consulting me. An exaggeration, I know.

'Yeah, okay, I'll call her next.' He says it with a very wide smile, but mine disappears, and he gives me a confused look.

'That's fine, Tom. Just take care of her, please.'

'I promise.' And with that he hangs up.

I feel like the sun is reflecting on his face because the smile he gives me is so bright and sweet it makes my knees weak. Still I don't smile. Instead, I get up from the bench we sat down before the call and walk.

'Hey, what happened? Is everything okay?'

'I'm fine, thanks. Can I have my phone back, please?' I didn't want to talk about it. I didn't want to think about it. I just wanted to walk.

He watches me as I walk away for a little while and then caches up with me. Not hard, my legs are so small.

We're nearly at the Waterloo Bridge when he grabs my hand. I try to get it free, but he tightens his grip.

'Tom, please let go,' I plead.

'I want to take you somewhere. Will you trust me?' Unfortunately, I do trust him, but I don't want to tell him that.

'I don't feel like going anywhere right now.' He looks down. I can see he's almost giving up, and at that moment, I feel a ping in my stomach. I don't want him to. He looks at me, takes a step forward, and lets out a long breath.

'Please?' Dammit, those are some serious puppy eyes. I put on my best smile.

'Where are we going?'

'I can't tell you that. It's a surprise.' He takes another small step forward, looks intensely at me. I can't look away again. Man, he's mesmerizing. I can't keep my smile away anymore. He leans down a little, and for a second, I think he's going to kiss me. Even if I wanted to, I can't move.

He kisses my forehead, and I smile against his throat, leaning into him. He's gentle and sweet and makes me think of later today. It's going to be hard to say goodbye.

He's got one hand on my lower back and the other still gripping mine, and I don't want this moment to end. I don't want to say goodbye. He starts leaning backwards, and I grab his back, pulling him to a hug. He lets go of my hand and pulls me in closer. I feel his breath on my neck, and it sends a shiver down my spine. I don't want to let go, and he doesn't move either, so we stand there in the middle of the sidewalk, linked by our limbs.

'You smell good.' I smile, but we still don't change our position.

'That's the idea of taking a shower.' I feel his chest rumble as he laughs.

'As much as I love to hug you – and believe me: I do – I think we should get going. We have to enjoy these last few hours.' That comment brings me back to reality and breaks off my trance. I clear my throat while I release him, and again, he grabs my hand as we continue walking.

'Promise me you'll try.' That came out of nowhere.

'Try what?' He chuckles but doesn't answer, and we keep our pace for a while. I continuously steal looks at him. After a while, he stops.

'Will you came up with me?' At first, I don't get it. Up where? Does he live here somewhere? Then I take a 360, and my eyes widen.

'Tom, I …' He doesn't let me finish, covering my mouth with two of his fingers, and I fight the urge to taste them.

'Before you say no, please listen.'

I nod lightly. 'Go on.'

He smiles and caresses my cheek with the back of his hand, letting his thumb softly sweep across my bottom lip.

'I know you're afraid, and before you ask, no, I didn't bring any "liquid courage". You'll have to do with my company.' He winks at me, and I laugh. He's so sweet to remember that. 'I promise I'll hold you the whole time.'

'Why?' He's taken by surprise with my question, looks up at my trap, and then back at me.

'I've been up there, alone, and with … people. It was never special. Yesterday at the balcony was. There was nobody else in the world I wanted there with me.'

I don't think that I've ever cried so much in my life as I did this weekend. When I feel my eyes well up, I do my best to stop it. *How is this possible? I hardly know him. I hardly know anything about him, and yet I feel so connected to him. I can't say no.*

Squeezing his hand, I pull him towards London Eye, and he wears the most beautiful smile. 'How are we getting a ticket now?' He laces an arm behind my back along my waist pulling me closer to him.

'Don't worry I got it.' Another squeeze and a wink, and I'm melting against him.

It has been a long time since I let a guy get this close to me this fast. It has been nothing but flings. I make sure to never let it go too long, didn't want to fall into another trap and end up being hurt again. For some reason, I was letting him get very close to me, too close. It was scary, but my heart was winning the battle with my head.

He takes me straight to the front and talks to the security guard. Even though it's Sunday, it's not busy, maybe because it's still early in the morning. They shake hands, and the guard gestures for us to proceed to the next cart. I feel my heart pounding in my ears, and my breathing quickens. The doors open. I look inside and look at him, big smile on his face and both arms reaching to me. I take both his hands in mine. He doesn't pull me inside, but I know I have to hurry getting in. The cart moves slow but doesn't stop.

It's a leap of faith and trust. I take it. The doors close, and we're alone.

'Close your eyes,' he says.

I obey and feel him turning me around so I'm in front of him.

'Walk slow and grab the rail.' His voice is low and soft but very commanding.

I'm still very nervous, for a few extra reasons. It has been a long time since I was this close to a man. In fact, it has been since Adrien, and now I find myself fawning over a man I hardly know. I've been trying to keep my distance, but it's so hard with him. I still don't know how is it possible to have such a strong connection with someone you barely know, and I don't want to get hurt again, the possibilities of that happening are … high.

He grabs the rail, putting each of his arms on my sides, trapping me in a cage of his body. I can hardly control myself. My whole body tingles, and a sigh escapes my mouth.

'Can I open my eyes now?'

He chuckles and leans forward, as if it was possible for him to be closer to me. I feel his breath down my neck and his lips brushing my ear. He's driving me crazy.

'Of course, you can.'

It's not an experience that you forget, and even though I was here yesterday, it is still an amazing view. I'm lost in thought, in awe of the sight. But when he blows next to my face, I jolt back to reality. My whole body lights up, I can't help but feel the heat. *What is this man doing to me?*

'How are you doing?' He has such a soft voice. *I'm hanging by a thread, thanks for asking.*

'I'm good thanks. I'll just keep looking out the window and forget where I am, no problem.'

He laughs in my ear. 'I hope I don't get forgotten too.' If only.

'I don't think that's possible.' My mouth speaks before my mind can catch up. *Get a grip, woman.*

He doesn't answer. He doesn't move. I feel his intense gaze on me, and we stay quiet until almost half the ride. He breaks the silence first.

'Could you turn around?'

I actually feel my heart skip a beat and flutter. My whole face turns pink, and I cough, trying to breathe and talk instead of stuttering.

'Tom, I don't think that's a good idea.' As I talk, I feel my heart sink to my stomach.

'I see.' That's all he says. Next thing I know, he lets go of the rail and moves his hands around my waist. For a moment, I think he's going to turn me around but instead, he hugs me tight and sits his chin on my shoulder. It's such a tender moment that I regret what I said before.

'You know it's not a bad thing, right?'

I get so confused that I turn my head to his and cock an eyebrow, big mistake that was. His mouth is right there, his juicy lips tease me, half parted, and I know he sees my desire when he licks his lips. Damn him.

'What are you talking about?' I try my best to look at his eyes, but still, that doesn't help much.

'The fact that you're attracted to me.' He kisses my cheek and tightens his grip around my waist.

'Wow, how humble.' I try to be sarcastic, and trust me: I'm usually very good at it. But he just throws me off my game. I fell the rumble of his laugh on my back, and I can't help but feel safe and comforted.

'It's true, and you know it.' This time, he's serious. I can't admit that to him. I can hardly admit it to myself, but this is dangerous territory, and I can't forget that, no matter how he makes me feel. I say nothing, and neither does he. We just stand there contemplating the view in each other's arms until the end of the ride.

'What do you want to lunch?' He extends a hand to help me off the cart, not that I need it, but I take it. Honestly, I do this to myself.

'Maybe we can go to a pub back there. The food is great.'

A grin spreads on his face. 'Another burger?' I see him wink and remember the bar encounter. That was fun.

'Maybe not a burger today. Maybe I'll get a steak.' *Is that my idea of flirting? And why the hell am I trying to?*

'Whatever you want, babe.' Another wink and he grabs my hand.

Another flutter in my chest. *'Babe'?' What in the world?* He's being very straightforward and pushy. I'm not sure I like it, but I follow. Once again, we walk side by side, hand in hand, in silence.

This weekend had certainly broken my routine and the feeling of helplessness, but tomorrow, everything is going back to the way it was before, before this weekend, before him. I have to do something.

We're seated in a booth, and I did go for the steak, and he decided to try the burger. 'You were right. This burger is delicious.'

I smile. He licks his fingers as he eats a chip, and I involuntarily lick my lips. I can't help it. I clear my throat and finally assemble the courage to ask.

'You said I could try. How you suggest I do that?'

He chokes on the burger, clearly not expecting my bluntness.

'are you okay?'

'Hum, yeah, fine. I just wasn't expecting that. Um, there's lots of things you can do to help.'

'Like what?'

He sets the burger down and takes a deep breath, I knew he understood me.

'Well, you can volunteer. There's lots of places that need help.' I know he can see the disappointment on my face, but I can't help it. He knows that right now that's not the kind of change or help I had in mind. Volunteering on a charity shop or soup kitchen won't change anything.

'That's clearly not what you were expecting.' He forces a smile. 'You have to be willing to make sacrifices to be able to achieve the kind of change that you want. It's not easy. You need a lot of dedication and, yes, like you said, money. Unfortunately, that's the reality of the world right now. But you can't give up. That's why I said you can try. If we all give up, the world would be in a much worse place right now.'

I keep silent, trying to digest all he said. I can see reason – I can – but doing that little isn't enough for me right now. I've done little my whole life. I've turned my head and given a blind eye. That is why I feel worse about all this. I can't help the way I'm feeling, and a decision or idea starts to form in my head.

He snaps his fingers in front of my face. 'Are you there?'

'I am.' My face is stern.

I can tell he's waiting for me to continue, but I can't really put my thoughts together, not enough to make a sentence anyway. I just smile. We finish our drinks, and when he doesn't let me pay my share, we find ourselves back by the river.

'What time do you guys have to leave?'

my feet stop. For a moment, I had forgotten what today was, what this afternoon was, a goodbye.

'Our train leaves at six.' I can't spend the next five hours with him just to say goodbye. 'Maybe I should be going back. I still have to pack.'

'Are you serious?' He scoffs, and his eyes really look hurt, but I can't meet them for long, so I gaze to the river and take a deep breath.

'Tom, maybe it's better if we say goodbye already instead of postponing it for later, don't you think?' His mouth is hanging open, he lets his head down, and I touch his arm, but he yanks it away. I can't help but feel my heart sink, though I still think it's for the best.

'Maybe you're right.' I can't say I wasn't expecting it, but no …'maybe we should just cut our losses. Come, I'll take you to your hotel.' There's nothing I would rather do, but I don't think that's a good idea. It'll just give us an excuse to go back to where we were before. It's not easy to resist his pull. So, very reluctantly, I turn to him and meet his eyes.

'I remember the way, thank you.' I really can't blame his next action. What was I expecting honestly? A gallant guy with no ego or pride for rejection? He pockets both his hands, stiffens his shoulders, which makes him look even taller and looks me dead in the eye, a lost vacant expression in his.

'Fine, goodbye.' He turns his back, and that is the last time I see Tom.

I cry the whole way back to the hotel, think it will be good to let myself dry before I go back to the girls, good plan. All their smiles crumble after they see my face, and it's a flood of arms and comforting words. They don't need to know what happened or ask questions right away. They know I just need a hug and space.

'Guys, I'm going to lie down a little okay?'

they all nod, and I'm surprised that Scarlett is still there and doesn't say anything.

Chapter 3

I die.

There's not much I remember, an explosion? The end of the world? I'm not sure. Other than my dream being black and white and Tom being there I don't remember it. I'm sweaty and panting when I wake up. My door is banging

'Come in.'

'How are you feeling?' Nat's look is concerned but very calm.

'I'm good. Don't worry.'

'Oh, I worry. You know I do. What time do you have to go?'

'I still have a few hours. Just thought it would be good to sleep a bit. Maybe I won't get too much jetlag.'

'That's good thinking.' I can tell there's something she wants to say, but I really don't want another speech on life.

'I'll just finish getting ready and check I have all I need, and then we can maybe get a coffee?'

'Honey, listen ...'

I lift my hand as I get out of bed. 'Please don't, not again. I'll be fine I told you.'

'I know you will. You're a very strong person, and I believe in you. I just wish you had given him a chance.'

'Not this again. You know as well as I do that wouldn't end up well, and I really don't want to talk about it anymore.' I try to convey an assertive tone to end the conversation, busy myself finding clothes to put on but she keeps going.

'But Scarlett spoke to him. You should hear ...'

I bang my hand on my dresser a little harder than I wanted to. 'Enough, Nat.'

She jumps. 'I'm sorry. I won't bring it up again.' The last thing I want is to hurt Nat, but I can't really talk about this anymore, so I hug her.

'I'm sorry, hon. I just don't want to hurt anymore. I just want to forget okay?'

'Of course,' she says with a squeeze.

First, I have to stop in Thailand, an extra shot that can only be administered there apparently, and need to collect an extra visa permission before I go to Cambodia.

It took me two months to get all visas and shots I needed in order. In that time, I worked every single shift I could, every odd job, to get some extra cash. I decided I wasn't going to quit my job. Guess I got chicken in the end. Instead I took a sabbatical. That's actually a funny idea, a sabbatical from retail sales. I'm nervous and scared, being out there around the world on my own, but this is something I have to do.

This isn't like coming to Gatwick or Birmingham. There's a lot more guns. Everything is checked more carefully, so intimidating. I would like to think I'm prepared enough. I did an insane amount of research. I exercised and controlled what I ate, since I have to be used to eating less. Never know what might happen.

There are so many people in Thailand I feel lost right away. I've never been in New York, but it can't be worse than this. It helps that most people speak English. I couldn't learn all the languages in two months, but I brought a few small dictionaries. We'll see how that goes.

It's so hard to explain. You would have to see it to believe it. We know and see things on TV, but we're human. We choose to turn our heads and change the channel. The floor is dust. The air is dust. The water is brown and contaminated. In the worse regions, houses are barns, and there are no beds. Some sleep on improvised hammocks, some on donated mattresses on the floor, others on the actual floor.

You would think the elders would be the ones sleeping more comfortably, but that's not what happens at all. Wonder why. Not worth saving those almost lost? It breaks my heart. But I made myself promise I wouldn't cry in front of anyone ever again.

You hear some celebrities go to Cambodia and adopt children and shine some light on the conditions. But I don't think the cameras show everything. This is nothing like I have ever seen. Nothing like I had imagined either. No children screaming constantly like those at the supermarkets in the UK because they want *that* chocolate. These suffer in silence.

I stay in Cambodia for four days. Better start slow. After finding an office there, I offer my services, anything they need. I cooked. I clean and try to teach some kids English. Not easy. I wasn't made to be a teacher.

Every day very early, I take the walk to the pit of contamination. The only place that village can get water just a few hours away. Even though I ask, right now there is no way to clean the water. They will never get better. Things will never get better.

I have to stop in Saudi Arabia before going to Africa, so I decide to go through Yemen, right in the corner, no harm. Yemen's situation is different. War blazes, drones, bombs, shootings, politicians trying to get accords done. All they really want is control, excuses to plant air defences that later can be used as offences. I'm shoved, yelled at, searched, and questioned, but I'm grateful they don't take my camera. After hours, I'm finally let go and told not to come through here again. I'm not a journalist.

It's been seven days, and I already can't believe all that I've seen. Got to call Nat. I promised I would check in. She even made me take a current picture and give her my itinerary. Although I told her that could change, she still insisted.

'Well, finally.' She's pissed.

'Hello to you too.'

'You should have called two days ago. We were worried. Are you okay?'

'Yes I'm all good. Things are tough, but I'm good. And you guys?'

'Oh, we're good. You know, all the same.'

'I hope not. How's married life?' I sound amused, but I actually want to know.

'It's the same. I've lived with him before, you know. I just wish you hadn't left right after the wedding.'

'I know, hon, but I had to. I hope you're happy, and I'm sure soon you guys going to have a mini you.'

'I hope so, hon. It's not easy.'

'I know, babe, but you have to keep positive. It will happen. Listen, hon, I wanted to ask you something.'

'Okay, what is it? What do you need?'

'I just wanted to know. Um … do you still talk to Scarlett?'

'You don't?'

'Yes, of course, I do, but I'm asking about you.'

'Why?'

'Well, I didn't want you to tell her anything I'm doing. She might go and tell him, and I don't want that.'

She's silent for a long time. 'I haven't told her about you, but she has asked, and so has he.'

'I don't want to know about that.'

'I know. Listen, hon, I have to go back. You be careful out there and don't forget to call.'

'I won't, hon. Thanks. Say hi to the girls for me. Take care.'

I always wanted to go to Kenya. This shouldn't be a vacation for me, but I can't help it. That's my next stop before going to Somalia.

There are national parks and lakes. It's beautiful. I hop on a tour jeep. After I explain I want to get to Somalia, they look at me strangely but give me a fair price. Walking around with money in my boots, it's definitely the weirdest thing I've done. There are lions. Rhinos. Elephants. The wildlife is incredible. Have to pinch myself just to make sure I'm not dreaming. On the outskirts of Somalia, the jeep driver advises me to hide my camera. He says journalists are not always welcome. Be careful. I'm scared, but I walk.

The country has been scorched by war, hunger, and climate change. Help cannot get quick enough here.

I come across a camp. Tents are put up, hundreds of them on top of each other, and people have no place to go. I'm scared of staying here and think of going up to Ethiopia, but I can't go back now. All eyes are on me, hungry beggars and guards. I spot a brick building and walk towards it.

It's a distribution centre of same kind, I think. There are armed guards at the door and lots of beggars around. As soon as one of the guards sees me, he sprints in my direction. Somehow I feel like it's better not to move.

He grabs my arm and shouts in Arabic. All I can say is 'Sorry.'

He keeps shouting at me, and I keep saying, 'Sorry. I don't understand.'

I hear the other guard shout for him, and he turns to me and says, 'Wait.' Does he speak English? Was he just trying to scare me? When he arrives at the same spot he left, the other guard walks towards me.

I gulp hard. His face his stern, serious. He holds his gun with both hands in front of him.

'Who are you?'

'I'm—'

'What are you doing here?' He interrupts. It's annoying.

'Are you a journalist?' This time he waits for me to answer. I don't know what it is, my shorts, backpack, or hiking boots that gives people a journalist vibe.

'No, I'm just a tourist. Violet.'

'A tourist?' He gives me a stink eye, full of doubt, but I nod. 'You don't look like a tourist. What are you doing here?'

I'm amused now. 'And what does a tourist look like?'

To my surprise, he smiles and gestures for me to follow. As we're approaching the other guard at the entrance of the building, he says something in Arabic to him. The other grunts and narrows his eyes at me. No idea what's happening, so I just stand there, skipping my eyes from one man to the other.

'Come.' The second guy says while he opens the door. *Should I go? What is worse, refusing to follow or leaving?* I walk behind him.

Before climbing the stairs, I take a peek. Downstairs, there's loads of boxes, loads of supplies, lads of a lot of things. Why is there so much misery outside? I feel my arm being yanked. I had forgotten about the guard.

'The curiosity of a reporter is unbelievable.' He's not shouting. He doesn't have a joking or sarcastic tone in is voice. Instead he's serious and sombre.

'I'm not a reporter, I told you.'

'Sure.' That's all he says, and he keeps 'helping' me up the stairs until we reach a door. Upstairs is all closed doors. Offices, I assume. We turn right. He knocks on the second door twice. A tall, blond, middle-aged woman opens the door.

She looks me up and down and talks to the guard.

'You reporter?'

I let out a sharp sigh. 'I said already no. I'm a tourist.'

'What is tourist doing here?' We're still standing at the door. Her hand remains on the doorknob.

'I'm travelling the world, trying to help people any way I can.'

She cocks an eyebrow and swings the door all the way open. 'Sit. You leave.' She gestures for me to take the chair. I oblige, and the door closes behind me.

'You rich tourist?' I can't help but laugh, but she keeps serious, and my laugh falls very quickly.

'If I was, I would be going around with my own guards.'

This time, she does smile. 'Yes, I guess you right. So what you think you can do for us here?'

'I don't know.' Seeing the expression on her face, I keep going. I tell her everything, that I wanted to do something to help the needy. I tell her about Cambodia and what I did there and all the places I still want to go. There is a silence for a long time, but I don't say anything else.

She gets up and stands looking out the window. 'That's ambitious for you. How you think you can do all that? Just you. No money?'

'I can try.' In that moment, that's the only thing that comes to mind, and I can't help but smile.

She turns to me with a dry smile. 'Okay, you can stay if you like. But no pictures.' From her tone, I hear it's a big deal. 'You help people around if you want, but you not interfere with anything you might see. Understood?'

I nod, keeping my eyes on hers.

'Is there any place around I could stay?'

'End of the corridor to the right. You can stay there while you here.'

'Thank you. Can I go now?'

She shoos me out.

I wanted to look around, maybe go around the village, but that didn't seem like the good move right now, so I head to the room. Once inside, my first instinct is to lock the door.

'No key?' I keep my eyes on the door. No bolts, no key. It doesn't look like I'll sleep much.

Reluctantly, I turn my back at the door to take in the room. There's a small bed with a bedside table and a dresser. I move to the window and drop my bag to the floor. There's misery everywhere, pain and hunger I won't be surprised if some of the people loitering on the floor are dead. Maybe I will.

I planned to get up early, but that decision is stolen from me when I hear a knock on the bedroom door. At least, they knocked.

'Good morning. You ready?' the second guard looks at me up and down. I can't help but notice how cute he is.

I clear my throat. 'Do I look ready to you?'

He just keeps looking at me. I start getting uncomfortable.

'I'm sorry. Can I help you with something?'

He moves his eyes to mine. 'I'm going to take you around the village today.'

My mouth parts a little. 'The lady said I could go around the village as I please as long as I don't take pictures.' My hand is still on the doorknob. We haven't moved an inch.

'Yes, you can. But today is the first day, and there are a lot of guards around, and they don't know who you are. Today you'll stick with me, and you'll be okay.'

Somehow I don't feel okay. I feel very unease maybe I shouldn't have come here. 'Give me ten minutes.' I close the door before he answers.

But I still hear him retort, 'Sure.'

I get dressed quickly. I really don't want to leave my things here, especially my camera. I have a feeling it might disappear, so I do the stupid thing and hide it under the pillow. I mean, why not? Who's going to think of that?

Once outside my room, I tell him that I still need to use the bathroom, and he gestures across the hall without saying a word. He's looking at me weird.

As we walk through the village, I try to take in all that I see. It's hard. There are mainly women on the dirty paths, but there are also children. Dust covered and hungry children. How is this possible?

'Why don't you help these people? Look at the children.' I'm almost crying but try to keep myself strong.

He stops at my brute words, grabs my arm, and pulls me towards an empty warehouse. I try to cut loose but no luck.

'You can't talk like that here.'

'Why?' I know the answer but still ask. He lets go of my arm, lets his gun down together with his head. I wasn't expecting that reaction. I can't read that expression, so I wait for him to talk. He turns to the door but doesn't move. He's in pain.

'It's been two years, and since then, I keep telling myself things will get better. That I'm actually helping.' He scoffs to himself and turns around. 'Listen. You really have to be careful. Don't talk like that. Don't interfere. You'll get hurt.'

I take a step back. 'Is that a threat?'

He steps towards me, and I step back again, so he stops and smiles. I'm surprised.

'You don't need to be afraid of me. I'm not going to hurt you. I'm trying to help you.'

I weigh what he says. Somehow I do feel safe with him and can't understand why.

'What happened two years ago?'

He immediately turns his head, and his expression hardens. 'It doesn't matter. Come. We have to go I have stuff to do.'

This time, I grab his arm. He looks at my hand and then at me and raises both eyebrows. 'What are you doing?' His voice is soft and low but very aware that I grabbed him. *What* am *I doing?*

'I know you won't hurt me.' I sound smug but let go of his arm. 'Why are you escorting me around?'

'I've told you it's dangerous.'

'And you think I can't take care of myself?'

He laughs hard.

'What?'

'You probably can, yes. But why can't I help?' He shrugs.

'I didn't say you couldn't.' I find myself flirting. 'But you need to understand that this is my nature. I want to help any way I can, and honestly if I die in the process, I'm okay with that.' I'm surprised at how serious I am. I really mean it.

He tilts his head and steps forward. 'You really mean that?'

'I do.' I nod.

'You're crazy.'

'Thank you,' I reply with a wink, and we stand there for a while. He takes another step forward. I'm nervous now.

'Two years ago, I came here with my sister. We wanted to help. Just like you.' I can tell it's hard for him to talk about it, and I can see where this is going. 'She was very ... spirited like you,' he says with a smile. 'Always trying to help and interfering. Rules are very strict here, and when people break them, the consequences are ... severe.'

'Like death severe?' I so hope the answer is no, but he lowers his head.

'Sometimes.' *Why does he look ashamed?*

'What happened to your sister?'

'An old lady was caught in a warehouse trying to take food.' He's looking at me now, and I let him continue without interruption. 'My sister found her first and tried to help her escape.' He stops, taking a deep breath. Clearly, this next part is difficult to get out. 'They were caught by the guards and taken to Carla.'

'Who's Carla?' I know but I ask.

'The boss.' The way he says it sends a cold shiver down my spine. 'She sentenced both of them to death, and I couldn't stop it. I failed Veronica, and I can't forgive myself.' He sits on one of the crates littering the floor, head in his hands.

I take a knee in front of him. 'Why did you stay working for her?' There's a lot of things I could have asked, but I can't understand that.

He looks me in the eyes and takes both my hands, giving them a light squeeze.

'Because I thought I owe her that much. I thought I could stay and help people like she wanted to. Turns out I'm only good to follow orders.'

I shake my head and squeeze his hands back. 'If that were true you wouldn't be here helping me.'

He smiles, and I can see the hurt in his eyes. He's in so much pain that I can feel it.

'So I remind you of your sister?'

He nods. Not looking at me.

'And you think I'll get myself killed?'

'I don't think. I'm sure. You're just like her, wanting to make a difference anywhere you go. Well, sometimes you can't. What can just one person do? Look at me. I haven't changed anything since I got here.'

And again only one thing comes to my mind. 'We can try.'

He looks at me as if I haven't heard a thing he said to me just now.

'I understand, and I am sorry what you've been through. I promise I will be careful, but I won't stop it. I need to do this.' I try to be as serious as possible. But we're still on the floor, holding hands.

'For who?'

'What?'

'Who are you doing this for? For you? So you can feel better about yourself?'

Now that hurts. I can't say if it's true or not. All I know is I felt I couldn't live with myself anymore without doing anything. And that's exactly what I tell him. After what's seems like an eternity, he gets up and holds a hand out to me.

'Come. There's a lot to see.'

He shows me everything, the worst parts of the village where most homeless wait for food, water, salvation, death. He takes me to a river nearby and tells me a lot of people get water from here, but just like Cambodia, the water is dirty and gets everyone sick. There are hardly any doctors around. So there's only one end to that story. The last place he takes me is a cemetery. It's odd, but I don't say anything. He stops in front of a grave.

'This is Veronica.'

'Loving sister and friend,' I read and look up at him. 'Where are you guys from?' I can tell they are not from here.

'Finland.' Not expecting that I'm not going to lie. 'Ever thought of going back? Leaving this place?'

He shrugs, and I can tell he wants to.

'It just doesn't seem right. Leaving her here. After everything. And there's really nothing to get back to. No family left.'

I get it. I do. But he's doing nothing to honour her memory. I can't bring myself to tell him that, so we walk back to the centre of the village.

'I have to go and … do my duties.' I don't want to ask, so I watch him walk away. Still don't know his name.

I take a 360 from the centre of the village. I've never felt so powerless and useless in my life, so I go back to the river.

There are kids there, playing in the shallow water. They are laughing, enjoying the little they have, and here I am feeling sorry for myself. They jump in the water and play with tree leaves, pretending they're boats. I wish I had my camera with me. I sat there and watched them for a while smiling. At one point, a lady came to me.

'Beautiful, no?' I still get impressed that a lot of people speak English, broken but understandable.

'Very.' She must me at her late forties. Maybe the kids are hers.

'Children are precious gift. They always happy. You have children?' I lower my head before responding.

'No.'

'You lost children?' I'm stunned. How can she possibly tell?

'How do you know?' And then I understand. I can see it in her eyes. She has lost too.

'You bear pain like me. It's easy to lose children here. Very hard to survive for them. Very hard for us to forget.'

'How many have you lost?'

'Two. But feels like more.'

'What do you mean?' I don't understand.

'All children here are mine and everyone's. We try take care of each other. When children die, we all in pain.' Now that's a heavy thought.

'I was lucky.' She looks straight at me now, such a confused look on her face so I explain. 'Mine had just been born, didn't get to meet her properly.' She softly sets a hand on my back just below my shoulder and pats me.

'You no lucky. You same like me, mother with no children.' I can't cry. That is exactly how I felt. I just couldn't say it. At the moment, I feel like I came here to help these people, but they're the ones helping me. And just like that, I hug her.

'You have to go.'

'What do you mean? Go where?'

'Leave this place. You get hurt.' She speaks in very hushed tones, as if she's afraid someone will hear. I too look around.

'I'll be fine.' I don't know if I'm trying to assure her or me.

For the next couple of weeks, I help people with distributing food and more blankets. There are always new arrivals here. It seems that there isn't enough for everyone. They must have something. Probably are just rationing the supplies. I hope.

After dinner and cleaning up, I decide to go take a walk by the river. The air is much fresher now. I must have walked a few hours before noticing how dark it was getting. So I turn around to head back to the village. I scream. Believe me when I say I'm not a screamer. Even when I see a spider, I just calmly remove myself from the room. But, man, did I jump now.

'What the hell are you doing? Trying to give me a heart attack?'

He chuckles. 'No. I couldn't find you anywhere. Thought you left.' He shrugs as he talks to me, looking at the river. We stay in silence for a while.

'Hey what's you name by the way?' Can't believe I haven't asked him yet.

'Mike.' He doesn't look like a Mike.

'Really? Mike and Veronica?' He cocks an eyebrow.

'You have a problem with that? It's who we are.' I don't know if he got upset, if he was serious or pulling my leg.

'No. No, it's just don't look like ...' *Just stop talking.*

'Like what?'

Now my face is scarlet, I'm sure. 'Like a Mike?' It's more of a question than anything else. His expression is very intimidating. But he laughs, and I relax a little.

'You think I look like I belong here, don't you?'

Tomato red now. All I can say is, 'Maybe. Sorry.' He keeps laughing and looking at me, and again I notice how cute he is, how his body is toned under that uniform, and how that rough but tidy beard makes him look sexy.

'Well, it takes a few years out of you being here and seeing ... so much.' I don't want to feel sorry for him, but I can't help it. Still, I decide to not make a comment on it.

'I'm not leaving yet. I haven't done anything.' I start retracing my steps as we talk.

'That's not what I heard.'

'What do you mean?'

'Everyone in the village is talking about you and all your help since you arrived. Even Carla said it would be good of you would stay here ... hum ... longer.' I steal a look at him quickly and trip on a branch lying on the ground. Mike's strong arms catch me. His arms are so firm, but his touch very gentle when he holds me up. I clear my throat, but my voice still comes out very breathy.

'Um ... thank you. I guess my clumsiness still follows me.' We both chuckle, and I try to avoid his eyes.

'How clumsy are you?' I haven't heard this voice before. It's soft and low and very suggestive.

'Um ... very. I'm actually surprised I haven't killed anyone yet.' He joins me in my laugh. 'That you know of.'

That did it. That made me stop laugh and think to all the times I could remember that my clumsiness hurt someone, and I turn to the water. There's a bench, and I sit. After a little while observing me, he comes to the bench and sits beside me and drops a hand on my knee.

'I'm sorry. I didn't know. I didn't mean to joke about it.'

'It's okay,' I joke as well. 'It's nothing really.'

'Come on. Tell me. You can talk to me.' I think back to the cemetery and the warehouse, how he opened up to me about his sister, and I take a deep breath.

'I was maybe about twenty-five. I was riding a bike on a sidewalk, and to my right were some people sitting on a bench and to my left was a crosswalk.' I stop close my eyes and swallow hard. He moves his hand to my shoulder, and I carry on. 'There were some people waiting for a green light.' Another blink of my eyes and it's like I'm back there.

'I looked back for like a second, and if you ask me now, I couldn't tell you what I was looking at. Somehow, while I was lost in oblivion, I had swerve to the left, and some people jumped to the street to get away from me. Everything happened so fast, but I was still seeing it all happening.' A tear strays down my cheek, and he wipes is with his thumb. Such a small and tender gesture. 'I was seeing it all happening beforehand. An older lady stayed behind, and a lorry was coming.'

He yelps.

'No.' I look at him as to tell him I'm not done.

'I threw myself on the floor and went for her arm.' Another harsh breath and I can see in his eyes he's expecting the worse. 'I grabbed her.'

'You saved her?'

'I saved her head.' He looks confused. 'She lost a leg.' I can't meet his eyes I'm so ashamed.

'But you saved her. She's okay.'

'I ruined her life. It will never be what it was like for her. Ever. Just because I was in cloud town.'

'You're being too hard on yourself. Accidents happen.'

'Yeah, but this one was caused by me.' He doesn't say anything anymore. He just grabs both my shoulders to turn me toward him, and he hugs me. I feel such comfort and so safe that for a moment, I wish I could forget everything and live here in his embrace. At least, I don't cry.

'I went to visit her at the hospital.' I don't let go of him or open my eyes. 'She never wanted to see me. She never forgave me. How could I really expect her to after what I did to her?'

'How long has it been since you spoke to her?' *God, how long has it been?* Sometimes I feel like it was yesterday when I felt her crushing rejection and hate towards me.

'About seven years.' I speak to the sky.

'Don't you think that maybe by now she has forgiven you?'

I can't help but let hope fill my chest. But I saw her eyes that day, the hatred and pain.

'I don't think so.' He hugs me tighter. 'I think you should find out.' I can't think of that right now. All I can feel are his arms around me, his strong back under my hands. Without a thought, I breathe him in.

The second I do it, we both tense. *What is wrong with me?* He still doesn't let go. He grabs tighter, and all I want to do right now is kiss him.

'You want to go get a drink?' I feel his soft voice falter, as if he's implying a lot more than a drink. I let go of him to find his eyes.

'I didn't know there was a bar here.' An expression of surprise covers my face. On his, a cocked smile stares at me.

'There isn't.' It actually takes me a little while to understand what he's saying. It has been a long while for me. He's so nice and sexy I don't think I'll be able resist him if I go to his room.

'Let's go.' *What am I doing?* I can see he wasn't expecting that, but without a word, he offers me an arm. I take it, and we walk.

We leave the crisp air of the river behind, and I still don't know where we're going. We just keep walking away from village until we arrive a little house. Well, more like a shack.

'You live here?' He nods. 'Why don't you stay where I am? There's lots of room that could be put to some good use.' I know he understands my innuendo. I still can't get past all they have hidden away and not sharing. He bows his head as we enter into his leaving room/kitchen.

'I didn't want to stay there.' His words are cold. There is something else, but he doesn't want to share, so I don't press.

'At least, you got a place for yourself.'

He turns quickly to me. His hazel eyes are getting darker and angrier. 'What are you saying? That I'm selfish? That I could put all those people outside in here and I could take their place? Is that it?'

I can see he's hurt but, no, that's not what I meant.

'I'm sorry. I didn't mean that. I was just trying to change the subject.'

He's pouring the drinks. Rum, I think. I take the drink he offers me.

'You didn't do a very good job then.'

'I'm sorry, Mike, really.' I try to put a hand on his arm, but he waves it away.

'You have no idea the things I've done for these people. If Carla knew, I would be dead already.' He's sitting on a chair at the back of the house's patio, and I follow him. I can't help but be surprised by what he said. I thought he was doing what Carla says, just following orders, and he catches that with a scoff.

'Right. You're quick to judge without knowing what is actually going on. You don't know everything you know?'

That is probably a rhetorical question, and I really wouldn't know what to say, so I just give him a nod, just my way of saying how selfish I am again. Judging, like he said, and I too have a room that I'm not sharing with anyone. Not sure that I could, though.

We sip our drinks in silence, and with every passing minute, I feel a crushing guilt. Still don't know what to say. Somehow just feel like sorry won't be enough so I keep silent. I start losing myself in thought. The things I've seen since I left Warwickshire. Never thought a year ago I would be here, trying and really failing. I know I'm looking for something, some way to actually help people, not just for a few days but actually make an impact and change their lives for better. Will I ever be able to do that?

I'm brought back to reality by a waving hand. 'Earth to Violet.' He keeps waving, and I grab his hand.

'I'm here.'

'Are you sure? Where did you go?' We're still holding hands.

'All over. Nowhere. I don't know.' I'm feeling broken right now, and I think he can see that. He lets go of my hand and cups my face with both hands, gently lifting my head so I'm looking at him. No more words. He just kisses me. Soft and gentle at first. I grab his neck, deepen the kiss. His hands roam over my back, and I feel the heat of his body.

In less than two minutes, we're in his room. Clothes cover the floor. I've never done this, but there's no turning back now. There's a need we both share. It's hungry, demanding but caring. Even though we start slowly, we quickly lose ourselves in each other and lie on the bed, breathless. I speak first.

'Well, I haven't done that in a while.' I laugh as he turns on his side to me. 'Really?' I'm not exactly offended, but what does he think? I scoff.

'Do you think I bang someone on every village I stay?' My voice comes out a little sharper than I intended. But I'm not taking it back. He tucks a strand of hair behind my ear, and I struggle not to melt into him.

'I didn't mean that. Sorry. It's just you're a very attractive woman. That's all.'

I turn to him and suddenly feel very exposed, so I grab a sheet to cover myself.

He chuckles. 'It has been a while for me too.'

I can't help it. I cock an eyebrow. 'Really?' My sarcasm is implied, but he jumps on top of me, setting his weight on his elbows so he doesn't crush me and starts kissing my mouth, my forehead, my cheeks, down my neck, and he settles on my breasts.

'I think I'm going to live here now.' I start chuckling. 'Forget the world outside and just stay here.' I know he doesn't mean it, but I can't help it, and my body stiffens. 'Please don't judge me.'

His face is still buried between my breasts, so his voice is muffled, but I still hear the resentment and regret it. Just at that moment, I do something before I understand what I'm actually doing or if that's even what I want.

'I understand you stayed for your sister. But there's lots of places that need help. You could come with me if you wanted to.' *What am I doing?* I don't want to be with a man right now, especially if I can't stop thinking about Tom.

'Do you mean that?' His eyes search mine.

'Sure. Why not?' I shrug.

'Somehow I have a feeling you don't really want me with you.' I don't say anything, but I feel my cheeks burn and betray me. 'I do think you're right, you know?' My eyes almost pop out of my sockets, and he laughs.

'I just don't think I'm ready to leave yet. But I know I should. I'm just not ready.' I relax.

'Well, if you ever do take my number. Maybe we can meet up sometime. I mean that.' I make sure my eyes are on his. I really do mean that.

He kisses me again and says between our glued lips, 'I will.' And with that, he ravishes me again. I wanted to go back to my room, but I couldn't resist his plea. 'I need you tonight.' How can I argue with that? It has been a while since I felt so safe and cherished that I fall asleep in his arms, and I have the best sleep that I've had in months.

I wake up to the smell of coffee. I think I'm dreaming, so I run out of the room before I wake up.

'No way. Is this for real?' He laughs and swings a cup under my nose. I try to grab it, but he moves it up. So I frown.

'How about a good morning first?' He pulls me close with his free hand and kisses me, soft and long.

'That's torture and coercion, you know?'

'Now you can have your coffee.'

'Thank you.' I kiss his cheek, have a sip, and let out a loud moan. I can't help it. Can't remember the last time I had coffee. He looks at me sideways.

'You keep that up, and I'll take you back to the bedroom.'

I feel my face burning and try to ignore his comment. 'How the hell did you get coffee?'

He moves some toasts and butter to the table and holds a chair out for me to sit.

'What a gentleman.' He sits beside and presses a kiss to my temple.

It's such a tender scene I can't help but feel a fuzzy, warm feeling in my stomach.

'I know it seems selfish, and it probably is. But I don't think those people outside need coffee or the butter.' He shrugs as he talks.

'You're probably right.' But I still can't help but feel guilty. 'You're so not like I pictured you.' His knife stops on its way to butter the bread.

'And what were you expecting?' He raises a single eyebrow.

I smile. 'Well, a big mean, macho military man of course.'

He grabs his stomach as he laughs. 'There's a lot of testosterone on that statement. I'm not sure I'm that macho.'

I join him in laughing. 'Oh you are.' With that comment, we find ourselves on the kitchen counter, hungry again.

He speaks close to my ear. 'I've never wanted anyone as much as I want you.' His voice is low and husky, and it sends thrills down my back, but sadly, I can't say the same to him, so I smile.

'You can have me.' That's all the permission he needs. I was never one to be interested in sex. But that felt good. He pants against my shoulder. I kiss him and hop off the counter.

'You kill me.' His phone rings. 'Shit, I'm late.'

'What time is it?'

'Nearly nine.'

I almost drop my coffee. 'What? I missed helping with breakfast. I didn't know it was so late.'

'I guess we lost track of time,' he says with a wink. I smile but get up quickly and start getting dressed.

'Whoa. Calm down. We're already late. It won't change anything getting stressed now. Take your time. Take a shower if you like. I have to go, sadly.' He moves to me slowly.

'You want me to stay here. Alone?'

He chuckles, tucking some hair behind my ear again. He does that a lot and makes me feel very vulnerable.

'I'm not holding you captive. You can leave whenever you want.' With that, he kisses me again and leaves.

I take my time with the rest of the coffee, do the dishes, and make the bed. Before I leave, I decide to call Nat. It hasn't been long, but so much has happened. The phone rings four times before I give up and make my way back to my room to change.

After ten minutes of wandering around, I realize I don't know where I am. He guided me to his shack yesterday, and I really didn't pay much attention to the route. Even when I take a look around, I can't see any of buildings. I hear a commotion and start getting scared. I'm going up a dirt path, lots of bushes around. I still hear the commotion but can't see anything. Ten more steps and I recognize the sound – a slash and a scream. It can't be what I'm thinking. It can't.

I hear Carla's voice and stop. She's so close. I look around and see her through the bushes. Witnessing that scene breaks me. I cover my mouth to muffle my yelps. There's a woman tied to a post, bare back covered in blood. One of the guards is whipping her. I'm seeing it and still can't believe it. Another slash. Another scream. Another yelp. What do I do? I want to help, but how can I? Carla is talking.

'You done with stealing?' Her voice is cold and unapologetic. The woman doesn't answer. 'I think she needs more incentive.' I see the guard drop his head. 'You got problem?' He turns to her, and my hand drops from my mouth.

'Yes, I have problem.' His voice is mocking her. 'I think she understands. She's had enough.' She moves to him very slowly, very intimidatingly.

'It's enough when I say is enough. You understand?' If I wasn't so close, I wouldn't understand what she was saying in that low, intimidating voice. He nods. What does this woman have on him?

All of a sudden, all heads are turned to me. It takes me a second to realize that my phone is ringing and another to have a guard grab my arm and pull me out of the bushes. He drags me and plants me in front of Carla. Mike can't even react. I try to free my arm, to no avail.

'Is this how you're helping people?'

'I never said I helping people. You did. What are you doing here? You take pictures?' She crosses her arms and moves towards me.

'No, but I really should so I can show what you're doing to these people.'

'You bitch. Get her phone.' She slaps me, but I don't back down. The other guard start toward me, and I show him my palm.

'No need. I'll get it.' Taking the phone out of my pocket, I say, 'I'll show you, but I need my phone back. Please don't break it.'

She laughs. A very dry and loud laugh. 'You know me well. Maybe you get some intel, no?' She's not looking at me. She's eyeing Mike, but he doesn't meet her eyes. 'Show me.' She's still looking at him as if trying to make a point, so I move to her, grab my phone as hard as I can, start sliding photos, sorting them by date to be faster.

'Okay. Now you can leave. We have business to finish.' I don't move my feet. Instead I look at Mike, but he turns his gaze away. That's okay. I think I can hold my own.

'I'm not going, and you're going to leave this poor lady alone. She needs a doctor.' I was expecting another fake laugh. Instead she slaps me, and again I don't let it affect me, but my arm is itching to respond.

'I told you not interfere. I let her go, you take her place.'

I don't even think. 'Okay.'

Both Mike and the victim shout, 'No!'

This time Mike moves to me. 'What are you doing? Trying to kill yourself?'

'I'm doing something. And you? Your job?'

'Please don't do this.' His eyes plead.

'I won't back down. You can hit as hard as you want.'

He scoffs. 'I'm not going to hit you.'

'Oi. Excuse me?' Carla's voice is accusing. 'You will do what I tell you to.' He turns to her, whip still in hand and his gun strapped to his back.

'I'm not going to hit her. You can forget that.'

'Well, if you won't do your job, there's someone else to do it.' She nods at the other guard, and he moves towards Mike. He whips the deadly rubber close to him as a warning, and stops looking at Carla. She lets out a frustrated shout.

'I have to do everything.' She lunges for Mike, and the other guard moves as well. It all happens very fast, and before I realize, I have the gun in my hand pointed at Carla and the other guard has the whip around his neck.

'She not shoot me. You let him go, Mike.'

'I don't think so.'

'I will kill her, Mike.'

'I don't think so.' I sound confident. I just hope I keep it going. Don't know if I would really and am not sure if I want to find out.

'So how do we solve this? You can point that gun at me forever.' And just then, I know what I want.

'You will leave this place and these people alone.'

'If not me, another will come and do same,' she says with an evil laugh.

'Do you want to find out?'

This time, she takes a step back.

An idea is flicking in the back of my head. A bad idea. *What the hell am I thinking?*

'I won't shoot you.' All eyes flick to me.

Carla's mouth curls into a snide smile. 'I know you won't.'

And Mike shoots me a confuse look. I'm not stopping now. I can't. I move towards the injured woman still tied to the pole. Keeping my gun on Carla, I untie the woman slowly and move her off the pole. I want to clean her wounds and her tears, but I can't stray from my goal. I crouch behind her and hold the gun in her hands.

'It's up to you. Remember all she's done to you, to all your children, and you decide.'

The woman doesn't look at me. She keeps moving her gaze between the gun and Carla. No one else says anything, and all we hear is Carla's voice coming from her half-open mouth.

'You think this starving vagabond woman shoot me? They know they need me.'

I pay Carla no attention. 'What's your name?' The woman turns her head slightly to me, my hands still on hers holding the gun. 'Ramira,' she says. Somehow I have a feeling these names aren't real.

'Well, Ramira, it is your choice. Whatever you decide, we do.' And we're silent for a while. Not even looks are exchanged. Finally, Ramira starts to get up, waving my hands away, refusing my help. She holds the gun, facing Carla.

'I want her to die. I want her to suffer.'

Carla's eyes look like they'll leave their sockets, and I find myself saying, 'Good.'

Ramira continues. 'I can't kill her.' She lowers the gun, and I swear I hear a breath escape Carla's mouth, so I move to take the gun from Ramira, but she takes a step away.

'Ramira, what—?'

'You can't kill her too.'

'You know she wouldn't think twice about killing any of us?' I'm frustrated now. How can she not see?

'She will go away from village and not come back.'

Carla scoffs.

'She won't agree to that. She will come back.' My voice is more cautious now, but I'm still surprised I want to be the judge and executioner of this woman. Ramira looks at Carla, gun still down.

'You go and take your friends.'

Carla sneers. 'We will come back.'

'When you do, I not kill you. He will.' She gestures to Mike, and we're both surprised, gasping at her. I see Mike blush with shame, regret, and I feel sorry for him.

Mike lets go of the other guard and gets the gun from Ramira. I move to get the guards gun, and we start hearing a commotion around us. The rest of the guards are approaching, and I do the logical thing. In seconds, I'm standing next to Carla, gun against her head.

'Baby, don't do it. Not worth it.'

'Ramira, don't worry. I told you it was your choice, and I'll respect that. But I won't die for her.' The guards have us surrounded, but we do not step back. 'You guys put your guns down and move there.' I gesture to the path leaving the village about twenty steps away from me. I just hope that'll be enough. They look at me, puzzled, and turn at Carla, but she nods. They all move, and I nudge Carla to join them. She complies.

'You know there always people to take. If not me, another.' I can't help but smirk at her.

'We'll be here. Don't worry.' As they walk away, I take a deep breath and hear a crash behind me. Ramira is on the floor.

'I'm so sorry.' Mike's eyes are desolate.

'Is okay.' Her smile is so kind that I ache.

'Go get help. I'll stay with her.'

'Okay, take the gun.' I look at Mike and then the gun and shake my head. 'Come on. They could come back. Just take it,' he shouts, and I startle. I can't meet his eyes, but I take the gun.

'Just hang tight, Ramira. Help is on the way.' I hug her and lean her on my lap. She swipes her hand across my face. Very softly.

'You're too kind," Ramira says. 'You need to be careful.'

'I'll be okay. Don't worry about me, Ramira.'

'Oh, baby girl. All that makes me worry because you're very nice, very kind, but really have to be careful.' She keeps cupping my face gently, and I feel loved.

'Don't waste your breath on her, Ramira. I have a feeling she won't listen or change.' Mike's tone is light, like he's trying to make a joke, but I still can't bring myself to look at him. I felt so safe with him last night, like I could trust him with my life. How could he be doing these kind of things? After everything he's been through. His sister? I can't understand.

The doctor brought help and a gurney. But before he moves Ramira, he examines her back carefully. She winces at every touch, and I see Mike's eyes are fixed on his shoes.

'She'll be okay. The cuts aren't too deep.'

Ramira holds her hand up.

'My dear, Mike was being kind to me.' I can't help let a tear roll down my face. Even though I know he was going easy on her, I can't help looking at him differently.

'All right," the doctor says. "I'm taking her now. If you want to visit her, please come tomorrow. I want her to rest.'

We both nod and watch them go. Mike starts to move towards me, and I can't help but take a step back. He stops.

'I not going to hurt you. I would never hurt you.' He holds a hand out, but I don't take it. I look down and realize I still have the gun, so I plant it in his hand. He sighs. 'I hope someday you can forgive me, and I promise to only do good now.'

Finally, my eyes meet his. 'Have you forgiven yourself?' He can't keep his gaze on me. I turn my back and start walking towards town.

I thought I would start seeing people running around, pillaging food, but still no one moves. Maybe they are too afraid. Or too weak. Once in my room I start gathering my things. I'm almost throwing my belongings in my backpack, which is highly ineffective. Half my stuff won't fit that way. I keep thinking, *How is it possible for people to be so horrible? So inhumane? What am I doing here?* Then it hits me. These people need help, real help, the kind of help I cannot offer, and right now, there's only one person I can think to call. But I can't call him. I can't. I cry myself to sleep, can't even tell for how long.

I wake up to a knocking on my door. I want to scream, *Go away*, but I get up instead to find leaning against the door frame a very dishevelled Mike. He looks like he hasn't slept all night, so I open the door wide for him to come in, and I go back to bed.

'I know what I did was bad and unforgivable and for a while I kept telling myself it was okay. In a way I was helping. I see now I was doing the bare minimum and making other people suffer.' I hold my hands up because I know I'll soon start crying, but he keeps going. 'No. I need to get this out—'

I cut him off, shouting, 'So you think you have the right to speak your mind so you can sleep easily?'

I'm expecting him to shout back at me, but all he says is no and sits next to me on the bed.

'I never meant to hurt you, and I didn't want to hurt anyone. But I did, and maybe I'll forgive myself. Maybe I won't.' He holds my chin and makes me look at him. 'But I hope you will one day.' Somehow I find myself smiling at Mike, and then I hug him. We stay like that for a long time until I break away.

'I can't stay here. I'll be leaving later today.'

He nods and lets his head hang down. 'I understand … but maybe just a little longer?' His eyes are on mine, pleading. But I can't change my mind. I don't want to. I'm not finished.

'I'll leave today.' He nods again. 'These people here need help, and I hope you'll be here for them, but—'

He cuts me off and stands. 'I'll be here yes. I'll do everything that I can to help everyone and make things better. You have to believe me.'

'I know you will. But honestly, I don't think it will be enough. They need a lot of help right now.' I move to him and slowly slide my palm along his right cheek. He leans into it, but after a beat, he scoffs, waving my hand away.

'And you're leaving?' He has no right to be pissed at me, but I need to let it go.

'I know some people that might be able to help. I hope.'

'Fine.' I move towards him again, but he steps back. I stop and smile.

'I'm going to make some calls, visit Ramira, and then I'll leave.' I wait for a reaction, but his eyes are trained on the floor. 'I hope you'll be okay. If you need anything, you can just call me.' I have no answer from him, so I go and start changing clothes.

'Are you serious?'

I shrug. 'What? It's not like you haven't seen me naked before.' He turns around, and I chuckle while I change.

'Okay. Mr Prude, I'm all decent.'

He turns. 'Don't smile at me like that. I don't deserve it.'

'No, you don't. But I believe in you, and one day, I know you will.' I'm caressing his cheek, and he pulls me towards him. It's said that a nice strong hug can heal any pain. Whoever came up with that was so right. Again, I want to stay here in this moment and forget everything, the whole world. But I can't. 'So I have a call to make.'

'Say goodbye to me before you go?'

I was hoping this would have been the goodbye. It's just going to get harder, but I nod, grab my bag, and make way to the improvised hospital. I stop in the middle of the village. It still looks like nothing happened. I finally get my phone out, and on the third ring, Nat answers.

'Violet Smith," Nat says. "I was about to call all embassies in the world.'

I can't help but chuckle.

'I'm not joking. It's not funny, V.'

'I know, Nat. Calm down. I'm fine.'

'Are you sure? Everything is okay? Why didn't you call sooner?' She's going crazy with the questions.

'Nat, I'm fine, and I have to save money and battery, babe. For, you know, an actual emergency.' I almost spell out the word.

'I'm sorry. We're just been worried.'

'I know. Sorry. All is … going, and you guys?' I'm sighing.

'Well, you know, same old.' I've known her for a long time. She's hiding something.

'Nat, what is it?'

'Do you have time for gossip?'

I chuckle. 'Yes, spill.'

'Okay. Do you remember the party we went on my hen night?'

'How could I forget?' I try to keep images of memories coming to my mind.

'Well, turns out Charlotte kept in contact with Charlie.'

'You serious?'

'Yup. They kept going out, and now they are seriously going out, as in together going out.'

'Wow. That's amazing I'm happy for her.' Silence fills the line. I actually think I lost her when she breaks it.

'Are you okay?' I guess she knows me pretty well too.

'I need a favour.'

'Do you need money?'

'No, Nat, I'm good.'

'Are you really? Tell me.'

'I'm good. I need help with a village.'

'What?' She's confused.

'I'm in a village in Somalia I'll give you all the details.'

'You're in Somalia? And you need help?' I keep humming. 'And you're still telling me you're okay?'

'The people in the village need help. They will die without care or food. And they also need medication.'

'Babe, I love you, and I love what you're doing really. But what am I supposed to do?'

'I'll send you an email with all the information.' I take a breath. 'I need you to get the information to Tom.'

'Tom? Are you sure?'

'Yes. Send it through Scarlett maybe. Don't mention me.' Another deep breath.

'How am I not going to mention you? I can't do that.'

'Just try. If you can't, then you can't. We just need to get these people help as soon as possible.'

'Okay, I'll just send what you need.'

'Thanks, hon. I have to go now, okay?'

'Okay, babe. Be safe and send news more often okay? Love you.'

'I promise. Bye, hon.'

Chapter 4

On my way to Zambia, I stop in Nairobi. Capital of Kenya. It'll give me a chance to take a proper shower and get some more cash.

It wasn't easy saying goodbye to Ramira. She kept telling me to go home. Be safe. I just hope she is safe. Mike, on the other hand, wanted to handcuff me to a pipe. I hope they'll get all the help they need.

All I want to do after a thorough bath is sleep. A long. Long sleep.

The next day, I wonder Nairobi. It feels strange seeing a modern city after all the places and misery I've witnessed. I came to know that there's a national park where they take care of endangered species. Breeding them and giving them shelter. There's also an elephant orphanage called David Sheldrick Wildlife Trust, I think. Once there in the middle of the animals, I can't help but think that maybe this is what I should be doing, saving animals. Most humans have lost their humanity, do not deserve salvation.

After spending the day with the animals and finally taking some pictures, I ask at the hotel what the best way to get to Zambia is. And by best, I mean safest. I'm told that is too far I should stop somewhere on the way there. The safest is Tanzania. Precisely the centre of it. The receptionist carries a tone as if that's the only place to be.

Early morning, I hop on a tour jeep to Tanzania. The driver talks all the way explaining customs, buildings, plants, and the way the animals move. I keep taking pictures and listening. We stop in Babati. There's another national park with some tents we can sleep in. I just hope we won't have any four legged visitors, but the driver assures us that it's safe.

I wanted to walk. I really did, but they all said it was too far and too dangerous. It's only three days, I keep saying to myself. Only three. But I stick with the jeep. The silence is bliss, just animal sounds and some hushed voices. Seems like no one wants to make a noise.

I wake up in the middle of the night, panting and cursing. Another nightmare. Another death. Again, Tom is there, and there's an explosion or something. Why is he there? V, it's a dream. Calm down. I try to go back to sleep but no luck. Keep trying to remember the dream, but I can only get flashes that I can't really make sense of.

The next day, we set out after ten in the morning for some reason. And in a little over six hours, we arrive in Tanzania. We're dropped in Dodoma and given a few masks since Tanzania is heavily affected by malaria. I get all the supplies I need and make sure I'm charged up before I make my way to Iringa. I figured I would stop there before carrying to Zambia.

After a very picturesque five-hour walk, I arrive at Iringa. The town is nested by a cliff and overlooks a big valley. There's lots of sights to visit in Iringa, but I don't plan on staying so I get a room for the night.

For the next day and a half, I make my way to Zambia stopping in Mbeya to see the beautiful wild flowers and the national park. It's a sight worth seeing. Then I visit Kasama. I couldn't miss the largest rock art in Southern Africa. Next stop I make is Serenje, and I regret not checking my email in Kasama. There is absolutely no reception here. The only interesting thing about is the fact that there's a train line, which would have been good for me to have found out earlier.

I keep repeating to myself as I enter Zambia, *No pictures at movements or law enforcement. No medication on me.* I just can't believe that homosexuality is illegal. How is it possible that people can't still live free? After checking in a little hotel in Lusaka I finally check my email. Nat has answered

Hey, hon,

I hope you're okay. By now you must be nearly in Zambia. I read on it please be careful. You'll be happy to know that Tom got an army of people to the village. Things are getting much better there. I don't know many details, but at least, it's good news. Tom keeps asking for you, asking what you were doing there, and, hon, I'm tired of lying to him. I think he deserves to know what you're doing. I'm not saying to tell him where you are, although he wasn't happy you were there alone. But tell him something. He's worried. We all are. Anyway, keep in touch and be safe.

Love you.

I take a very slow deep breath. Hold it in and exhale slowly. I'm so relieved that they got help. I'm imagining Ramira by the river with all her kids.

Can't really blame Nat for spilling to Tom he would eventually find out. He meeting Mike should be fun.

Hey Nat,

Hope you guys are okay. I'm so happy that they are getting help. I can't thank you enough. Actually, thank Scarlett and Tom for me, and, yes, you can tell them. It'll be fine.

I'm in Zambia now but don't think I'll stay here much longer. Things are … strict, and you know I'm not the kind of person to keep my mouth shut. So I might make my way to Zimbabwe tomorrow. Take care.

Love you.

I know I can't stay here. There's not much I can help with in the city, and like Mike said, I'll most definitely get myself killed. Better keep on moving.

There are so many issues in Zambia I don't even know how they manage.

From child malnutrition or lack of education to child marriage and poor sanitation. At least, UNICEF is working deep in the country to save as many children as possible, but there's never enough help.

I try to take a main road. It's a dirt road. But seeing as it's the only one, it's the main road. I'm definitely not taking any trails here. This time, I won't go through any big city. No point in doing that. I have a map. Yes, a paper map. Better to save battery on my phone. The plan is to settle for a few days in Mutimutema, a small village with tobacco farms. I keep being told that is going to be difficult and dangerous, that the road connecting Masuka to Mutimutema is being rebuilt. But I mean I'm walking, and I'm not going that way. To get there, it'll take me over four days. I'll have to stop in a lot of places.

So that's what I do. Sometimes I run when I hear weird noises. I even hide in between bushes other times. There's a lot of borders and checkpoints. Most times, it's very intimidating, but I can't freak out. That's worse. After going through Chirundu and Magunje, I'm told the next place to stop is my waypoint. That is going to be a very long stretch. I should have brought a tent. So I decide to email Nat. It might be a good idea that someone knows my exact location. You never know. She has responded:

> Hey babe,
>
> Hope you're okay and safe. Things in the village are getting much better. Tom is trying to get a school built there, and the water is all clean. Darling, I gave him your email. I hope you don't get mad at me.
>
> Love you. Be safe.

I have tears running down my cheeks. Finally, I helped someone or, at least, tried. I scan my emails, but there's nothing from Tom. Was I really expecting him to write? Can't think about that now.

> Hey Nat,
>
> I'm really happy that the village is growing into a town I'm sure it is in great hands. I thought I would let you know where I am. Just an update. I'm going to Mutimutema in Zimbabwe I'm in Magunje today. I hope day after tomorrow I will be there. Love.

I hope I didn't sound too scared. Because I really am.

Halfway there, I keep debating with myself. Should I keep to the road, or should I take detours sometimes? Every (rare) time I see a car or van coming, I move to the trails. People get kidnaped here, but if I keep to the trails, I might find some lost tribe or something. I'm scared. Movies mess us up. Thank God I found a place to get a tent. It's a day and a half there. I have to sleep somewhere.

Chapter 5

The smell burns my eyes. I can feel it burning my nostrils as I inhale. What you read in the news is not what you see, the subsided growth of the town, the monetary investment made to boost the tobacco industry, especially the green leaf tobacco making it the biggest currency in Zimbabwe. I researched all of this while I was in Magunje, but getting here, seeing all this, I feel like the earth is turning slower. Like all of it just stops. It's hard to describe. There are fields until the eye can see. There are old people, children, and women working. There are guards around and a cloud of smoke engulfing them. I can't move. I can't think or say anything. Three months ago, I was arguing because I didn't want to go to a privileged, celebrity-filled party. Could I have been anymore selfish?

I wake up with a horn and a shake of my arm, an old lady is gently pulling me to the side of the field toward a guard. I keep asking if anyone speaks English, but no luck so far. I have a feeling some of these people aren't working here on free will. I head to a big cabana. Looks like a compound of some kind.

'Hello, miss. Are you okay?' Wow. Wasn't expecting to be greeted like that.

'Hi. Yes, I'm good. I'm Violet. I'm just travelling around seeing the world, you know?'

'And you came here?' They exchange looks, and I chuckle a little.

'Well, yeah. I'm on my way to Gwanda. Came from Magunje. I'm a little tired, so I thought maybe I could rest here.' I try to convey a tone, making sure they know it's a question.

'You came from Magunje? That's far.'

'Actually, I came from England. That's further.' They laugh and nod. I have no intention to go to Gwanda, but somehow I don't think they need to know that.

'There are no places available here.' I nod. 'But you have a sleeping bag so you can stay here. Sleep on the floor. At least, it's safe.' For some reason, the way he says it sends shivers down my spine.

'Thank you. Is it okay if I cook something? I have a little stove.'

They look at each other and smile. One stands and walks towards me 'Come. I'll show you where you can set up your things.'

I thank him, and we walk inland. Only then, I notice that this isn't a village. It's a well-set-up organization – planting, harvesting, processing. And it looks like there's a building for everything. There are people everywhere, carrying bags on their backs. There are little buildings around I assume are houses. He leads me to a large building. Once there, I see it's like a mess hall, long tables with benches.

'I'll ask the cook to make something hot for you. In the building next door, a lot of people sleep in hammocks. You can set your sleeping bag there on the floor okay?'

I nod. 'Yes. Thank you so much. You sure I can eat? Won't they need it more?' I gesture out towards the building, to all the silently suffering people.

He looks out and then at me. 'We have enough. Don't worry.'

I nod again and walk towards the cooking station. He stops me. 'You're welcome to stay. But if you're going to stay for long, you'll have to work.' He holds my shoulder while he talks, very slowly, not dropping his gaze from mine.

'I don't mind work. Anything if I can help.'

He drops his hand and his already dark eyes turn pitch black. 'We have a system here. It works, and things are the way they are. You're not to interfere or do anything differently. You understand?'

I get a déjà vu feeling. I've heard that before. I know what it means. 'Okay. No problem.'

My eyes burn. My throat hurts from coughing so much. How can people live like this? It's been five days, and Frank, one of the guards, keeps telling me that's normal. I'll adjust. I just feel like I'm dying slowly. I've seen things, things that make me want to interfere, but I can't. At least, not yet.

I've been doing what I'm told. Trying to keep my head down, but it's so not easy. I think I might have stumbled into a human trafficking organization. Where do all these people come from? I've seen people arrive and people leave. It has been only five days.

'Today I need you in the processing building. We're a few people down,' one of the guards tells me, and I'm left thinking, *Jeez, I wonder where they went.*

'Sure, no problem.' There's not much more I can say. For now, I need the access. I've been trying to get into the building at night, but security runs so tight that makes me wonder how I'll ever help anyone. I know that something happens here. People go in, but they don't always come out. Let's just hope I can do something before I disappear as well.

A lot of the workers speak Spanish, so I can understand a little, but anytime I ask them something, all they say is no and scatter away. They're too afraid. I don't know if I'll be able to come back here tomorrow, so I need to find something today. Consuela is the only one who talks to me. She's also the one who pulled me out of the road when I first arrived. She's my only option.

'No, senorita. No puedo.'

'Consuela, please. Tengo que saber.'

She cries and keeps looking around. 'Moriremos.'

'No. No dejare. Quiero ayudar.'

'No puedo ayudar. Tengo hijos.' She calms down and points to a door.

'I understand.' I nod. At least, that's something. I can't put someone in danger just to help me help them. That doesn't even make sense. This smoke is making me crazy.

On the afternoon shift, I see the guard distracted. Testing the product, I guess. So I move to the door. It's hard to conceal a gun working here, but since Mike gave it to me, I've always had it on me. Just hope I won't have to use it. I find the door is unlocked. After peeking through, I slide in. They might be trafficking humans, but this isn't it. There are rows and rows of tables covered with crates. Guns. Maybe they are trading them? Need to take a closer look while there's no one around. Some crates are open, and at first, I don't really know what kind of weapon that is. It's not guns, so

I search for labels. It's mines. Like landmines. Angola is just next door. They must be supplying them. I hear voices, and apart from a big loading door, there's just one exit. Where I came through. The room comes to life, and I try my best to stay behind some crates when I hear Frank's voice.

'We need to get them out. It's been too long.'

'If you do that now, they might find it suspicious. I think we have to wait longer.' The door opens again.

'So when will it be ready?'

'Tonight. I think,' Frank answers calmly, as if he were trading cards. What can I do? Think. The room turns dark again, and I move to the door. Shit.

I hear Frank coming back, and I hide under a table. Lights on. Can he see me? He speaks low. 'Yeah, it's me … tonight, yeah … to Angola … no to Jamba first … I don't know we have to move fast … yeah, okay.' What is he planning on his own? I don't know what to do, but I have to take a leap.

After dinner at the mess hall, I go to take a pretend walk around the village, something I do every day, so not suspicious. I see Frank going into the building, so I follow. He turns.

'Miss Violet. Out of your usual path tonight, no?'

How am I going to approach this? Smile on.

'Yeah, just to be different.'

'I have work to do. Anything I can do for you?' Now or never. I take a look around to make sure we're alone.

'Actually, yes.' Raised brows invite me to continue. 'I was wondering what you guys are doing with these landmines and how I can help.' It takes him a beat. Out of the daze, he grabs my arm and drags me to into the back room. It was not a good idea to hide the gun on my ankle.

'How do you know about this? What do you know? Someone sent you?' He points the gun at me, at the mines, and all around, but speaks in a very low voice.

'I don't know anything. I just found the room. What are you guys doing? Killing more people? More children in Angola?'

'It seems you know a lot.' He narrows his eyes and glares at me.

'I don't. Just heard your conversation.' Is it wise to tell him the truth? He lowers the gun.

'Okay. You can't tell anyone, and you can't do anything—'

'But these people clearly need help.'

'Shss. Keep your voice down. Listen. I know they need help, and right now, you just have to trust me because I don't have time to explain. They'll be here any minute.'

'Dude, I don't know you I can't trust you when all I see is you hurting people and people disappearing.'

'You've never seen me hurting anyone, and, yes, people are going, but right now, please, you have to go. Please.'

It's not like I really trust him, but if he was going to hurt me or turn me in, he would have, right? No sleep tonight.

Next day, I go back to the processing building. Frank is patrolling here today, so I try to get him to talk, but the whole day he keeps telling me not. 'Not now. Later.' Maybe I made a mistake trusting him. I'm so restless. Don't know what to do so I go for my walk as always. I guess later is now because Frank is behind a building, gesturing me to follow.

'Finally. Are you going to tell me now what's going on?'

'Yes. But first you need to keep your damn voice down. We can't get caught.' He's still grabbing my arm pulling me around the building, and he seems annoyed with me. *He's* annoyed.

'Okay, sorry. But you got to start talking because I'm a bit confused.'

Letting go of my arm, he sighs heavily. 'I don't even know where to begin.'

'Usually the beginning is a good start.' I don't mean to be snarky or disrespectful really. I don't. But that's how he takes it.

'You're such a smartass. You don't know anything.'

'Well, tell me then, and I won't have to make assumptions.' Another heavy sigh and he looks away.

'I work with NATO. We try to deactivate as many mines as we can on the way, and there's people on the other side trying to do the same. But it's never enough. So you see we need to be careful and quiet so we don't get caught get it?' His eyes are bulging, a warning.

'Okay. But what's happening to the people? They come; they go. What's happening?'

'When we ship the mines, we also get some people out. But it's not easy, and we have to do it a few people at a time.' He lowers his head.

'Is that not a good thing?'

'It would be if we could get more people out then the ones arriving.'

'Oh. Where do they come from?'

'Hum … kidnaped, I guess … tricked …' He seems almost broken.

'How long have you been doing this?'

'Three years and it still feels like the first day. I haven't changed a thing.' The look in his eyes makes me feel so powerless. He looks so defeated. Looks like he's fifty, but I suspect he might be younger than that.

'At least, you're trying. That's all we can do we can try and make a change, but we don't control everything.'

His look softens a little, and he gives me a nod. 'You seem a little too wise for your age.' He chuckles. 'But you know I'm tired of trying tired of doing the bare minimum.'

'I know how you feel believe me.'

So I tell him everything, what I was doing before and the disappointment in myself for doing just the bare minimum. I tell him about the party (minus specifics of Tom) and the charity table. I tell him all about the village in Somalia.

'I guess you're tougher than I thought.' He's teasing me, but I smile.

'Yeah. So what happens to the mines that you guys can't get out?'

'Um … unfortunately, I think they get to Angola and … are put to use.'

I start pacing. He's right we have to do something more. Back and forth, I go.

'Will you stop that? You're making me nervous.'

'Frank. Let's say you have someone in those camps in Angola, someone trained to deactivate those mines. That would help, right?' He's looking at me, and I can see gears turning.

'Maybe, yeah, but we would have to train someone, and the only person here that knows how it's me, but I'm not leaving these people, Miss.'

'Stop calling me that.' I so hate it. Then a smile spreads across my face.

'You're right. This isn't working. We have to do more.'

'And that's amusing to you?'

'Listen. It wouldn't be weird if I left.'

'What do you mean? Do you know how to do it?'

I laugh. 'Ah. No but you could teach me, and then I can go there.

We keep in touch so I know when new shipments are coming, and I'll get more help in I'm sure.'

'Help from the same person that helped you in Somalia?' He looks at me weird. Like he doesn't believe me. Like I'm crazy.

'If he's available, or maybe someone else.'

'You know someone else?'

'No, but he does.'

'And he would help you with something like this?'

'I think so yes.'

'And you trust him?' So many bloody questions.

'With my life. Listen, I'm offering to do this. Why are you giving me such a hard time?'

'You need to understand this isn't about you or me. It's about them.' He takes a step back and breathes to the sky, then gestures to the cabanas.

'I know it is. If I didn't know that, if I didn't care, I wouldn't be here, don't you think?'

He eyes me for a long time, and I start pacing again.

'We'll start tomorrow, but we have to be careful. Any sign of suspicion, we abort, and I'll try and find out the exact places where the trucks go now. They keep changing.'

I nod.

'You can't change anything in the meantime, okay?'

Another nod.

'I'm serious, V. You can't interfere with anything and jeopardise all of this, understand?'

'Okay. Okay, I get it.'

And that's what we do for the next two weeks. I have so many near misses that I start having dreams of sea of landmines. Frank teases me every time I cut the wrong wire, every time I forget a step. Makes me want to punch him, especially every time he scares me when I'm trying to concentrate.

'You keep forgetting steps.'

'I know. I'm trying. It's not easy. You don't make it easy.'

'It's not supposed to be easy. You have to concentrate even with distractions. It's been two weeks, and you should be able to do it by now.'

'I am.' We keep arguing for the next half hour. I don't even think I'm paying attention to what I'm doing anymore.

'Stop yelling at me. Stop asking me things. No, I'm not done.' I'm waving my arms around so ferociously that he grabs both of them mid-air.

'Stop that. You'll make even more noise.'

'Sorry, but you're driving me crazy, man. Can't you lay off for a bit?' He chuckles.

'Of course, it would be funny to you.'

'Do you know how long it takes for a proper trainee to learn this?'

'Yeah, I know. I'm trying my best, okay? You don't need to be a dick about it.' I didn't mean to say it really, but I couldn't stop myself. The man has been driving me crazy for the past couple of weeks. He had it coming. No jerk eyes, a yell, or even slap. Instead, he laughs.

'Good for you. It takes months for a normal trainee.'

'What? I still have to do this for months? We don't have time for …'

He cuts me off with a raised hand. 'No, you won't have to.'

'I don't get it. You're getting someone else? Just give me another chance. I know …'

Another raised hand. 'Damn, you talk, woman. You don't have to because you're ready. You have been for a while actually, but we didn't have all the info on the villages, so …'

'You decided to have a little fun with me. I could have gotten us killed.'

'Hardly.'

'What do you mean?' He looks so guilty.

'For that to happen, the mines need a key component, which is only installed when they are activated on the ground. These are harmless.'

My jaw is on the floor. I'm so pissed that I throw a mine at him.

'Are you crazy? What if I had dropped it? You can get us caught.'

'Calm down I knew you would catch it. So what now?'

'Now we get you out.'

'I can just go. I mean, I did say I was going to stay for a while and then carry on. Everyone knows that.'

'They'll never let you go now. You've seen too much.'

'Seriously?'

He nods, thinking.

'We're sending people tomorrow. You'll have to be ready by midnight. Meet me at my bunker an hour before, okay?'

I nod and feel a tightness on my stomach, and he squeezes my shoulder before we put everything back and leave.

The day crawls, but my fear increases. One false move and not only are we both dead but also the people in town. I need to say something to Nat, but I can't tell her everything. She'll get worried, and this time, she really might call all embassies. I have to keep it light, but before I get to open a new email draft, Tom's name sits there. In my inbox below Nat's. My heart stomps. My breath catches. I open Nat's first.

Hi darling,

It's been so long without news ... I hope you're okay. Tom told me not to call your phone. I don't really know why, but I trust him, I guess. You should talk to him. Please answer back soon. I miss you. Love you. Be safe.

I know why he told her not to call my phone. Mike must have told him everything.

Hey hon,

Sorry it has been so long. There's not much reception here, and I couldn't top up my phone. There's a lot to do here in Mutimutema, but we're so close to Angola that I might go there. I'm not sure. I'll let you know.

I hope things are good there, and I miss you guys too. So much you have no idea. Thank you for keep talking to me. Helped keep me sane. You're a lifesaver. I hope you know that. I love you really. Thank you for everything. Talk to you soon.

Is that an obvious goodbye? I hope not. With palpitations, I open Tom's email.

Hi Violet,

It's been a while. You know, when I said you could try, I didn't mean what you're doing. J But I guess that's the kind of person you are. We're all very proud of you.

I think you'll be happy to know that I finally got enough financing to build the school. Yesterday, actually. Scarlett and I bothered so many people that they couldn't say no. We start construction in a week. It's incredible, the growth of the town. I need to get some pictures to you. Or maybe you could come and see.

It took me about two hours to write this email. I kept deleting and rewriting. I wasn't sure what to say. I miss you.

I really hope you're being safe. Mike told me all the things you've done, and Nat keeps telling me more. Like I said, we're very proud, but please be careful – the world can't be changed in one day. Anyway, if you ever need anything, please call me. My number is at the end of the email. If you come back to Somalia, I'll be there in a week. Maybe we could talk? I'm working with the charity this month. It's amazing the things we do; you should see it. Take care of yourself and please be safe.

Tom

I don't even know what to think. He misses me. The town is growing, and I would really like to see it. He misses me. He wants to see me. He misses me. I haven't seen him in over four months, and I still can't stop thinking about him or fantasizing about meeting with him in Somalia, but that's not going to happen. I have things to do. What do I say?

Hello Tom,

I know it's been a long time. I'm sorry. But I hope you better than anyone will understand. The world is crazy. Sometimes I still think I'm dreaming because the things I see can't possibly be true. You were right. If I let it, it'll crush my soul, but I have a motto that I've been passing around: 'I can try.' Thank you for that. It's been keeping me sane.

I don't even know how to thank you for helping the village. Really. Really, thank you. You're their saviour. I would love to visit them again and see how they are doing, but I don't think I'll be able to anytime soon. There's a lot of places I would like to visit still. Like Angola, maybe. Might go there soon. I'm not sure yet. Right now, I'm helping in a town in Mutimutema. There's a lot of good people here, but there's so much suffering it's hard to watch. Hopefully, we'll make a change here as well.

Thank you for all your help and for writing.

Take care,

V

I so wanted to tell him, 'I miss you too. Can't wait to see you.' How complicated would that be? I have to focus on the objective – helping these people and the ones in Angola. That's all that matters right now. I hope he understands that. But my fingers are itching. I have his number. What harm will do for him to have mine?

Hey Tom,
It's V. Saw your email today. Thanks. Just thought you could have my number as well. Please do not call. Thanks.
That's okay, right? Not too forward. I have to turn off the phone now. Can't take any risks.
Ryan comes to get me. He's been working with Frank.
'You ready?' He smiles at me.

'As ready as I'll ever be.' I let a scatter sigh out.

'That wasn't very convincing, doll.' He always calls me that. Such a sweet old man.

'Wasn't I supposed to meet with Frank?'

'Yeah, but he's busy now. Come on.'

'Let's do it.' As we're about to leave the cabana, another guard is walking by. 'Hey, what's up, Ryan?'

'Not much. Just checking on things.' Ryan stands at the door frame, and I'm behind the door.

'Yeah. Hey have you seen V? Didn't see her out for her walk tonight.' Shit. I guess we forgot that little detail. Tell him I left. Something.

'I don't know haven't seen her.' He shrugs as he exits.

'I got to go now. Lots to do.'

'Yeah, I know. It's you and Frank tonight, right?'

'Yup.'

'All right, have a good one.' I hear Ryan moving on down the path. He left the door open, and the other guard steps inside. And stops on the same spot Ryan was standing. Please don't come in. He turns and closes the door behind him. I breathe out, but what do I do now? I didn't hear him move. I think he's still outside. Then I start hearing a noise, not exactly knocking more like scraping. Might be someone in their sleep. I try to ignore it, but it keeps happening. Thank God for Ryan. Never noticed there was a window at the end of the cabana. Backpack goes first.

'Thanks.'

'Sorry, doll. He's not supposed to be there, and I have a feeling he's going to keep looking for you. We have to hurry.'

'Okay. What are you going to tell him tomorrow?'

'I know nothing. If you're not there, you must have left in the middle of the night.' He winks at me and carries my backpack.

I'm in a dark truck. There's a few people with me and a letter from Frank to his contact. We are going to Jamba. Between somewhere there and Luiana, someone will get us out and steal some landmines. Same as always. Most people will have places to go. From there, I'll be dropped with some of the landmines to Muie. There are a lot of places that still have landmines, but we will start there. It will take a long time to get there, and we can't take main roads. Let's do this.

Chapter 6

Sometimes I feel like we're climbing mountains with the jeep, and I keep thinking we're going to flip over, but the driver seems to be in total control. He's even got time to take a hand off the wheel to smoke. I'm freaking out.

Flashing light and a jolt. I wake up.

Sweating. Panting. And screaming. 'Calm, Miss. Is okay. We almost there.' It takes me a minute to calm down. We didn't turn over. I just died again. Why do I keep dreaming this? Tom. Bomb death. Actually, I start getting worried. I'm carrying landmines. I'm going to be working with them. Have I been having dreams as a premonition? Is that how I'm really going to die? That's crazy. I don't believe in that, and it's crazy, right? Must be the lack of fumes in my head. I must be detoxing.

It takes us about eight hours to get there. Everyone is very friendly and helpful. I drop my backpack and start helping unload the truck when a hand settles on my shoulder heavily.

'You must be Violet.'

'Yes. You're Mark?'

'Yeah.'

'Frank asked me to give you this.' I hand him the letter, and he slides it in his pocket. He clearly isn't as old as Mark, but working in this place seems like it taken a lot out of him. His curly light blond hair accentuates all his harsh lines from constant worry and long hours. This isn't a life for just anyone, how long will I last?

'You're not going to read it?'

'Not now. We have guests. I'm sure you're hungry and maybe need some rest.' He smiles at me before walking away, and gratefully, I follow.

There isn't a gun in sight. I see authority figures, but no one carries a gun. This is new.

'So I'll get something for you to eat and—'

'It's okay. I have some crackers, and it's late.' He watches me as I reach my backpack to fish the crackers. 'See?'

'Crackers are for parrots. I'll get the food. You settle in there. First hammock to the left is yours.' He laughs.

'Wait, a hammock?'

'You don't know what that is?' He raises his eyebrows in disbelief.

'Yes, I know, but I've never slept in one.' My tone is both sarcastic and embarrassed.

'There's nothing to it, doll. Just lie on it.' Mark isn't as old as Ryan, but I still find it sweet to be called that. I stand in front of the improvised bed. 'Just lie on in. There's nothing to it.'

I have played on a hammock before, but I have a feeling I won't be very comfortable sleeping on one. I sit on it, have to start slow, and Mark comes back, speaking in hushed tones.

'Here, doll. Have this and then have some rest. We'll do a tour tomorrow.'

'Thanks, Mark.' A lovely bowl of hot soup. I'm in heaven, and I know I'm having selfish thoughts but can't help it. It's been a while since I felt such comfort.

There's good reception here, so I fish for my phone. Email and text Nat answered fast.

> How long have we known each other? Really think about it. Must be what? Seven or eight years? I know you even when you're writing to me. I can tell when you're happy and when you're scared, and I can also tell when you're trying to say goodbye to me. I won't take it. You better keep writing me and being safe, or I'll get on as many planes as needed to go and get you. So this is me saying until next time, babe. Take care.

I'm crying and smiling to myself. Of course, she saw right through what I wrote. Guess I was kind of expecting that.

Hi darling,

Yes, it's been about eight years, and you never disappoint. I promise I won't do it again. Sorry. Everything is good and hope things there are great. Kisses to the girls. Love you.

Next I open Tom's text. Very short.

Hey V. Thanks for the text. Saw your email will get back to you when I can. Take care.

Cold and short. Shouldn't expect more really. He sent me such a vulnerable and honest email, and I brushed over it. Over his feelings. Again. I can't think about it right now. There's a lot for me to worry about, so I sleep – on the floor.

Mark shakes me awake. 'Why the hell are you sleeping on the floor?'

'And good morning to you too. This thing doesn't agree with me.'

'The hammock?'

'Yeah. I don't know how people can balance on that.'

'You're joking, right?'

'Yeah, of course,' I lie. 'I just became used to the floor.'

'Okay, let's go then. There's a lot to see after breakfast.'

'All right. Mark, I meant to tell you. I have a gun. Should I give it to somebody?'

He turns to me quickly with bulging eyes. 'Why do you have a gun?'

'Whoa, calm down. I needed one. I've been in a few dangerous places. I had to be able to protect myself. Don't you think?'

His shoulders relax. 'Yeah, I guess. You can leave it in the office when we go there.'

Four weeks go by, and another shipment comes in. More people are free, but we weren't able to recover nearly as many mines as last time. I've been trying me best to deactivate as many mines as I can, and there's a lot of them, but we're finally getting to a low number. I even have been travelling to neighbouring villages and towns. There are so many amputees waiting for prosthetics. There's never enough for everyone. It's never enough what we do. I've been much more comfortable disabling the mines. I haven't even been wearing the suit anymore. Mark keeps yelling at me, which reminds me of Frank and relaxes me more while I work. Unfortunately, last week, we had an accident. A little girl was playing football too close to the minefield. I can't even think about it anymore. She lost her right leg, and I blame myself.

Why the hell haven't we built a wall around the damn field? Why haven't I thought about it before? I run to the town office. Only when I see people screaming do I realize I'm running with a mine in my hand. What the hell am I doing? Trying to hurt someone else?

'It's okay. Safe. Not armed.'

Lauren is standing by the central office door. Arms crossed shaking her head. 'I don't think that's what you're supposed to do with that. Do you?' She smiles at me. It has been nice to have another woman to work with for a change. She's very nice and patient. She runs this town with such poise it's incredible.

'Hey, can I talk to you for a sec?'

'Put that where it belongs and then meet me inside.' I chuckle as she gestures to the mine in my hands. Once the menace is properly stored, I go back to Lauren.

'What's up?'

'We need a wall.'

'What? Like keep-the-Mexicans-out wall?' She making fun of me, but I keep serious.

'We have to build a wall around the minefields. We can make it safer. Isn't enough to get rid of the mines. It's taking too long.'

'You're always wanting more, Violet. It's incredible.'

She's shaking her head at me again. People do that a lot. Am I that unreasonable? Don't really know what to say, so I just keep looking at her and nod.

'Even if I wanted to, I can't. We don't have the resources for that. All our partners think we have more important issues right now. Besides, there's not many mines left.'

I can tell she doesn't agree. 'That's bullshit.'

'Violet, it's not. We're trying …'

I cut her off, standing. 'No. Not that. I know you're doing what you can. I mean, I don't know. I'll have to think about it.'

She comes to me and puts a hand around my shoulders. 'All we can do is try our best. You told me that. Just be patient. We'll get there. Now leave me the hell alone. I have to prepare for visitors.'

'Anyone important?'

'You mean anyone that maybe can help?'

'Maybe.'

'I don't know. We'll see.' She laughs and nudges me out of the office.

Another week goes by, and I find myself collecting bricks over time. Have to start somewhere, right?

'How do you think you're going to do this? It'll take you years this way.'

'Mark, I just need help.'

'Baby doll, you need to accept defeat sometimes. Can't change everything at once.' He grabs my shoulder and gives it a light squeeze.

I'm so tired of hearing that. I know it's true, and he's trying to make me feel better, but I'm tired. Tired of waiting for better times and change. Tired of being so optimistic saying, 'I can try.' I've been trying for months and haven't changed much. Can't do or change anything without help. I need to punch something.

I take Lauren's advice. She told me the other day I needed a day off. Don't even remember what that is anymore. I miss walking by the river in Somalia. Unfortunately, there isn't any river for miles here, so I've been going away, getting to know the area better. Muie is very little, but we have Lumbala nearby with its own airport. We get all our supplies through there. Just not enough. Never enough.

I'm walking back through Cangamba when my phone rings. It has been such a long time since my phone rang that I don't recognize the sound for a second. It's surprising to have such good reception with so many mountains around. Nat's name flashes on my screen.

'Hey, Nat, are you okay? Something happened?'

'Yes.'

'What? What is it? You had an accident? Are the girls okay? What—'

'Will you let me talk?'

'Sorry. Go on.'

'Well, I'm pregnant.'

I stop in my tracks, yelling and jumping. 'Oh my God, honey. I'm so happy for you. How are you feeling?'

'Still the same. It's still new. It's like, when I stopped thinking and stressing about it, it just happened. I'm so relieved.' She lets out a slow and long breath, and I cry missing her hugs.

'I'm really happy, darling. I wish I was there with you.'

Silence fills the line for a while.

'You can, you know? Maybe you have done enough. Maybe it's time for you to come home.'

I shake my head as I talk. 'I can't, hon. There's a lot to do, and we're really helping people.'

She knows by now she shouldn't press. 'Okay. Have you spoken to Tom?'

I wasn't expecting her to ask. 'You know that I have, missy. He said he has been talking to you.'

'You know. It came to a point I couldn't bullshit anymore, and honestly, I didn't want to.'

I start to laugh.

'Good to know I amuse you.'

'You do.'

'So?'

'So what?'

'Oh, come on. Just tell me. What have you guys been talking about?' She's so excited her voice is shrieking in my ear.

'Nothing much really.' I want to tell her. Tell her everything, but I can't hardly think about it. It hurts. 'I've messed up, babe.'

'What do you mean?'

'With Tom. I've messed up. I keep pushing him away.'

'Why do you do that? It seems to me you guys really like each other. Why don't you want to give it a chance?'

It's the first time we speak about it. I can tell she's being cautious with her hushed tone.

'I'm afraid I guess.'

'I understand. You've been through enough but do you really think that he's like that?'

'I don't know, but it's not just that.'

'Then what?'

'I'm finally doing something important with my life, and I think if I

92

would even give this a thought I might lose myself again. I can't let that happen.'

We've been talking for a while. I've almost walked back to Muie.

'So you're afraid, if you guys get together, you'll just go back to your old life and not help anyone else. Is that it?'

'You know me so well. I guess that's it … maybe?'

'Babe. That will only happen if you want it to. No matter how much you love someone, you can't lose your identity in them, and I'll be honest with you. I don't think Tom would let that happen. He's just not like that.'

'You're starting to get really wise, big momma.'

'Only now? How dare you.'

'Sorry. Sorry.'

We both laugh for a while, and she updates me on the other girls.

'Well, I'll let you go. Just think about what I said okay?'

'Okay, honey, I will and congratulations again. Send me pictures.'

'I will. Love you.'

When I raise my head from the phone, I'm back in the middle of town. It felt good talking to Nat about everything, but I'm still so frustrated with what I can't do that my fingers start to itch again. Gotta punch something.

There are no gyms here obviously, but I have an idea. Behind the main building sits the warehouses. I spot Lauren going in with some people, and judging by the parked cars, I would say these are the visitors, but I can't meet anyone right now. Can't punch someone if you want them to help, right?

Who would know that rice bags were good to punch? I punch until my hands are red with bruises. Until I can't take it anymore. Until I break and cry. By the time I walk back to wash my hands, the cars are gone. Guess I missed my chance to grovel for help. At least, I'm, oh, so much calmer now.

The rest of the afternoon goes by quickly. I don't work on the fields but do odd jobs around town. Eat. Help clean up and go to bed or my very uncooperative hammock. Got to try again. I've been sleeping on the floor for so long. When I get there, everyone is already counting sheep. Here goes nothing.

'Shit.' Of course, I had to fall, but no matter, it's just the first try. This thing should come with instructions. If I turn to a side, I roll off and hit the floor again, but I keep trying for a few minutes until a voice interrupts me.

'What the hell are you doing? Trying to wake up everybody?'

Oh, he's nice.

'Look, man, I'm sorry I just—' As I'm turning to him and the moonlight hits his face, I start thinking I'm dreaming. I'll soon wake up with an explosion, I'm sure. But the end doesn't come. I just stare at him, mouth mute and half parted.

'What are you doing here?' His voice is harsh almost accusing.

'Me? What are you doing here?'

'I told you I was working with the charity for a while. I was coming to Angola.'

'Yeah, but I thought you were going to Luanda or something.'

'What the hell are you doing here? Can't you just sleep quietly like everybody else? These people need rest you know?'

What the hell? Is he serious? Why is he talking to me like that? He doesn't let me talk again. 'Just go to sleep and stay quiet.' He turns his back and goes to sleep on his swinging bed opposite me.

I have no reaction at all. He sounded like he hated me. I get that he might be hurt because I kept pushing him away, but I wasn't expecting this. Hell, I wasn't expecting him, what is Tom doing here? Could Nat have told him? That doesn't make sense, she doesn't know exactly where I am... Not wanting more verbal aggression, I sleep on the floor again. The whole night, I dream of him, how casual and sexy he looked in his black jeans and half-buttoned blue shirt. Damn, he looked good.

First thing I do when I wake up is glance at the bed. But he isn't there. Did I really just dream all of that? I feel like I'm going crazy. Better stop thinking about it and just carry on with my day. Enough time off.

I'm on centre field in the middle of the afternoon when I hear Lauren calling me.

'V, can you come here please?'

'I can't now, Lauren. What's up?' Can't raise my head, so I shout back.

'I would like to introduce you to someone. Some help.' She enunciates those last words, and I know what she means, but I still can't look up.

'Just give me a few minutes, okay? I'm alm—'

I'm cut off by Lauren screaming and a voice cursing next to me.

'Sir, you can't go there.'

'Are you fucking kidding me? You're the landmine specialist?'

It looks like I wasn't dreaming after all, but I'm used to being yelled at while I work, so I carry on, not looking up.

'What's wrong with that?'

'Can't you stop that?'

'No, I'm working.'

'I get that, but can't you just take a break? Can we talk?'

Is he serious? Now he wants to talk?

'You wanna talk, Tom? Talk I'm listening or you can wait until I'm done.' I try to keep impartial, but my voice is coming out impatient. Why is he so pissed?

'Are you serious?'

I don't answer.

'You're unbelievable.'

'What?' I get up with the mine in my hand. He looks at my hands and me and takes a step back. I laugh and move past him. While he follows me with his eyes, I go to place the mine in the crate sitting next to Lauren.

'Is this what you've been doing? Trying to kill yourself?'

Lauren keeps watching us, arms crossed over her chest, moving her head side to side as if she was watching a tennis match.

'I'm doing whatever I can to help. Wherever I go. Trying to help, isn't that what you told me to do?'

'I didn't tell you to do this. To risk your life with no regard for … anything else.' He's gesturing around, not quite meeting my gaze, and now I'm getting pissed.

'You know what? I don't need to listen to this. I'm helping, and if you excuse me, I have work to do.' I walk back to the field and hear him following me.

'Violet, stop. Let's talk.'

'I don't want to talk.'

'You're being selfish.' He stops and shouts it at me, and the whole situation is so ridiculous. We're shouting at each other in the middle of a landmine field.

'Are you kidding me?' I so want to punch him right now.

'I didn't mean it like that, obviously.'

'So what the fuck did you mean, Tom? What exactly are you trying to say?'

'I'm talking about you. About me. Us.' He starts towards me, and I take a step back, and he stops. He really went there. The last thing I want to do is talk about it, much less shout it with an audience.

'There's nothing to talk about. There's no us. There's nothing—'

He doesn't let me finish. He starts shouting again, and I step back once more.

'How can you say that? After everything? After all the moments we shared.'

'No.' I really don't want to hear it, so I keep stepping back.

'You didn't talk to me for months. I only knew a few things from Nat, and even then, she wouldn't tell me everything. Why?'

That's his last shout and my last step. I trip on a rock and fall flat on my ass. It's a funny situation, and even Lauren is laughing. I would be too if I hadn't heard a very familiar sound. Tom starts towards me.

'Come. I'll help you up.'

'Stop. Stay there.' I raise my hand flat.

'Are you serious? I'm just trying to help you up nothing else. Jesus.'

'It's fine. I got it. Just stay away.'

This time, he pulls back his hand and looks at me. He knows.

'Tom, stop. Please.'

But he keeps moving towards me until he kneels in front of me. 'What can I do?'

I smile and slide my right hand down his face, and he closes his eyes. 'I missed you.'

'I know.' He gives me a cocked smile, and, boy, how I missed that smugness.

'Now. How can we fix this?' He's rubbing his hands together and looking down between my legs. This is not the situation I was hoping that would happen in. The situation is ridiculous and uncomfortable, and I start to blush. Was hoping he wouldn't notice, but no chance of that, of course. He laughs and moves to kiss my forehead.

'Stop.'

'What?'

'Any change in pressure will set it off.'

He exhales. 'Sorry. I didn't know. So tell me: Who should I call?' He turns to Lauren. 'Hey, Lauren.' She was about to go back to her office.

96

Don't think she noticed what happened. She turns, and I watch their exchange, and he comes back to me.

'So you're the only one that does this?' I nod. 'Ever occurred to you to teach someone else?'

I know he's trying to lighten the mood, but I don't find it funny. 'Seriously? Right now?'

He holds his hands up in defeat. And we sit there in silence for a little while until I break it.

'Okay go put on the suit.'

He looks at me confused.

'The anti-mine suit. Maybe I can guide you.'

'Look, I don't know what I'm doing.' He's shaking his head.

'Okay, so go get Mark. Tell him—'

'No. No. That's not what I'm saying. I don't know, and if I put on the suit, I don't think I'll be able to see or move properly to help you.'

'Fine. Now listen: you have to do exactly as I say, okay?'

'Of course.' And then I do the only thing I can to give him access to the mine. I spread my legs, and a huge grin spreads across his face. Why did I have to wear shorts today?

'Tom, focus.'

'Oh, I am. Believe me.' He moves in between my legs, and I can't help but smile and shake my head. My heart races and not because of the bomb beneath me.

'I'll help you on one condition.'

'You're joking, right?' He shakes his head. He's so close. 'So you'll let me die if I refuse?'

'Of course not. But I might make you wait a bit longer.'

'That's cruel. I can't believe you're blackmailing me.'

'I am. So what's it going to be?'

'What do you want?'

'What I wanted since we met. At the party. At the balcony. At the London Eye.'

'And what's that?' I missed that intense gaze of his. It makes my heart race, and my breath catches.

'I want my kiss.' This has been a long time coming, and he's right. It already belongs to him. One look is all it takes. He caresses my cheek and slides his thumb along my bottom lip, and for a second, I forget where I am and start leaning into him. All I can think about is kissing him. Thankfully, one of us has a grasp on reality. He lightly presses my shoulders back.

'What are you doing?'

'Sorry. Forgot where I was. You have that effect on me, you know?' He tilts his head to the side, smiles, and kisses my nose. I can't help but laugh. 'Is that it? That's the kiss you've been waiting for this whole time?'

He looks me deep in the eyes and very seriously and slowly says, 'No. But the kind of kiss I want involves movement, and I don't think that's a good idea right now.'

I shiver and blush at his words. This man drives me crazy.

'Okay. So go get my extra tool bag. It's by my bed, and bring one of the deactivated mines from the crate.'

After a few minutes, he comes back and puts the bag next to him.

'There's a flashlight in there if you need. You see the mine has an opening panel on the side. We access the wires from there. You see it?' I explain him as he manoeuvres the deactivated mine and tell him everything he needs to know. Step by step. 'Any questions?'

'Not right now.'

'Okay, so take a look and see if you can open the cover.'

He grabs the flashlight and a knife and buries his face between my legs. I blush again. After a few seconds, he goes around to look at my back.

'Not enough of a view at the front?' A couple more seconds and he looks at me, worried.

'What? You can't open it?'

'The thing is, the cover is to the other side. I don't know …'

He lowers his head, and I touch his arm. 'It's okay. Don't worry.'

'Wow, you're very calm for this situation.'

'Well, the man that trained me deactivating the mines was constantly screaming at me while I was doing it, so I got used to working in the chaos.'

'I still can't believe you have been doing this. You're amazing.'

'Okay, don't go all mushy on me. You need to twist it.'

'What? Are you crazy?'

'Don't call me crazy, and it's okay. You just have to make sure you don't apply pressure down. Just twist it.'

'Oh, it's that easy is it?'

The pain on my lower back is killing me, but I reach for his hand. 'You'll do great. Just remember to remain calm, and if you start trembling, just stop and collect yourself, okay?'

He nods and puts the tools down. I can feel his warm breath in between my thighs. It's weird to feel like this in this situation. I take a shaking deep breath when I feel his hand brushing my thigh.

'You know. This is definitely not how I imagined being in this position for the first time.'

'You have imagined it?'

I look down and laugh. His face meets mine. I feel myself panting, and by the way his chest is moving, I would say he feels exactly like I do. His voice comes out low and rough, and he doesn't break eye contact with me.

'I think I need a break.'

We both smile and keep our eyes connected.

'This isn't as easy as I thought.' He caresses my cheeks again and grabs the tools.

'What are you doing?'

'I'm going to remove the cover. That's the next step, right?'

'Yeah, but you still have to twist it.'

'It's done.' And he busies himself at my centre again.

'Wow, that's some good work. I didn't feel a thing.'

'Don't have too high hopes for me, I see.'

'No, I mean. That is something hard to do, and with my weight on it, I didn't feel a thing. That's a compliment.'

'You're not that heavy. Now is the hard part.' He shrugs, and I wait for him to finish.

After guiding him again on all the steps, isolating and protecting all wires, after a lot of deep breaths and scares, he says he's done.

'What's the next step again?' We're both trembling. I can feel while I hold his hands.

'Tom, listen ...'

'No. No goodbyes or messages for family and friends. We'll be fine.'

'Maybe we should rethink that kiss.'

'We have time.' He looks at me with his oceanic eyes, leans in, and kisses my nose again.

'All right, go back to Lauren.'

'I'm not leaving you.'

'Tom, come on. Be serious.'

'I am.' He grips my hands and touches his forehead to mine.

'You're crazy. I can't let you get hurt because of me.'

'So you're just going to sit there forever? This isn't where I imagined living.'

'Tom, this really isn't the time to joke. Go back to Lauren.'

'You know it sounds like you're sending me back to my ex. It's weird.'

'You're weird. Pass me my phone, please.'

'Why?'

'I want to call Nat.'

'You have no faith that I done everything right, do you?'

'It's not that.'

'I'm offended.' He puts both hands to his chest.

'Stop the drama, please.'

'Fine, but you can't tell her what's happening.'

'Why would I do that? I never told her any specifics of what happened to me.' I was going through the phone as I was talking, and he covers the screen with his hand.

'What happened to you?' He looks genuinely concerned.

I smile softly wafting his hand. 'Nothing I couldn't handle.' And I wink at him.

I almost had it. Was so close to pressing call before he saw and grabbed the phone from my hand.

'Ah. You can lie. You tricked me.'

'No, I was just calling someone else first.' I have a sly smile on, and I stick my tongue out at him.

'It looks like I found my queen of mischief.' How can you not melt at this man's feet?

'Keep my phone then. Give it to Lauren for all I care. If you won't let me make a call, I won't need it.'

'Do you think I was born yesterday?' He was almost up when he sat back down.

'So close.'

'I'm not leaving you. Close your eyes.'

'Why?'

'Will you just trust me and do as I ask?'

I oblige. Can't argue with him anymore.

'All right, now extend your arms to me.'

'Tom…' I keep my eyes closed and my arms at my sides.

'Please, Violet. Let me.' His pleading breaks me, and I can feel him smile.

'I'll count to three, okay?' He grabs my hands.

'Okay, let's do it.' I squeeze tight. We both take deep breaths, and I open my eyes.

'Hey, I asked you to keep your eyes closed.'

'Tom, if I might die, I'll have enough darkness. I'd rather see you.'

'Just come back to me.' His smile broads slowly, and I do just that. I take a leap into his arms.

I don't wake up.

Not with a jolt of a dream. Not to an explosion. Instead, I keep my eyes closed and my arms tight around what I last saw – Tom.

'I think we're safe now.' I hear it. I do, but I still think I'm dreaming, so I hug my bed, and it laughs.

'Are we dreaming? Are we dead?'

'If we are, darling, I'm in heaven.' His belly rumbles beneath me. And he kisses the top of my head, and I meet his eyes. He brings me to a sitting position. I can't take it anymore, so I hold his face with both my hands and give him what is his.

And there we sit in a lost village in Angola in the middle of a landmine field, kissing. All the light touches we had, the teasing words, and the intense looks have spilled into this kiss.

'Do you guys think that's the best place to do that?' Lauren's voice brings us back to the present. I blush when it dawns on me that I'm sitting on his lap, and I leap up. He laughs and follows me.

'You guys okay?'

'Yeah, Lauren, we're fine.' I let a sigh out.

'You're never that careless.' She whispers the statement. Can't really say anything, so I just smile. Lauren stands there, arms still crossed, watching us walk away.

'Hey, can you slow down?' His legs might be longer, but I'm on a mission. Why am I feeling so pissed? Finally, he catches up to me and grabs my arm. 'Can you tell me what just happened?'

'Tom, what are you doing here?' I can see that my words hurt him, but I can't let myself get lost and drown in this man again. I have a job to do. I'm nowhere near finished.

'Are you serious? Why are you being like this?'

'Like what?' A bitch? That's probably it.

'I thought we just shared a great moment. Dangerous but great, and now you're being cold and distant again. Why? Why do you keep pushing me away?'

I don't want to tell him what's on my mind, so I turn and keep walking. 'Where are you going?'

'To take a walk.' He doesn't follow. Why do I feel a pit in my stomach? I don't want him to follow me. I don't want him here, do I?

I always wondered if I would ever see Tom again, and if so, what I would tell him. What I would feel. Now I know.

It's almost dark when I come back to the town, and the first thing I do is go to the field to collect the deactivated mines and tools we left behind.

'Should you be there in the dark?'

I almost drop the bloody mines when I jump at his voice. 'Tom.'

'What?' He's teasing me, and I'm trying so hard not to smile at him. 'Are you okay?'

'I'm fine and you?' I fail miserably trying not to smile. He lowers his head and chuckles.

'So ...'

Bang.

'Maybe we ca—'

Bang. I start hammering the crate every time he speaks.

'Please—'

Another bang. But he doesn't stop. Instead, he steals the hammer from my hand.

'Hey, I have to finish.'

'You have finished. You've put enough nails that crate will survive until Narnia.' Unfortunately, I smile again.

'Please can we just talk?'

'Okay, talk.' I try to look everywhere but him, but I feel his eyes following me.

'Here? Now?' He moves slowly to me and puts the hammer on top of the crate.

'Unless you want to wait a few months.'

He doesn't find that funny.

After watching him pacing for a while, I lose my cool. 'Can you stop, please?'

'You said a few months. Still plan on being here then?'

I can sense his cautious tone. I can't lie to him anymore. He's very patient, waiting for my answer, studying me almost like he's trying to read my thoughts.

'Okay. Okay, we should sit.'

'Where? In the middle of the death field?' He takes a spin and gestures all around, and that brings me to our earlier kiss, and I shiver.

'Come. There's no one in the mess hall right now.'

We sit on opposite sides of a table for a while. I don't know where to start. It's not like we haven't seen each other in years, but I've lived through so much since that it feels like it.

'Nat's pregnant,' I blurt out. Any chance to delay the inevitable.

'Really? That's amazing.' He gets his phone out of his pocket and starts typing.

'What are you doing?'

'Texting Nat to say congratulations.' He doesn't move his eyes from the phone.

'Oh, I didn't know you guys spoke that much.'

'I speak more with her than with you.' Still with his eyes trained on the screen, he stops typing.

I know he's right, but it still hurts to hear something like that coming from him.

His phone buzzes, and he chuckles. Finally, he puts it down on the table and looks at me. 'Nat says hi.'

My gaze keeps moving between his face and his phone, and all I do is nod, and he sighs.

'So tell me what it's been like going around the world. What have you been doing? Apart from dismantling bombs, of course.'

We share a faint smile. Here goes nothing.

'It's been … surreal, to say the least. It's overwhelming. Sometimes I …' I can't finish my thought. It's too selfish. His hand covers mine, and I see it again. God, how I've missed those kind eyes.

'What is it? You can tell me.'

And just like that I feel disarmed by his light touch, by his soft smile and warm hands. I give and tell him everything since I left England. I tell him about Carla and Ramira. I even tell him about Mike, but something in his expression tells me he already knew. After I tell him about the situation in Mutimutema, he interrupts.

'So that's why you're doing this now?'

'Frank tried to talk me out of it, believe me, but I just felt like I had to do it. I had to help.'

'You had to try.' We both smile again, and he takes my hand to his lips. So gentle. So tender.

'You know how dangerous that all was? Human trafficking is serious. If they had caught you, the worst wouldn't be to kill you.'

'It wouldn't?' My brows almost join my hair line.

'No. You could have been taken. You would disappear in an instant.' He lowers his eyes, and I know he's thinking of the worst possible scenario so I stroke his face.

'It's okay, Tom. I'm fine. I've been lucky.'

'Only you could call yourself lucky in situations like those.' He chuckles and shakes his head.

'I haven't properly thanked you for what you did in Somalia. I still can't believe how fast you got there.'

'I just wished you had waited for me. It took me all of two weeks to get there. I didn't think you would be gone by then.'

'I'm sorry. I wasn't done. I had to keep going.' I see him swallowing hard, opening and closing his mouth a few times, trying to find the right words.

'What is it, Tom?'

His eyes find mine again. 'And now?'

'Now what?'

He takes a deep breath. 'Are you done now?'

All that I've feared with him I can see in his eyes. I know what he wants, and I want to tell him just that: *Take me home, Tom.* But I can't go back. At least, not now. Can't allow myself to get lost in him. So I do what I've always done. I let go of his hand, get up, and start pacing in front of him. I can see his disappointment in his face.

'I don't feel like I am.'

'What are you hoping will happen? You getting a divine feeling telling you that you've done enough, or are you waiting to get killed?'

His tone is so harsh it makes me want to walk away again. But I have to stay calm. There's no point in arguing.

'Neither. As long as I'm doing something to help, I think I'll stay. If I was useless, I would have left already.'

I see him digesting this, and he's the one pacing now.

'So you're never going to go back home?'

'I didn't say that.'

'No. I think that's exactly what you're saying. And you're using the need of the world as an excuse again. Just to push me away. Again. Why do you do that? What are you so afraid of?'

'I did push you away before in London. But that's only because I had made up my mind I couldn't go back.'

'Why? Why can't you do this and let me in at the same time? Why are you so scared?' By now he has stopped pacing. He's staring at me, flailing his arms around, only the table between us.

I can't stop shaking my head a continuous no.

'Everywhere you go, there'll always be help needed. The world is filled with hard realities, and honestly, all the evil in it will make you exhausted or break you, and you will never go home.' He pauses for a while, trying to study and figure out my expression.

'Do you think I do the bare minimum?'

'What? No. Of course not.'

'So you think I help?'

'Yes.' Where is he going with this?

'Yet I manage to still have a life and be happy, or at least try.' He tilts his head to me, a wicked grin posted on his face. I should have seen it coming.

'I'm not you, Tom.'

'No, you're not.' He starts going around the table towards me, and I move in the opposite direction.

'Tom, stop.'

'You're so much better than me.'

'Tom, please.'

'So much stronger.' He doesn't stop.

'You're incredible, and I think you can do anything you want.'

'What exactly have I done to help anyone? I haven't really. You have. Not me.' Tears start to fill my eyes, and I finally stop.

'You have no idea the impact you make in people's lives, do you?' He shakes his head and smiles. My stare is blank, and he wipes the tears off my face. 'I have something to show you. I was supposed to send you this, but after your lovely email, I couldn't bring myself to write to you.' I feel the pang of guilt.

'I'm sorry, Tom. I didn't know what to say.' He looks at me, phone in hand.

'You know. Reading it felt like an old friend was writing to me. I read the distance and coldness of your words even after I opened myself to you. I even admitted how long it took me to write that email, and you just brushed it aside. I opened myself to you. I was vulnerable, and after your email, I felt unwanted just … overlooked and forgotten by you.'

I couldn't believe his sincerity. I heard the hurt and vulnerability in his voice, and I wanted to cry. For some reason, his words were making me feel more guilt, knowing I was the one who caused him so much pain. No more restraints.

I lunge for him and wrap him tight between my arms. His squeezes my back.

'Violet …'

'Shhh.' I don't want words right now. I just want his warm chest against mine I just want him. I feel him smelling my hair and kissing the top of my head. His grip starts to loosen.

'Please don't let go.' I feel his chest rumble with chuckles.

'Never.' If only I could stop time.

'Can I talk now?'

'No.'

'Okay, then can I kiss you?'

My lips instantly turn up with a smile, and I look up at him. He keeps a hand on my back and the other stroking my right cheek. My eyes. My nose (which makes me wrinkle it and he laughs). He moves his thumb along my jaw and settles on my lower lip. His eyes follow, and I keep mine on his. Waiting. He nudges my jaw, lifting my head, and his lips crash with mine.

Our first kiss was more urgent and desperate. Considering the life or death situation, it was understandable, but this one is soft, caring, like he's getting to know my lips before he introduces himself to my mouth.

I tug his back to me. Somehow I want him closer, and judging by the way he pushes me against the wall, I would say he got the message. My hands roam his back, his hair, face, chest. God, I've missed him, and I've wanted this for so long. Suddenly, it isn't my mouth he's kissing. He tastes my cheeks and moves to my neck. I can't stop him. I want this as much as he does. I'm his, and he knows it. He finds all the right places on my neck. I grab his hair and whisper his name, a moan escaping my mouth. That must have brought him back to reality because he stops kissing me. He's just panting against my shoulder now, covering me in shivers.

He holds himself against the wall, bracing his arms on each side of my face. He's looking at me so intensely, his eyes full of unspoken words. I know what he wants to say, what he wants to ask, but I can't, so I let my face look at the floor and a tear escapes my eyes again.

'Please look at me.' I do, and he kisses my tear away. 'What are you thinking?'

'I don't want to say.' I feel my cheeks burning, and he touches his forehead to mine.

'Come, sit.' This time, we sit on the same side of the table. With a hand, he holds mine, and the other fetches his phone from his pocket. 'This was when I arrived.' He starts showing me pictures of the Somali village, but it looks different from what I remember.

'Are you sure it's the same place?'

'Um … yes. Look, isn't that Mike?' He continues sliding through pictures, and there he is. It's Mike.

'It's just so different from what I remember. There are no people sitting on the street. When I was there, the streets were filled with beggars.'

'Mike had already taken care of that. He found a room for everyone and even started to assign jobs.'

'Wow, that's amazing. I really should call him.'

'Call him?' He stops shuffling through the pictures and looks at me.

'Um ... yes. Talk to him, see how things are going there, maybe talk to Ramira too.'

He scoffs. 'She hardly speaks any English, and I can tell you how things are going in the town.'

Is he jealous? I can't believe it. I feel a need to tease him further. 'Yeah, but I miss them. I really connected with the people in Somalia. I might go there sometime soon.'

'So you don't want to go home, but you'll go to visit them?'

I nod, not moving my eyes from his.

'Who exactly would you like to visit? I mean, who do you miss?'

Ah he's probing. I take my time, looking at the ceiling, trying to remember names of people I've never met and sigh occasionally.

'I really do miss Ramira. Even with poor English, she understood me better than anyone I ever met. It's like she knew me. And of course, I miss Mike. We shared quite a lot.'

I pause waiting for a reaction. He definitely knows, and I can see he's struggling to hide it but I keep going.

'We shared secrets, things we haven't told anyone, and has he told you I remind him of his sister? It's crazy ...'

'Okay, enough of Mike,' he blurts out, and somehow I feel like gloating. *Do it on the inside, V.*

'Tom. What's up with you?'

The hand that was holding mine now covers his eyes, and he shakes his head. 'Nothing. Maybe we should go to sleep.'

He starts to get up, and I put my hand on his shoulder.

'What is it? Just talk to me please.'

'You want me to talk?' His voice is snarky, as if he's about to throw something in my face, but I nod and keep eye contact.

'You ... you ...'

'I what?'

'Do you like him?'

'Who?'

'For fuck sake, Mike, obviously.' There is it. His face blushes, and I feel like are in high school.

'I just told you I miss him. Of course, I like him. He's my friend.'

'Friend? What kind of friend?'

I know what answer he's looking for, but I don't go there. 'The kind of friend who listens to your concerns and your dreams. The kind who confides in you and listens to your secrets too. The kind of friend who you trust. You know, a good friend.'

I'm still teasing him and being a bit too sharp. On top of it all, I wink at him when I finish talking. He bursts again.

'The kind of friend with benefits?'

My face hardens. I knew what he was insinuating, but I thought we were just teasing each other. Can't believe he said that, and by the look of regret on his face, neither does he. So I get up and pace.

'I'm sorry. I didn't mean it like that.'

'So what did you mean it like?'

He doesn't answer, just avoids my gaze. My turn to be snarky and direct.

'So since we've met, you haven't slept with anyone else?'

The scandalous look on his face almost makes me laugh.

'Why are you asking that?'

'Because you're trying to make me feel bad for sleeping once with a guy. It's not like were dating, you know?'

'I know that, but I thought that maybe I was more important to you …' He kind of trails off, and I'm not sure if he's finished, but I don't wait.

'You didn't answer my question.' My voice his low. He won't push it aside.

'What question?'

My blood is boiling. Words can't come out, but my stare answers him, and he lowers his head. 'I did. It was …'

'I don't need to know any details of who or where or how many times. I just didn't want you to make me feel ashamed and guilty for having sex for the first time in two years.'

I didn't mean to say it. I really didn't. But it just came out. I felt like I was on trial, had to defend myself.

At first, his jaw drops, and his eyes double in size but he doesn't say anything for a while. I start hopping from one leg to the other and feel myself blush again. I was expecting some more shouting or censuring me some more, but instead, he comes to me, hugs me, and kisses my forehead.

'You know, your first time should have been with me.'

The intensity of his look, the roughness of his voice, makes my whole body tremble and shiver. I think my heart actually skipped a beat.

'I love you, Tom.' I couldn't stop it. Almost hurts not to say it.

He touches his forehead to mine and closes his eyes. 'Finally.'

I start laughing but stop when I realize he's got tears streaming down his face.

'Tom...'

'You know. I actually had dreams of you saying that to me.'

'I had different dreams.' I wipe the tears from his face, and he starts wiggling his eyebrows.

'No. Not even close. Can't tell you how many times I woke up sweating and shivering from dying.'

'Wait, what?'

'For months, I've been dreaming that I die with an explosion or something like it, and you're always there. Always.' I let my head hit the wall remembering all those times I woke up with a jolt.

'Yeah, that's it. You're not working with mines anymore.'

Can't help but laugh at that. I actually never thought too much about it, but even before working with the mines, I was already having these dreams. Maybe it was a premonition.

'By the way, I love you too.' My smile spreads from ear to ear, and I pull his face to mine. My hands roam his full, fluffy, wavy hair and rugged face, and he squeezes my back and starts moving lower and lower, and I let myself go pulling him harder towards me. His hand slide down my legs, and suddenly, they are wrapped around his waist, and he's moving me to the table, never stopping the intense kiss we're sharing. I'm trying to think, trying to be rational, but I've denied this so many times, for so long that I really don't want to stop. We keep kissing, grabbing, and squeezing, and he starts kissing down my neck, and a moan escapes my mouth again – louder and more rushed.

We're both huffing and panting, and he starts to slow down until he stops and lays his head on my chest, and I hug him.

'Are you okay?'

He still doesn't talk, just moves his head up and down against my chest. I feel the cloud starting to clear, and I can't believe we almost did that on top of a dining table in the middle of the mess hall. So I let a long sigh out and close my eyes.

'I can hear your brain thinking,' Tom says.

'It's your fault.' I can't help but chuckle, and he pulls his face from my breasts to face me with a raised brow.

'How come?' he asks.

'You're the one who stopped. You know my brain starts to think when it has nothing else to do.' I smirk and wink, and he moves up my body, kissing on his way to my face.

'So you don't want me to stop?' He keeps kissing.

'Now that I thought about it ...'

'Oh man. I made you think.'

'We need to go to sleep. It's late.' I kiss his cheek with a smile.

'I know, but we aren't finished talking.' He keeps kissing, and I start falling into him again.

'We really have to go to bed, Tom.'

'Just tell me to stop.'

'Tom, please.' My mind is drowning with desire and lust. I have to get him off me.

'You don't have to beg, baby. I'm coming.' He starts blowing raspberries against my neck, and we both start laughing. He gets off me and extends a hand.

'Come, I'll help you up.'

'Hum, that's okay. I think it's best if you don't touch me for a while.'

'No chance in that, love. I'm not keeping my hands off you from now on.'

I know he meant it as a joke, nothing more, but my stupid brain starts thinking again. I actually think the air got colder, and judging by the look on his face, he knows exactly what I'm thinking. He raises both hands slowly as if he was approaching a wild animal.

'Babe, I didn't mean anything by it. Please don't jump to conclusions.'

'Don't worry. I know. I'm not running, just want to go to bed, please. I'm tired. We can talk more tomorrow, okay?'

I can't help but laugh at his cautious tone and movements, and he nods suspiciously.

'Hey, if you want, we can go to Lumbala or something.'

'And what do you plan to do in the city?' He raises an eyebrow and looks at me sideways.

'Get your head out of the gutter. We can go climb the mountains if you want.'

'You sure you can take some time off from your busy schedule?'

'Ah. Yeah, there's hardly any more mines for me to deactivate. I've been going to neighbour villages and towns. I really need to call Frank about it.'

'Oh. So you're almost done here?'

'Tom, please, we have time to talk tomorrow, okay? Let's just go to sleep.'

He has a blush creeping on his face but just nods, grabs my hand, and we walk towards the sleeping buildings.

'Are you going to make noise while you try to sleep again?'

'I tried many times. I can't sleep on this thing. Every time I move, I roll over. I'm sticking to the floor.'

'So because you like to sleep on your side, you've been sleeping on the floor this whole time?'

'Yeah. It's fine. I'm used to it by now. It's not that bad.'

'Make sure you don't have any commitments for two days. I'm making a plan.'

'For two days? I don't know. We both have stuff to do.'

'Stuff that I'm sure it can wait. But tomorrow morning, we go talk to Lauren, okay?' He's very softly caressing my cheek and then kisses me. 'Goodnight. See you in a few hours.'

I'm tired. My brain is drained, so I just mutter, 'Goodnight.'

I can't believe how long this day was. It felt like days filled with so many emotions. I would sleep for days if I could, but the thought of spending tomorrow with him excites me. I missed him so much, and there's still a lot we need to talk about. I've set my alarm for eight thirty. Thought I deserved to sleep a bit longer, but I'm awoken by a nudge instead. His eyes are dark and half hooded. Best way to wake up ever. He kisses my nose. I smile as he hugs me.

'Morning.' His rough morning voice gives me goose bumps. 'How'd you sleep?'

'Like a rock, and you?'

'Okay. I'm sure I'll sleep better tonight.'

'What do you mean?' That was weird.

'No time to talk now. Let's go.'

Most people who know me know that I like quiet in the morning. Too much talk makes me feel cranky, and it seems like Tom has caught up to it maybe because my answers started to be more like grunts, then words, because we both fall into silence. We have breakfast, and he just follows my movements as I help clean up everything, but when I move to carry on with the rest of the morning tasks, he stops me.

'No, no, no. Let's go talk to Lauren and then get on with our day, okay?'

Right now that's all I want, to spend time with him, so I just nod.

'Hello. What can I do for you today?' I've never heard Lauren being so formal. Maybe it's because of Tom, but before he says anything, I jump in.

'Have you talked to Frank?'

'Not recently why?'

'Well, you know the mine situation. I think they might be shipping it somewhere else. We're not receiving nearly as much as before, and only a couple of people made through last time. We need to talk to him. Call him.'

'V, you know I can't just call him. I'll text him and wait for him to get back to me.'

Tom's been watching us patiently, giving me an occasional sideways look, but he breaks the silence.

'Right. So if that's out of the way, I think it's my turn.'

'What? What did she ask you?' Lauren's eyes widen and target mine. Her eyebrows shoot up.

'Hey. I didn't ask him anything.' Honestly, there's a lot I could ask him, but apart from transportation to school and more prosthetics, there's not much he can do for us right now.

'No, I want to ask if there are any pressing matters for Violet or me to attend to for the next two days. We would like to take some time off, please.'

'Didn't you just hack a day off?' If I could, I would wipe the smug smile from her face. She's just teasing me, but Tom cuts me off.

'She did, but I think I kind of ruined it, and I would like to make it up to her. So?'

'Of course. Apart from town chores, there's not much for her to do anyway. You guys have fun.' She winks and leans back on her chair. My whole face is red when Tom grabs my hand, thanks her, and leads me out. This is really happening, and I feel like a teenager with butterflies in my stomach.

'Do you want to change before we go?'

I look down at myself. I might not look great or like I'm going to a ball, but I didn't think I looked that bad. Tom walks slowly towards me, smiling softly and shaking his head. He puts his hands on my hips, pulling me to him, and brushes his lips to mine.

'You look great. Beautiful as ever. I just want you to be comfortable and take a change of clothes as well.'

'Okay, what exactly are you planning?'

'You'll see. Just hurry so we can enjoy the day.'

Chapter 7

Next thing I know, we're in Lumbala checking into a hotel. I take a sweep of the room and watch Tom drop the bags down. There's only one thing on my mind right now, so I look at the bed and back at him. I turn a crimson tone, but I don't care I just want him, so I wrap my arms around his neck and kiss him like there's no tomorrow. In less than two minutes, we're rolling over each other on the bed, and this is all I can think of, all I want, but it seems that Tom has different ideas because he stops kissing me and gets off the bed, holding an arm out.

'We have to stop.' He's breathing heavily and stepping away from the bed. 'I have plans for today. We need to go.'

'You're joking, right?'

'Come on, we have time for that later. I want to go out and do things with you.'

'Well, I wanted to do things with you here.' I gesture to the bed as I get up. 'Tom, I think we had enough foreplay.'

'What … Violet.' He chokes on his own breath and words.

'What? Are you going to say you don't want to?'

He moves so slow and, oh, so sexy, puts a hand on my hip, and the other slides down my cheek and along my jaw, and he kisses me. So soft. So tenderly that my knees shake.

'Trust me: there's nothing I want more right now, but I really did make plans for us. I want you to have a little fun and forget the world's problems for a few days, okay?'

'You, sir, are weird. So where are we going?'

'Not telling. Just dress comfortably and wear those boots you love.

Maybe those jeans too.' He's pointing to what I'm already wearing. Nothing special about that.

'You know that I haven't worn a dress in half a year, right?'

'You have a dress?'

'How dare you? I'll have you know that I too had plans for these days, but they didn't actually involve boots.' I swat his arm.

He laughs and kisses my nose. 'Come on. Get changed. We're losing daylight.'

Okay. Can't believe I shaved my legs for this. I missed him and wanted him for so long. How does he have so much self-control?

Jeans on and boots marching, I follow Tom, and for a moment, I think we're going back to Miue. I've walked this path before, but he takes a turn, and we find ourselves climbing the mountains.

'How do you know your way around so well?'

'Have you heard of Google Maps?'

I laugh and slap his bum. He stops and looks at me, surprised, and trust me: so am I, but all I can do is shrug. He shakes his head, and we keep climbing.

Good thing it's not summer, because it's midday, and the sun is sky high. At times like these, I really miss sunglasses. Despite all the anguish and misery around us, the top of the mountains feels like it's a whole different world. It's green. It's brown and blue. It's beautiful and peaceful, so I close my eyes and take a deep breath. Better take it all in while I can. I might move soon.

All that fades away when I feel Tom's lips on mine and arms snaking around my waist. This man really sweeps me off my feet.

'Sorry to interrupt your thoughts there, but I couldn't help myself. So?'

I raise an eyebrow at him.

'Do you like it? I mean here. The view. The company.' He's leaning his shoulder against me, and I chuckle.

'Yes, Tom. I've always loved it here.'

'What? You've been here before?'

'Well, yeah, it's not that far from Muie. I like to come here sometimes and clear my head.'

'Oh. That's nice.' I can see the disappointment spread on his face, and I can't help but feel an elation, and smile and nudge my shoulder at him.

'This time, it's much better. I have great company now.' He chuckles and nudges me back, and we stand quiet for a little while until he breaks the silence.

'Come. I want you to do something.' He starts to climb a higher point of the mountain and stretches his hands to me.

'Um. I think we're safer down here.'

'Seriously, you play with landmines but are afraid to come to the top of a mountain? Chicken.'

'How dare you, sir?' I gasp but take his hands, and we both laugh.

'Here's what I want you to do …'

'Just so you know, I'm not getting naked here.'

'Will you get your head out of the gutter? No. I want you to close your eyes and scream.' His mouth hangs open for a second.

'Um … why?'

'Just try it, okay?'

'You should know I'm not a girly girl, so I don't scream like one. I'm not even sure I can scream.' This is weird to me, and I'm trying to relax as I joke, but he doesn't reply or even look at me.

I've never done something like this. It's weird and I'm uncomfortable. I'm pretty sure all that comes out of my mouth is a squeal, and I start giggling at myself, but when I look at Tom, he seems to be so far away in concentration that I don't think he noticed my fit, so I try again. I close my eyes and take a few breaths but no screams come out. I've seen so many movies with scenes like these, and there's always some kind of catharsis. I just need to get there. It's not like my life was horrible. Hasn't been great either, but I always put that aside when I think of all the things I've seen since I decided to try.

My problems are nothing when I remember all the horrible things Carla was doing in Somalia. At that moment, I feel something in me. Images of Ramira tied to the pole while she's being whipped. I see Mike's eyes when he's telling me what happened to his sister, and I see the charity's table at the party in London. My chest fills to a point that I think it's going to explode, and I let it all out.

Never in my life have I screamed like this. I screamed for Ramira, for all the children she lost. For Mike and everyone who has died or lost a limb in the landmine fields. I scream for my mother and the deceit I've been through. I actually thought I was going to end up in tears, but luckily, that didn't happen. I've cried enough in front of Tom.

When I open my eyes, Tom is looking at me with a soft smile, and I feel my cheeks burn. Still, I reciprocate his smile. I can tell he wants to talk, but he's fidgeting and holding himself back, so I grab his hand to go back down. We walk atop the mountains for a while.

'Thank you for that. I've never thought of it, but it was really helpful.'

'You're welcome. I'm glad I could be helpful.' He's still holding back, waiting for me to talk, and I think now is better than never.

'Do you remember when we were having lunch in that pub after London Eye?'

'Um ... yes. Of course. Why?'

'Do you remember what you told me then?'

'Hon. We spoke about a lot of things. Did I say anything wrong?'

'No, silly. You said that if I wanted to achieve the change I wanted or any at all, I had to be willing to make sacrifices. Do you remember that?' I chuckle a little.

'I do. But do you think you have to sacrifice your whole life?'

'No, I don't.'

I can actually see his chest decrease in size as he lets out a breath. I chuckle a little and carry on.

'I know I shouldn't, and I won't sacrifice my life, but there's still a lot of things I want to do. Like I told you, I don't think I'm done.'

I feel him tense beside me, and he's squeezing my hand a little, but he keeps silent, so I keep going.

'Listen, Tom, I'm not saying I'm never going back home. I'm just saying I don't know when I'm going. Can you accept that?'

He stops walking and gazes at the view. Now is my turn to tense up and wait for him to open up to me.

'You know I'm very proud of what you're doing. Worried but proud. It really is amazing. You're amazing.' He gives me a cheeky smile, and I blush a little. 'I just thought that maybe I could be more important to you more than all of this. Someday, I mean.'

I can see the pain in his eyes and disappointment in his words, and all I want to do is hold him, but we have to get this out.

'Tom, you're important. You gave me the push I needed to make this possible.'

'Yay, me.' He raises both fists to go sarcastically with his remark.

'I'm serious, Tom. You helped me, and I'm really thankful for that.'

He shrugs a little and gives me a soft smile. All I want is to grab him get on a plane and take him home. It's a nice dream.

'Things in Muie are much better. There are hardly any more mines, and the injured are getting the help they need. Now we just need to find out what's going on in Mutimutema and go from there.'

'So you're going to do somewhere else?'

'Yeah, I think so.'

'Is home that somewhere else, by any chance?'

'Tom, I've been away from home not even six months. It really hasn't been that long, and I want to do so much more.'

'Well, it feels like ages ago to me. I've missed you, and I haven't been able to stop thinking about you. Do you think we have any chance? Any at all? And I don't mean right now. Sometime in the future maybe?'

All I want to say is yes, no ifs or buts. Just move on with my life. With him. That's what I want, but not what I can do right now. I feel like my brain is having a fight with itself, trying to find the right thing to say to him. I can't say no, and I feel Tom's eyes on me, so I avoid his gaze and start walking away, but he grabs my arm and hugs me. I wasn't expecting that.

'Sorry, baby, I didn't mean to pressure you. I just had to get it out. I brought a couple of sandwiches. Shall we take a sit?'

Wow that took an odd turn, but I still go with it, and we start to eat in silence.

'It really is a nice view.'

'Tom...'

'Don't say anything, please. I'd rather not have any kind of answer than hear a no, okay?'

'Okay.' And we fall into silence again.

'Tom...' He lets his head drop, clearly waiting for rejection. 'How about we keep in touch for a while?'

'What do you mean?'

'I'm not going to lie or make excuses okay? I'm not going back home and settle down right now, but I want to, someday, and be with you, but it's not fair of me to ask you to wait for me. I just—'

'What if I want to wait?'

'Wait, really?'

He just shrugs and nods.

'Even though I don't know when I might go back home?'

He turns to me. 'Listen, I don't know. I'm not sure. All I know is that I miss you and I love you and I want to be with you. I know right now it's not what will happen but if I'm willing to wait, that's my problem, right?'

I'm not sure what to say. It's really not fair of me to expect him to wait for me, but I so want to.

'I love you too, and I missed you like crazy, but are you sure you want to do that?'

'Let's just do what you suggested. We keep in touch as much as possible and go from there. What do you say?'

He caresses my cheek with his long palm, and I lean into it and sigh. He kisses me, softly and slowly, and I melt in his arms.

'Yeah. Let's do that,' I say with a big smile.

He smiles back and hugs me tight. Yeah, we'll take it from there and see how it goes.

We walk back do Lumbala hand in hand and at the same pace. It feels nice and safe, and I don't want it to end, but we seem to reach the hotel faster then I wanted.

'Okay, so here's the plan. We take a quick shower and go out to dinner I've made plans.'

'Really? Plans as in diner reservations?'

'What's wrong with that? No need to make fun okay.'

'Not making fun. Just surprised that's all.'

'Sure. Sure. I'll take a shower first, and then you can go, okay?'

'Wait, what?'

'You can choose what to wear while you wait.' He gives me a cheeky kiss and winks at me.

'Or maybe I could join you in the shower.' Apparently, my very suggestive tone makes him laugh. Not my intention at all. 'What's so funny?'

'Nothing, but I'm going to shower alone, okay?' He kisses my forehead grabs his bag and goes to the bathroom.

I just stand there looking at the closed door. What's up with him? I thought he wanted me as much as I want him, but apparently, I was wrong.

'Can you close your eyes?'

'What. Why?' I find myself getting confused with his voice coming through the door, scared he would just walk in.

'Well, I want this to be like a date, and I want you to see me when I see you. So now can you please close your eyes?' This is bloody romantic and weird too, but I smile and close my eyes anyway.

'They're closed.'

'You sure? No peeking.'

'Come on. They're closed. How am I going to take a shower now?'

'Don't be a smartass. I'll leave for a sec, and then you can go.'

I hear the door open and wait for the room door noise, but instead, I feel his lips on mine, and I smile.

'Just give me a sec, and then you can open your eyes, okay?'

'Yes, sir.' He kisses me again and leaves. I find myself giggling in the middle of the hotel room, grab my bag on my way to the bathroom, locking the door behind me. I feel queasy and nervous and butterflies in my stomach. I have to talk to someone so I text Nat.

Hey Nat,

Hope you're okay darling. How have you been feeling? Any chance you can talk now?

My heart is almost leaping out of my chest. I'm so nervous, but Nat doesn't answer, so I go and take my shower. When I come out, I see a missed call from Nat.

'Hey, hon.'

'Hi. Finally, you talk to me. How's it going?'

Her question is very insinuating, and I know exactly what she's asking.

'I'm good. How're you feeling?'

'Well, so far, so good. No morning sickness yet, so that's good.' She doesn't say anything else. I can sense she's waiting for me to talk.

'So … you know Tom is here.'

'Yes … and …?'

'Well, we've been talking.'

'Yes … and …?'

I chuckle a little. She really wants me to get to the point.

'So we decided to take a couple of days off work and spend some time together and talk.'

I can hear her gasp, but she doesn't speak.

'And we've been talking, and even though we want to be together, I'm just not ready to go home yet.'

'Why not?'

'Because I don't feel like I'm done.'

'When do you think you'll be done trying to save the world, V? Because you shouldn't put your life on hold because of that, and you also shouldn't make Tom wait for you either. It's not fair.'

'I know it's not, and I don't want that.'

'So what are you saying exactly?'

'I told him exactly that. It's not fair for him if I make him wait until I'm done.'

'What did he say?'

'He said that maybe he wants to wait.'

There's a moment of silence, and I can feel everything she's not saying.

'Hon?'

'Yeah?'

'I know it's not fair, and I don't intend to lead him on, but I really miss him. So we kind of came up with something.'

'Oh?' That's her reply. Filled with judgement.

'We're going to keep in touch as much as we can and go from there.'

'Okay.'

'Please. Come on be honest. Am I being stupid and reckless?'

'Hum, yes and yes. But if that's what you both want, then you should go for it.'

'Really? No more judgement?'

'Oh, I'll still judge, but I can also support you. That's what friends are for. I just want you to be careful, okay?'

'Yes, hon, I'll be careful.' I was so deep in conversation with Nat that I startle when Tom's voice comes through the bathroom door.

'Hey, babe, are you okay?'

'Yeah, I'm fine.'

'Okay, listen. Our reservation is in thirty minutes. I wouldn't want to be late.'

'Oh, sorry, lost track of time. Just give me five more minutes, okay?'

'Five minutes, sure.' If I wasn't on the phone with Nat, it would be five minutes, and his sarcastic implication would be wrong.

'Hey, hon, I don't have much time.'

'So you guys are going out? Like a date?'

'It's weird, but yeah. He made all these plans.'

'Oh. Saucy.'

'Well, I wanted to talk to you because I'm nervous.'

'Why are you nervous? You like him, and he likes you. What's the problem?'

'Since we saw each other, we've talked, and we argued, and we … kissed.'

'Ah. Finally. Something juicy. Spill.'

'There's not much to spill. We did make out. A lot. But nothing else happened, and I've shamelessly thrown myself at him, but he never lets go. What you think the problem is? Does he not want me?'

'How can you say that? He's there with you and, by the sound of it, making real efforts to make you feel comfortable and loved. Just because he hasn't slept with you doesn't mean he doesn't want you. Maybe he's just trying to take things slow and be a gentleman.' The butterflies in my stomach settle down for a little while.

'Okay, hon. Thanks for talking to me. I really have to go now.'

'Fine, but tell me later how it went, okay?'

'Of course. Talk to you later.'

'Bye, hon.'

Somehow I managed to get ready while talking to Nat. Minimal make-up. Which I'm still surprised Lauren had. Now just need to put my dress and shoes on.

'Hey, Tom?'

'Yeah? Are you finally ready?' He's teasing me, and I'm rolling my eyes to the mirror.

'Yes. Can I come out?'

'Wait.'

I hear some shuffling, and then he tells me to come out. I was expecting him to be outside the door, but instead, he's nowhere to be found.

'Tom?' No answer, but there's a knock at the door, and I'm getting more nervous. Where did he go? Did he order room service? We don't need reservations for that. Another knock. Might as well open it.

I cannot believe my eyes. My jaw is on the floor, and I feel my knees weaken at the vision in front of me.

'You look beautiful.' I still can't talk, so I just smile and accept the bouquet of white tulips he's holding out to me. Tom looks so good and sexy I just want to drag him to the bed. But Nat's voice lingers in my head, so I swallow hard and hug the flowers.

'Thank you. You don't look so bad yourself.' I wink so he knows I'm teasing, and he laughs. 'Why did you do this?'

'I wanted it to feel like a real date so. You ready to go?'

'Just a sec.' I go back inside to put the flowers in the vase sitting on the dresser and grab my jacket.

We walk out of the hotel and through the street, hand in hand and in silence. I feel tingly and nervous and wonder if this is what it would feel like to be with Tom always.

'What are you thinking so hard about?'

I'm not sure what to say. Don't want to give him false hope, but I can't keep my feelings from him anymore. 'About you. About us.'

'And is that a good thing?' He quirks an eyebrow at me.

I chuckle a bit and lean into him, letting my head rest on his shoulder and sigh.

'Yep. Never a good thing when you get to thinking.' He gives me a tight squeeze, and we both laugh.

In a couple of minutes, we're sitting in a beautiful and cosy Chinese restaurant. It reminds me of a place I used to go with my friends from school. Mainly red and candlelit with golden partitions throughout the room. I can't help but feel nostalgic.

'So tell me. What were you thinking?' I look at him from the top of my menu, and the way he looks and smiles at me makes my heart flutter, but I still want to tease him.

'Why wouldn't I be thinking of something good?'

His brows shoot up in surprise, but he recovers quickly and gives me a devilish grin. 'Because whenever you start thinking like that, it's only about consequences and finding the problems. I don't think it's easy for you to see just a good thing without ...' He trails off, and I'm surprised by his honesty, so I complete his thought.

'Without obstacles.'

He nods and smiles. 'I guess I can be a little pessimist sometimes.' He raises a single brow again.

'Sometimes? I think that's your go-to move whenever you're experiencing something good.'

'Wow. Don't be gentle or anything.'

'I'm sorry, babe. I just think we should be honest with each other from now on. Don't you?' He gently places his hand on mine and gives it a light squeeze. His eyes not leaving mine. I don't drop my gaze, but even though I agree with him, I don't think I can tell him everything.

'Yes, I do.' He shakes his head. 'What?'

'I might not know you very well, but I know you well enough to know that answer was very short and not entirely true.'

'Are you saying I'm lying?'

'No. I'm saying you're hiding something.'

I start shifting on my chair, uncomfortable with his honesty, and he notices. 'Okay, listen. I know I'm coming out a bit heavy and serious.'

'A bit?' I interrupt, but he just smiles.'

'I just think this is best, us being honest with each other for once.'

'Tom, I don't know if I'll be able to tell you everything when I'm out there.'

'You think I'm going to get mad?'

'I wouldn't say mad but maybe a little freaked out. I've seen and done some dangerous things, and I don't think that will change.' I put it all out there, and I kind of expect him to get a bit mad at me, but he's silent for a while as we keep eating until he finally speaks.

'If we do this I expect you to be honest and tell me what's really happening with you.'

'And if it's something dangerous, you'll be able to just accept that?'

'I'm not saying I'll like it, but I'll have to live with it and trust that you're being safe.' He sighs.

'You're being very understanding right now.'

'You don't believe me?' I think for a while. I fish for some way to make him understand my point of view. 'Do you remember when I told you about Carla and Ramira?'

'And Mike, yes.' He wants to tease, but now's not the moment, so I give him a pointed look, and he raises his hands.

'I didn't tell you everything that happened.' I trail off a little, afraid of his reaction.

'There's more?'

I nod and take a sip of my tea.

'I held a gun to Carla's head.'

'You did what?' His eyes almost pop out.

'Tom, calm down. I'll tell you everything, but you have to promise to keep calm and not flip out, okay?'

'Okay, I'll be calm.'

'And …?'

'I won't flip out. Really, I won't.' I'm still not convinced, but I tell him everything—Ramira tied to a post with a bleeding back. I tell him how I was willing to take her place and how I put Carla's life in her hands. When I finish talking, we keep silent for a while. The waiter delivers the bill, and after Tom pays, we walk out.

'Did you wanted to kill her?'

I stop walking and keep my eyes on the floor. My cheeks flush and shame fills my eyes. All I do is nod. Tom walks to me very slowly and wraps his arms around me, and I squeeze tight.

'It's okay. We all do things we're not proud of, but we have to learn to forgive ourselves. Don't you want Mike to forgive himself?'

'Of course, I want to. Despite what he has done, I still think he's a good person and deserves forgiveness.' I push back a little from him to look at his eyes.

'So if he deserves it, so do you.'

'I just never thought I would be capable of doing something like that. I really hated her. I wanted her to suffer.'

'You're just trying to protect those you love. I understand that.'

'Thank you, I guess.' I'm still talking to his warm chest, and I don't want to let go.

'I can't believe you went through all of that. What else are you hiding from me?'

'Trust me: that was the most dangerous thing I've done. The rest was nothing in comparison.'

'Still, I want you to tell me.'

'Hum, okay. I've travelled from Somalia, passed through Tanzania. I went through a lot of small villages and towns on my way to Zambia. There's way too many issues there, and I'm sure if I stayed I would get myself killed for sure, so I made way to Mutimutema.'

'Where you met Frank?'

'Right. It took me about four days to get there, but thankfully, nothing happened on the way. I can't say I wasn't scared at times, especially every time I was at a border or checkpoint. When I got to Mutimutema, I felt the world stop. The tobacco fields were everywhere, and it seemed like everyone was smoking it. The cloud engulfed the entire town. It was painful to breathe and to watch.'

'Yeah, I remember you yesterday talking about human trafficking as if nothing.'

'Tom, I know it was dangerous. I don't want you to think I was doing things just because. I know how dangerous it was, but if I didn't know how to handle things or I didn't think I would be able to do it, I wouldn't have done any of it.'

He hugs me again. 'I just want you to be safe. That's all.'

We've been talking and walking for a while, and when I look around, I have no idea where we are.

'Hey, Tom, where are we?'

'Ah, finally a place you haven't been to.'

I laugh a little and look around the beautiful park we're standing in. I guess Lumbala is bigger than I thought. There's a little river crossing the park. Beautiful flowers and a field of trees letting rays of moonlight through, it's almost magical. He raises a hand to me.

'Come. Let's do this like Notting Hill. Let's sit on a bench.' I laugh to the sky, but I take his hand, and we do just that. We sit side by side, but then I remember and lay my head on his lap. A sweet smile spreads on his face, and he runs his hand through my hair.

'You know what I've been trying to figure out?' He keeps caressing my hair and hums for me to continue. 'I know I've seen it somewhere. A movie or something, but I can't remember.'

'What are you talking about?'

'Your little move of picking me up for our date. I know I've seen it ...'

'You can't remember?'

'No. I feel like I've seen it loads of times, but I just can't place it. Come on, tell me.'

'I was hoping you wouldn't recognize it. I thought it was such a cool move.'

'It was a cool move. Very romantic. Now tell me.'

'Fine. It's from *Friends*.' As soon as he says that, my brain clicks, and I see the whole scene happening.

'Wow, I can't believe I didn't remember.'

'Yeah, well.' He just shrugs and looks at the sky.

We have talked so much about so many things that the silence feels peaceful and comforting.

'Let's just forget the world and stay here.' His eyes quickly leave the sparkling sky to meet mine.

'Are you sure you should be saying that to me? Because I'll chain you to my suitcase and take you back home with me.' I start laughing hard but stop as fast when I see the serious look on his face. I can't make him feel bad for saying that.

'Maybe one day you will.' I give him a quick wink. He lifts me to his lap and kisses me. This kiss feels different. It's slow and soft. He kisses my cheeks and nudges my nose with his. There's no urgency just tenderness.

'It's getting late. We should get going.' My heart leaps and starts racing at the implication of his words. I might be nervous, but I wanted this since I've seen him, so I let my body take control. I stand in front of him with an outstretched hand.

'Let's go then.' He gives me a shy smile and takes my hand. In no time, we find ourselves at the hotel room door again. He's fumbling with the key, and I can't help but find it funny. I guess we're both nervous. But I can't wait any longer. As soon as we're inside, my arms fly around his neck, and my lips crash with his. Our arms roam our bodies. Hands squeeze and try to tug the clothes out, but suddenly, he starts to slow down and pushes me away.

'We should slow down a bit. Talk some more.' We're both panting, and I can see the desire in his eyes as well. Why is he hesitating?

'I think we've talked enough, don't you?' I try to pull him to the bed again, but he takes a step back.

'What's going on, Tom? I thought you wanted this as I do. I mean yesterday in the mess hall …'

'I know. I know.' He lets out a deep breath and collapses on the bed.

I don't know what's going through his head, so I sit next to him and wait.

'I planned these two days for us so we could relax and get our minds off the world's problems.' He looks at me flushed.

'Okay …'

'I planned and made reservations and kind of forgot a small detail …' He trails off again, and his cheeks turn pink.

'Tom, are you going to tell me what you're talking about, or are you going to keep talking in code?'

'I don't want you to think I don't want to be with you, because trust me: I really do.' He hugs me tight and talks to my ear. His lips brush my ear, and his rough voice makes me shiver. 'But I kind of forgot a little accessory for that.' It's so cute that he's so embarrassed.

'Okay, Mr Crypto. Can you stop being embarrassed and tell me what you mean?'

'Yeah, I see you didn't remember either. I forgot to get condoms, okay?' This time, I flush. He paces for a bit and stops in front of the window. I lace my arms around his waist and hug him from behind.

'So shall we go to sleep then? Big day tomorrow.'

'Really? You're not upset?'

'Of course, I'm not upset. I just want to be with you. However that is. Now let's go to bed.'

His chest feels strong and warm, and I feel safe. A dreamless night is a bliss.

I'm awoken by the smell of coffee and warm pastries. The room is so lit up it looks like the sun is inside.

'How early it is?' I'm trying to cover my head with a sheet, but he pulls them off me.

'Come on, sleepyhead. Let's enjoy the day.' This man has the nerve to not come prepared for a night together and walks around the room half naked. My eyes keep trailing him as he's bringing the breakfast tray to the bed. 'You need to stop looking at me like that.'

'And you need to stop walking around half naked.' He laughs and hands me a coffee cup. 'So what's the plan for today?'

'I didn't make specific plans for today. Whatever you want. We can go for another hike, and there's a cinema here if you're interested. What do you think?'

'Nothing says normal like going to the cinema, so let's do that.'

'Normal is what I need right now. Normal gives me perspective and hope. We spend our normal day talking about nothing, roaming through the city, hand in hand, visiting silly stores for nothing. We visit the movies and have pizza. Soon it's almost dark, and we're on our way back to Muie.

'We spoke about a lot of things, but I still want to ask you something.'

'Okay.' He speaks slow and tilts his head to me.

'When are you leaving?'

'Wow. Right to the point.'

'Come on. We've been avoiding talking about it, but we both know that you have to leave, so I just wanted to know.'

'I wish I could stay longer, but I have to go tomorrow afternoon.' He chuckles softly and pulls me to him. I feel a tug in my heart.

'That's soon.'

'I just came to see the town's conditions. We got word that was the first place to get a landmine specialist, and we were thinking on getting that person to other places. I just didn't think it was you.'

'You know, you're actually right. I should have thought of training someone else.'

'You're still in time you know?' I just shrug, and he kisses my forehead.

As soon as we're back to Muie, Lauren tells me that Frank isn't in Mutimutema anymore. She's been talking to Ryan. Apparently, Frank got tired of not seeing the changes he wanted and decided to take action. The problem now is that he stopped giving updates to Ryan, and no one is sure where he is.

'So since he went to Thailand, has he said anything else?'

'We don't know. Ryan said that's been nearly two weeks without news, and that's not normal from Frank. All we know is that he managed to find the exact place where they're keeping the people before they move them, and it's not just Mutimutema. They're even sending people to Europe.' Lauren sounds really concerned.

'These aren't good news, are they?'

'He would never go too long without giving news. Like I said, that's not normal. Something happened.'

Tom's looking at me like he knows what's in my mind, and I can't meet his gaze.

'You can't go alone.'

'What?'

'I can tell what you're thinking, and I get it, but this is way too dangerous you can't go alone. I told you before you'll disappear in a blink of an eye.'

'He's right V. I don't think there's much you can do this time.' Lauren is trying to warn me, but the gears in my brain are already turning. There's something. No one will like it, but there's something so I look at Mark.

'Doll, I see what you're thinking, but I'm not even in the circle. How are we going to get in?'

This time, Tom chimes in. 'Well, we can hope that Frank is okay, and when you get there, you can mention you've been working with him?'

'It's worth a shot.'

'V, this is very dangerous. Are you sure you want to do this?'

'No, Lauren. Not at all. But it's what I have to do. I owe it to Frank.'

Chapter 8

For the next week and a half, we make all the plans, and I also train one of the young guards how to deactivate the mines. Just in case. I leave all the steps detailed in paper with Lauren. Hopefully, she'll get more people learning. We kept talking to Ryan, but so far, no news from Frank. I just hope he's still there. Saying goodbye to Tom was definitely the worst part. I took him to Lumbala's little airport, and he made me promise I wouldn't die. He actually wanted me to text him every day, but we have to be realistic. So we made our promises, kissed a lot, and said goodbye.

It's known that Thailand is one of the biggest centres of global sex trafficking rings. I had never really looked into it, so I decide to do that before we leave. Just a little of research. It's all out there, and my heart squeezes at every single picture I see. Fortunately, there's been a lot of rescued victims, which gives me hope.

'I'm still not sure this is going to work, doll.'

'I don't know either. You know me. I kind of go with the flow, but I don't know much about this.'

'Doll, I don't think we should do this. We're going in blind. I have a bad feeling. Even Ryan said you're crazy and shouldn't do this. You should listen.'

I really should listen to all of them, but what's the alternative? Abandon Frank and move on with my life? I can't do that.

'You're right. We don't know what we're getting ourselves into, but, Mark, we have to do something. We can't just give up on Frank.'

'I know, doll, but we have to be smart about this. Here's what I think we should do. Instead of me pretending to work in a place that no one knows me just to get you in there, how about we watch the place for a while and then go from there? What do you think?'

'You're a very wise old man.'

'Old? I'm not that old.' We both laugh and fall into silence again. His plan sounds much better than mine. I should've agreed to it before.

We're on our way to Bangkok before we go to Nakhon Ratchasima, where Frank said he was last time he gave news, but we have to stop in India to get on another plane and collect some permits.

Tom made me call Nat in front of him before he left to make sure I wouldn't slip up anything, and she was very disappointed to learn that nothing more than sleeping happened between Tom and me. Even though I won't be able to, he texts me every day.

The latest one:

> Good morning, gorgeous. I hope you guys have a safe trip.
> Please let me know when you get there, and anything you
> need, just call me. Stay safe. Love you.

I love him, and I miss him, and that gives me another reason not to be reckless and go with Mark's plan.

We get on a cab right after we exchange money. The drive to Nakhan is about three and a half hours. It's going to be an expensive taxi ride.

Who would think that Thailand is one of the worst countries in Southeast Asia hiding horrible tales of human trafficking when you see all the beautiful monuments and spiritual sights? All the gorgeous beaches and embellished hotels hiding ugly truths behind its doors? I've only passed through here when I was going to Cambodia, but my stomach turns every time one of the thousands of pictures of caged human beings comes to my mind. I have my small foldable knife tucked away in my backpack, and I still don't think I would be able to defend myself for too long in the circle.

'Don't look so worried. We just have to stick together and be careful. We'll be fine, okay, doll?'

'I know, Mark. I'm just thinking of all those innocent people there suffering, and I'm going there for just one.'

'Well, that's not really fair. Do you know how many millions of people are trapped and lost around the world? Since you went to Mutimutema, there's a few dozen less to add to that count. That is a direct result from your help and actions. You should be proud of that, doll.'

'Mark, I had help. I didn't do anything by myself.'

'Who does? Everyone needs help, and working together is the only way we can make serious changes in the world.' I know he's right. What can I do by myself? But his words kneed my chest: *Millions of people lost in the world.*

'You're right. I can't do much for millions. I can help Frank and maybe a few more.'

'Yes, doll, maybe. Just one step at a time.'

We're dropped off in the middle of town. It's bustling with people and tents filled with random supplies and hagglers shouting through the streets.

'Come, stay close to me.'

'Where are we going? Don't we have to go the other way?'

'You're not the only one to do research. We're going to stay here. There's a place to rent some rooms, and it's safer.'

'That makes sense. Lead the way.' I clutch my backpack as if I was holding on for dear life. All around, I feel eyes on me. Let's just hope it's because we're tourists. Can't really attract attention to ourselves.

'We don't need to waste money, Mark. It's fine.'

'At least, we should get two beds.'

'Do you know how long I've been sleeping on the floor? The couch will be perfect for me. We have serious problems to worry about.'

'Fine. Fine.'

English really is a universal language. Good or bad, it's so much better than carrying dictionaries around, and I don't think I could have learned Thai in the short time we had. We need to look like tourists, but at the same time, we can't attract attention. How is that going to go? Sunglasses or no?

'Take that off. You look silly.'

'What? I'm supposed to be trying things out. I'm a tourist, remember?'

'Yeah. A silly one at that. Come on, we have to get going.'

We've been following people for three days. Sometimes Mark goes alone, not to arouse suspicion. We're sure that something is happening in Ratchathani village. On the third day of surveillance, we see a truck pull into a warehouse. Mark climbs a window, but he can only make up shapes and shadows. Too many shadows, but we have to start somewhere, so we're going in. We find a low window leading to some kind of office. It doesn't seem like anyone uses it, from what we've seen.

'We need to be quiet, and you do as I say, understand?'

I just nod. There's no time to be heroic right now.

The air feels saturated with sweat, tears from tortured souls. There's only a couple of lights on, and we have to feel our way around for a while until Mark stops abruptly and covers both our mouths. My heart is racing, and my eyes are bulging out of the sockets. I can't see what Mark sees, but I trust him and try to control my breathing. We keep crouched for a while, and then Mark takes a step forward, gesturing me to stay put. I'm scared for him, but I nod again, and he disappears into the darkness. I bundle myself under a desk in that dark room. I feel stranded with indecision. It's been a long time since Mark left, but I'm not sure if I should go look for him or not. I keep hearing voices and seeing shadows walk by until one stops by the door. I don't understand what anyone is saying. I can't even be sure what language they're speaking until suddenly I hear shuffling and the voices are inside the room.

'Are you sure it's here?'

'I think so. Or at least, it's the closest place she could be.'

Wait. I know those voices. Both of them. I quickly climb out under the desk.

'Frank?'

He immediately covers my mouth. I got a little carried away. I wasn't expecting to find him so soon if at all. We keep quiet for another second to make sure no one heard my frenzied greeting. He whispers to us.

'What the hell are you guys doing here?'

'You disappeared, stopped giving updates. We thought something happened to you.'

'Let me guess. It's your idea you're here.'

'Not just hers. Even Lauren was concerned. We're all involved. Since Ryan said you stopped checking in, we all started to make a plan.' Frank starts to shake his head, laughing softly, and Mark and I exchange a confused look.

'Well, that's nice of you guys, but I just lost my phone, and I couldn't remember the number to get back to Ryan. That's all.'

We're serious and holding our breath for a second before we all start laughing.

'Shhhh!' Frank is trying to quiet us, but he's still laughing too.

'I can't believe the danger you put yourself through just for me. You really are amazing. Thank you, Violet.' He's hugging me now and a tear escapes my eyes.

'A wise old man told me that everyone needs help. Even you and me.'

'Again with the old?' Mark punches me softly on my shoulder.

'And wise.'

'Guys, you need to leave. This is definitely more dangerous than landmines.'

'Frank, we're here, and I'm sure we can help.'

'There you go with your "trying" thing. This is serious, girl. Lives are at stake.' He's throwing his arms up and looking at me with contempt, and I really don't like it, but I have to keep calm. Mark remains quiet; he knows me well.

'Don't call me girl. I know what's at stake. I might not be able to do much, but I'm sure I can help.'

'You should know what her original plan was.'

'Mark. You aren't helping.'

'Let me guess. She wanted you to bring her in.' Mark just nods and smiles. They're both mocking me, and I'm starting to get frustrated.

'Okay, that's enough. I need to get back, or they'll get suspicious. Where are you guys staying?'

'We've rented a room in the centre of Nakhan.'

Mark gives him the details necessary to find us, and Frank helps us leave, promising he will find us tonight.

I know I'm way in over my head, but I can't just see and not do anything. Let's just hope I don't screw things over.

'Don't you think he should be here already?'

'I don't know, doll, but all we can do now is wait.' It's nearly midnight, and I'm starting to think that something happened.

'Did Lauren get the message to Ryan?'

'Yeah. They're all very relieved that he's okay. She told me we should go home and let Frank be, that he knows what he's doing.' Mark trains his eyes on his shoes. 'I'm thinking she might be right …' He trails off.

'What? And abandon Frank and all those people?'

'We're so out of our league here I don't even know where to start.'

'Do you think when I left England I knew where to start? I just followed my feet, and anywhere that needed help, I tried my best to be of assistance. We can't give up because we're overwhelmed.'

'Most people shut down when they're overwhelmed.'

'Well, I don't. I can't accept that.' He studies me for a while, and I see a shadow of defeat cross his face.

'No, you don't. I know you heard it before, but you amaze me all the time. I don't know where you get the strength to keep going and not think about your family or friends I can't do that. I'm sorry for being selfish, but right now, I can only think of going back so I can hold those I love in my arms.' My eyes start to fill with tears, and a wave of compassion invades my chest, and I sit next to Mark.

'I'm sorry. I don't mean to be inconsiderate. To be honest, I didn't know you had family. I'm sorry. But I don't want you to think I don't miss my friends and family. I just can't let myself think of them all the time. Otherwise, I'm sure I wouldn't be able to do any of this. I love them and miss them every day.'

'I miss Lauren.' He nudges my shoulder with his. My brows raise, and I giggle.

'Mark. Really? I had no idea.'

'No one does. We don't exactly live in a fairy-tale place. Anything can change at any moment so we didn't want to ... you know ...' he blushes a little.

'I do know. I really do.' We're interrupted by a knock at the door.

'It's Frank. Open up.'

'Finally. Man.'

'What? You think it's easy to sneak around when those people know who you are? Let's talk.'

'Why don't the authorities here do anything? Did you have a chance to talk to any of them?'

Frank starts shaking his head at me again. 'You're so eager, woman. I did ask around when I got here. Just to get a feel of things, but—'

'And how did you know they were here. How—'

'If you let me talk, maybe you'll find out.' There's the impatient Frank I know.

'Calm down, man. She's just trying to help.'

'It's okay, Mark. I remember this Frank, and I'm used to him besides. He's right.'

'What? Did you just say I'm right?'

'She's nice when she wants to be.'

'Can you guys stop talking about me as if I'm not here? Let's just get to the point, please.' I give them both a pointed look but can't help to smile.

'She even says please now.'

'Frank.'

'Okay. Okay, sorry. You know I always liked teasing you. How're you doing with the mines, by the way?'

'There's hardly any left that's why we wanted to talk to you to see what else we could do. Because not many people were coming through anymore, so I thought we could do something about it.'

'What do you mean, not many left? I can't even say how many fields of landmines there were. You're saying you got them all?'

'Almost. I trained another guy before I came to look for you. He'll finish. You know I like to keep myself busy. But enough of me. Tell us what's going on here.'

'I hope you didn't train him like I did you.'

'Of course, I did. How else is he going to learn?' The three of us start laughing, forgetting for a second the horrors past the door.

'Fine, so crash course. Source countries are where they get the people from. Transit, it's where they're held before they are sold to whatever destination, okay?'

'So what kind is Thailand?'

'Unfortunately, Thailand is a bit of everything, and that makes it so much harder to fight the problem, and the fact that a lot of the police are bought doesn't make it easier. After a few days, I managed to find someone decent, and he's using his contacts to get more help, but we really have to be careful. These guys move really fast, and if they suspect anything, they'll disappear in a blink of an eye.'

I hear Tom's voice echoing in my head saying the exact same thing. This is serious, and I can't let my clumsiness screw things up.

'Right. We have to be smart about this. Can't just go in guns blazing. How did you find out they were coming here?'

'Ah. The other guys in Mutimutema started to suspect things and wanted to send someone with one of the loads, so before things got worse, I volunteered. They're sending people everywhere, but I had to go somewhere. I couldn't go back, so I pretended I was escorting that group and ended up here. Honestly, I got lucky I wasn't discovered.'

'Wow, it looks like I'm not the only reckless one here. That was quite a trip, must have taken a long time to get here.'

'Not too long. They're well organized. We sailed to India, and then they took us to Vietnam. They have like a centre in Laos, and from there, people go all over even to Europe. So you have it all source, transit, and destination. I've been trying to gather as much information as I can, and my contact from the police has been doing the same, but this ring is very big. I don't think we have enough bodies to help.' Frank looks defeated, and it makes me ache.

We need more people to help. How am I going to do that?

'I see you thinking, and maybe you can help.'

'Really? How?'

'Well, that friend of yours that helped in Somalia. Do you think he can do anything?'

'I'm not sure, Frank. I would have to ask.'

'Something big is happening in a few days. With or without help, we're going in. I can't watch anymore.' He's up and starts pacing the room.

'Get all the information you and your contact have to me. I'll call Tom.' I get up as well and put a hand on his shoulder. He gives me a grateful smile and gets on the phone.

'Do you think Tom will be able to help, doll? This might be a little out of his reach.'

'I don't know, Mark, but I have to try, right? That's what we're going to do, but we need to be careful and not get caught.'

'Yeah, that would be nice.'

'Okay, Sam sent all he's got to you.' All eyes on me. The expectation is so high that I'm getting nervous.

'This is my number. Text me if you need anything. I have to get back, or they might come looking for me.'

'Please be careful, Frank.' He hugs me, gives Mark a curt nod, and leaves. I'm scared, tired, and nervous, but here goes nothing.

'Violet, are you okay?' Tom says.

'We're fine, Tom. Don't worry.'

'Sure, don't worry. You're calling me, so something happened,' he snorts.

'I might be calling because I miss you.'

'V, we don't have time for this.'

'Right sorry.'

'Is that Mark keeping you straight?'

'Yeah. Tom, I've sent you a detailed email. I need you to read it and call me back to tell me if there's anything you can do to help, okay?'

'Okay, I'll check it out.'

'No, Tom. Read it right now and call me. Please.' I hear the silence on the line. He understands my urgency.

'Okay, babe. Call you soon.'

'All we can do is wait, I guess. I'm going to shut my eyes for a bit. You should do the same, doll.'

I don't answer him. Just keep looking at my black screen. I'm tired, but I can't sleep. I might miss his call. What if he doesn't call? What if there's nothing he can do? What do we do then?

Am I falling? Am I on a boat? I feel the ground shaking. What is happening? Where am I?

'Violet. Come on, doll, wake up. Your phone has been ringing. Answer it.'

My brain feels lagged. I don't know when I fell asleep, but it was definitely not enough.

'Hello?'

'Hi, darling.' The line fills with silence, and I shake a little. What will we do if no more help is coming? There's no point in duelling.

'So ...?'

'Right to the point. Okay. You're very lucky I know so many people and have so many contacts. Did you know that?'

'Yes, Tom. You're an amazing star. Now can you help?'

'Ouch. I don't need my ego stroked, but I was just joking, hon.'

I'm being extremely impatient with him. I'm sighing, and I might be seeing my ears the way I'm rolling my eyes, and to add to my confusion, he's not upset. He's making jokes, teasing me, and speaking in a very calm tone.

'Tom, stop joking around. This is serious. We have no time to waste.'

'I know.'

'You do? It doesn't look like it.'

'I do. Trust me.'

I'm pacing around the room with Mark's eyes following me. I'm really going to lose my temper with him. I had already raised my voice and was probably a chuckle away from shouting. Still, I let out a deep and long breath.

'Tom, please. Did you read the email?'

'Your email? Yeah I did.'

'And?'

'Well, it was a very well-written and nice-structured email.'

My mouth hangs open and I don't breathe for a few seconds. What is he doing to me? Finally, I let it all out.

'Tom, for fuck sake, stop playing. Can you help with this or not?' Adding to my frustration, he starts laughing, and I let my hand with my phone drop from my ear to my side.

'What is it, doll? He can't help?' I shake my head. 'That's too bad, but we can help ourselves, right?'

'You don't understand. He's making fun of me.'

'What do you mean?'

'Did you not hear the conversation, Mark?' I don't even let him answer. Just bring the phone back to me with Tom's voice shouting through it.

'Hello? Violet?'

'Thanks anyway, Tom. I have to go.'

'No, wait.'

'What?' I almost hung up. Almost.

'I was just joking to get you to relax.'

'Do you think this is a time to joke?'

'No, sorry. Babe, everything is taken care of. I just wanted you to relax. Seriously.'

'What do you mean, "everything is taken care of"?'

'Like I told you, I know a lot of people through the foundation. Even if I don't know the right people, they do. So I made a few calls. They made a few calls, and all the right people were ranged until we got the UN engaged. They are extremely involved with human trafficking, and as soon as they got the email, they got on the move.'

I can't believe what I'm hearing. I actually thought, this time, he wouldn't be able to do anything. I must have been in a trance, stunned by the news, because Mark is shaking my shoulder, and Tom is calling me through the phone.

'Violet, are you okay?' Mark rarely calls me by my name, and I move my eyes to his.

'Help is on the way.' That's all I can say. Still not quite believing it, but Mark is smiling, and that soothes me.

'Tom?'

'Yeah?'

'I love you.'

'I love you too, baby.' He chuckles a little.

'So … help is really on the way?'

'Of course. Why would I lie? I wanted to go too, but Kyle said I was crazy.'

'Yeah, you are. So what's happening now?'

'I'm not sure of the details. Kyle is in contact with Sam. They worked everything out.'

'Okay.'

We're both silent for a while. Both afraid of what's coming next.

'You really are a knight in shining armour.'

'Hardly. But I'm happy to help and that you're happy too, but, V?'

'Tom, I know.'

'I know you know,' he says with a laugh. 'But please. Please be careful, okay?'

'I promise. I have to go now, okay?'

'Okay, babe. If you need anything just call. At any time. Love you.'

'I will. Love you too.'

'You guys are sickening cute. So all good then?'

'Yeah. I have to call Sam and make sure he has Frank in the loop.' I'm smiling and still looking at my phone.

'You look like you need a rest. Let me.' He sits me on the couch and takes the phone from me. I'm tired, but I'm too pumped to sleep.

'Hey, I'm going to take a walk.'

'Are you sure? You know this isn't a safe area, and it's late. You should stay here. Have some rest. It's late.'

'I'll just take a walk around. Be back in a jiffy.' I wink at him and grab my jacket, leaving behind a very sceptical Mark shaking his head.

I know I'm supposed to be inconspicuous, but having a yellow jacket isn't doing much to help that, or maybe their eyes are on me because they all know I'm a tourist, or, I'm just being paranoid and there's no one looking at me.

Chapter 9

The streets are bustling even at this late hour. How can so many people fit in such a small space? I remember from my research that a Buddhist temple was nearby, and even though it's late, I started to walk. Can't think of a better place to be.

All kinds of shops adorn the street. A bundle of colours and smells overwhelms me, and it really is a very interesting and beautiful country darkened by these horrible secrets hidden in plain sight.

I've been walking for a while, and I kind of lost track of where I was. Everything looks so similar, doesn't matter where I look. Only then when I reach to my pocket do I realize I didn't bring my phone. That's not good. I've swung my head around so much that I'm getting whiplash, but I notice a lady looking at me. There's nothing like asking a native.

'Excuse me. Do you speak English?' This tiny, dark-haired lady smiles at me as if I were her best friend.

'Yes. Yes. You need help?'

'Yeah. I was going to this temple, but I must have missed it or taken a wrong turn. I don't even know where my hotel is.' I laugh a little at myself.

'Okay. Okay. You know name of hotel?'

'I don't remember. I just rented a room.' I'm feeling really lost now.

'Okay, I take you.' To where? Still I follow. After a while and a few turns in all kinds of direction, I start getting more confused and restless.

'I'm sorry. Where are we going?'

'You want visit temple, yes? I take you there.'

'Oh, thanks.' She's so nice and has such a bright smile that I find myself grinning as well. Another while longer of walking and turns, I really have no idea where I am. At that point, I'm sure I'm nowhere near the centre of town, but no matter. The woman has stopped walking.

'So this is the temple?' I don't remember if I had seen pictures of it before. I had done so much research that all the images that I'd seen have started to blend together. All I see is an enormous red door and high walls. Maybe it's a small temple. I had seen all kinds of things in movies. Anything is possible.

'Can I knock?' She just smiles and nods. There's no knocker only a bell for me to ring. Should there be a bell at a temple? Well, what do I know? I just press the white buzzer and wait.

How could I have seen this coming?

All I see is dark. All I feel is a throbbing pain in my head. What just happened? It takes a while for all my senses to come back to me. The air is putrid with sweat. The foul smell of mould fills my nostrils, and I taste blood in my mouth. All I remember is a big red door opening, and then everything went black. I try to get up, but my head is pounding, and then I feel my hands tied behind my back. It's so silly, but at this moment, all I can imagine is everyone I know saying, 'I told you so.' And even in these circumstances, I'm laughing.

I don't know how, who, or where. Maybe they saw us snooping around and followed me, but right now I just want to know where I am and who I have to fight to get out of this one. I'm not sure if hours or days went by, but I was sitting on the cold floor against a wall in a dark room for what seemed like forever until light invaded and someone entered.

Suddenly, I'm being jolted upwards and dragged out of the room. The clarity burns my retinas and disorientates me even more. I'm tired and weak. There's not much fight in me. Before I know it, I'm dragged down some stairs and thrown on top of a pile of whimpering, scared, and filthy women. Everything clicks into place, and I know exactly where I am. How could I let myself get fooled like this? I keep hearing Ramira's voice in my head telling me that I'm too nice. That I need to be careful. I really have to stop being so trusting.

Someone walks around the circle of helpless women sitting on the floor and starts throwing pieces of bread at us. I thought I knew it was bad. I thought all the pictures I saw were the worst thing I had ever seen. How wrong was I?

That scene breaks me, and instead of joining the frenzy searching for food, I just cry. Silent tears stream down my face, and I bow my head. Not because of the predicament I'm in, but how insignificant and useless I feel right now. Someone nudges my shoulder, and when I open my eyes, one of the desperate souls offers me a piece of bread. My hands are still clasped, but they're at my front now, and with a grateful bow, I accept the bread. Funny how those that have little or nothing are the first one to give away.

Enough moping. Time to make a plan. I start looking around me, Taking in my surroundings. We're in a big room, right in the centre. These guys are smart. I see the stairs and know that's my exit, but there's no way I can ever get there, not without a distraction. But not much happens, and I feel like hours pass. Women sleep on top of each other, looking for warmth and comfort. How can I help them?

Somehow in the middle of hell, I too fall asleep, covered in limbs. There's no one around, and I can't hear a sound. Maybe this is my chance. Just as I was going to get up, doors around the room start to open, and more grimy bodies are thrown in the pile. Something is happening. It looks like they're rounding us up. I can't understand anything they're saying until I hear some faraway English coming down the stairs. My hopes rise up at the sight. I can't stop looking at him, but he doesn't turn in our direction. I guess he doesn't want to see anymore suffering. I keep swaying from one side to the other, hoping the agitation will catch his attention, but nothing. Finally, he turns around, and I perk up a little. He looked, but he didn't see. I guess we're transparent and look blurred to these guys, but I hoped Frank would recognize me. Still I keep following him with my eyes. Maybe it will open a whole on his back. All at once, he stops and turns. His eyes locked on mine, and his eyebrows shoot up. A silent question. I nudge my head, and he shakes his and goes back up the stairs. He's going to get help, right?

Infinite hours pass by. My legs are cramping, and I move to change position and stretch my legs. Only then I feel it – my knife. I have to be calm and choose the right moment. I make small movements and stop sometimes. When I reach my side pocket and my fingers wrap around my folded knife, I let a relieved sigh out. I'm not safe but feel safer when I have a weapon in my hand. Weird feeling to have.

Another long while. Minutes, hours, or days, who knows? The guys have been moving us around a lot from room to room. Maybe they're trying to confuse us, but I think the lack of water and food does that well enough. I had to put my knife away. Being manhandled so much, I couldn't risk them finding it. I tried very hard to keep track of the days, but some rooms don't have windows, and I'm so disorientated that I'm not sure anymore. I still can't believe Frank left me behind. How could he do that after we came back for him?

I start hearing commotion above. That brings me back from my self-pitying daze, and I search for my knife again. They're coming down the stairs. Door open. Women whimper. Doors close. A nearby door opens again. Women whimper again, and the door closes again. My heart is pounding. My palms are sweating, and I'm afraid I'll let my knife slip off.

Our door opens, and the women start to whimper. There's only one face I recognize, but this time, I'm not relieved to see him. Frank stands beside a few suits. If only they were lawyers to come and save us. But no. They're the devil's hand. He's trying really hard not to look at me, and I'm remembering Mike and how lost he was. Did Frank get lost too?

The suits are eyeing us like vultures with carcasses, and then they start to point. I guess the shopping has started. They sticker us with different colours for different buyers, like cows selected for slaughter. There's no talking in this exchange, only greedy looks. A greasy old man with yellow teeth points at me, and one of the guards speaks.

'No. She new. Not broken.'

The inflated man turns his angry gaze at the guard. 'I pay good money. I don't care the state they are as long as they're alive.'

'She not ready. You take other.'

'Listen. I've been doing this a long time. I've met all kinds of people, but I've never met a stupid person that doesn't know who I am.' The guy pockets both his hands and walks slowly to the guard. He lets the message sink in to make sure that everyone understands that he gets what he wants – no questions or arguments. The guard exchanges a look with Frank, and he nods. What the hell? Is he really that eager to get rid of me?

'Fine, we send her.'

A shiver runs down my spine, and my eyes search Frank's, but he doesn't dare to face me. The door opens, and everyone exits.

My mind goes to Tom. How I wish I could see him just one more time and how he warned me that if I got caught in this, the worst wouldn't be dying. The look on the greasy man makes me believe I will really disappear in an instant.

My eyes jerk open. No. That's not what I'll be thinking about. It's time for action. In no time I cut the bounds around my hands and stand by the door. I don't hear anything, but the girls are starting to go into frenzy, and I start to lull them to calm, trying to explain that I'm here to help and start removing stickers from their bodies. There's not much I can do for them here. There are no windows. How am I going to risk to get out of the room without being seen?

My conundrum becomes moot when I hear noise outside the door and the handle moves. All I can think of is hide behind the door. It's the guard from earlier. The one that said I wasn't broken, yet. He closes the door and starts to scan the room. Now's my time. I'm weak right now, but if I keep the knife close to his throat, he wouldn't dare to fight. I hope. I move quickly and quietly, and the whole time I'm praying that the girls don't start screaming.

'Make a sound and you die.'

'Whoa, calm down. There's no need for that.' He raises both his hands very slowly, and I press the knife harder, but something's not right. He's speaking a proper English now no broken words.

'What's going on? You don't speak the same.'

'Ah, Frank was right. You're clever.'

'Frank?' We're having this discussion, and I'm thankful that the girls are quiet.

'I'm Sam, Frank's friend. I've also been in contact with Kyle, Tom's friend.' He waits for my reaction, waiting for the message to sink in, and my grip on him starts to loosen until I release him and he rubs his throat.

'I have to say Frank didn't exaggerate. You're tough. As soon as he told me you were here, I wanted to get you out, but he said it would be risky and could break our cover. He said you were tough enough and could probably help us.' This is typical Frank, and now I'm feeling guilty of all the bad things I thought about him. That he had abandoned me.

'Yes, Frank. He's quite something. So what's the plan then?'

'Hey, where are the stickers?'

'I took them off. We're not cattle.'

'You're really crazy.' He looks between me and the girls.

'Yes. Everyone knows I'm crazy. Now what's the plan?'

'Violet, I can't let you get out right now. You need to understand that.'

'You're joking.'

'Shhh.'

'Sorry. Come on I can help.' I spoke a little louder than necessary.

'I'm sure you can, but I have orders to keep you safe. I don't want to be beaten up.'

'Did Frank said that? I'll be careful. I promise.'

'Not only Frank. Since you disappeared, everyone has been looking for you, and when Frank saw you here, they all said the same: "You keep her safe, or I'll kill you."' I laugh a little. I can totally see Mark saying that.

'That's a little drastic, but okay. Tell me what you guys have in mind then.' He was about to start talking when the handle moved, and before the door was open, he pushed me to the floor, gesturing to hide my hands.

'There you are.' Frank closes the door and looks for me in the puddle of women. I get up slowly. He doesn't talk or react at all for a little while until he moves slowly to me and wraps me in his arms.

'You're a sight for sore eyes. You're crazy, you know that? V, I'm sorry I turned my back that day. I had to.'

'I understand. Don't worry.'

'I never thought you would come here on your own. You really shouldn't have done that.'

'What? I didn't.'

'So how did you end up here? Mark said you left for a walk and never came back.'

'I did leave for a walk. I wanted to go to a nearby temple, but I got lost and when I wanted to find my way back, I realized I didn't have my phone. I had left it with Mark so he could sort things out with Sam and Kyle. When I started to look around, a lady saw me and asked if I was lost. She said she would take me to the temple because I couldn't remember my hotel name. She took me here. Big red door was the last thing I saw before I was smacked in the back of my head.'

'Wow. Damn phones, right?'

I can't help but smile. 'Frank, we've been here too long.'

He nods.

'Just tell me the plan.'

'Everything is happening tonight. We were waiting for the buyers to come so we could get them too. In less than an hour, everyone will be safe, but you need to stay here and do as we say, okay?' My body twists and cringes, but I agree with a nod.

'I'm serious, V.'

'Okay, I get it.' And I sit back on the floor. All the girls are looking at me, and I find myself making conversation, asking if they speak English, saying that we'll be safe, and asking them to be quiet.

Since I can remember, I've felt a void in my life, like something was missing and only at Nat's bachelorette party did I get a clear sight of what that was. At that moment, the idea of helping started to form in my head, but only when I was having lunch with Tom after we went to London Eye, did I made my decision on trying. Never for a moment had I thought I would be in a situation like this or even the one in Somalia. I really didn't think I would ever be holding a gun.

Screams and thumps jar me from my thoughts, and the girls start to get agitated.

'Please calm.' I plead the best I can. We have to remain calm. I start hearing a soft sob, silent painful cries, and my eyes fall on the youngest of the group. She must be fourteen or so, and it breaks my heart. A child should not be aware of this kind of evil in the world. She's biting her lip, trying to keep quiet, and I hug her. I try to shush her and tell her we'll be okay. I'll protect her, but will I really be able to keep my promise?

The door opens abruptly. The girls start to scream, but they look at me, and their screams turn to whimpers, and a wave of affection runs through my body. Unfortunately, that feeling vanishes quickly when I don't recognize the guards that are rounding us up out of the room. I clasp my knife against my palm. We're back in the main room. More whimpering women join us, and a large door opens at the back of the large room that's when I spot a truck outside. Now I'm the worried one.

I keep looking around, but there's no sign of Frank or Sam. What do I do? *Think, Violet.* More women are brought from upstairs and thrown into the pile. The frenzy starts to grow and chaos breaks out when some women try to run through the open door but are shot. My eyes widen, and I stop breathing for a while. I had not noticed any guns. How had I not seen any guns? Finally, I catch my breath. Got to do something. I was about to get up when more bodies poured down the stairs. These were different. They had uniforms and guns. More guns and red gloves. That's flashy. Aren't they supposed to stay inconspicuous? So not the point right now. How does my mind wander like that in these situations?

This was it. The help we were waiting for. They start fighting with the guards, and the girls start to run in every direction. I'm also running around, kicking guards down. Those times punching rice bags really paid off.

Suddenly, my eyes lock on the young girl being dragged through the back door, and my feet move before I think. The confusion is so widespread that the girls started to pour through the city. The guards need to get them to be able to help them. The young blonde girl is kicking and screaming, and I finally get close enough to run my knife into the man's leg.

'Ahh! You bitch!' He lets go of the young girl, and I seize her arm.

'Run!' She looks at me and back at the cursing man. 'Go,' I scream at her, and the guard lifts his gun and shoots at the young girl. I don't think. I just jump.

It takes me a while to understand what happened. The girl isn't running, and I'm stabbing the man's chest, but I can't keep going. Not because I don't want to. I do. Along with Carla, I want him dead. But I'm feeling weak and dizzy. I start to think it's because I'm dehydrated, being locked away for so many days of neglect, but that isn't it. I couldn't grip the knife anymore. My arm isn't moving and it's starting to throb. I collapse on the floor.

I only see flashes now. Darkness. Faces. Lights in my eyes. And a young girl sobbing on my face.

Chapter 10

For a while, I actually thought I would die with a mine exploding in my face. Having so many dreams about it I kind of started to accept it. It started to feel familiar. This, on the other hand, doesn't. I peacefully went to sleep and was swallowed by darkness. Not that I like pain, but it would make me feel alive. Pain would tell me if I was dead. If I would ever wake up from this darkness.

I dream of the day I met Tom, of his sweet voice and kind eyes, of his electrifying touch on my skin. Every touch that day made my body feel like it came to life, like it had found the piece it was missing. I dream of his intense gaze on me when we were dancing. The way his look kept drawing me in and how I got lost so easily in him. Never have I felt so connected to someone, especially someone I hardly knew, but I'm nothing but grateful that I met him.

Is the ground shaking again? Is this hell? I wasn't expecting golden gate doors, but I didn't think I would end up in hell. Maybe a between place or something. Maybe this is limbo because nothing happens. The floor doesn't crack to swallow me, and the clouds do not part to clear a path to the sky. This will be me, lost, till the end of time, not dead nor alive.

I have no idea how long it's been until the sky is finally begins to clear. Maybe the tally was made, and I got in heaven after all, but it doesn't feel like it. I don't feel at peace or safe. I don't feel happiness. I just feel pain, burning lights shining in my eyes and a sharp sting on my shoulder. This is definitely not heaven.

I can move. I can breathe, but I'm scared of opening my eyes. What if this is the dream? Being alive when I'm actually lost. I have to try.

I feel pressure on my forehead. A touch on my shoulder and light voices. Then a finger opens me eyelid, and I jerk my head away.

'It's okay. You're safe. I just want to check your response.' It's a man's voice, and he's talking to me. I'm not dead.

'What happened?' My voice is weak and groggy. 'Where am I?'

'You're in the hospital, Violet. You've been shot, but you're okay now. My name is Marshall. I'm the doctor taking care of you.'

'How long have I been here?' My vision is blurry, and I can only get shapes at first. I blink rapidly to try and get the fog out of my eyes.

'You've been here two weeks.' He's looking at my vitals and writing down, and I'm getting impatient. Why can't men multitask?

'Two weeks? Was I in a coma or something?'

'Something, yeah. You weren't in a standard coma. You just wouldn't wake up even when we tried to shake you awake last week.' He laughs a little. I guess that explains why I felt the floor shaking.

I start scanning the small room, I'm alone, no other patients, just me a solitary plant in a dark corner and a few noisy machines. Some of them are hooked to me with wires that come to my chest, another comes to pinch my index finger. I'm not sure how to phrase my questions. I guess I'm a little scared of asking, so I keep glancing to the grey-haired doctor and looking away. He sits slowly on the side of my bed.

'What is it, Violet?'

'I just … I have so many questions I don't know where to start.'

'I'm sure there's a lot you want to know, but I only know about you. You were shot in the shoulder trying to protect a little girl. You arrived already unconscious. You had lots of worried visitors. They even wanted to camp here. I had to kick them out so you could rest.' He smiles softly at me like a father would smile to his child.

'I hope everyone is okay. Can't wait to see them.'

'I'm sure, but you're still healing. You have to take it easy.'

'That was never my strong suit. When will I be able to leave?'

'It depends. Are you going to take it easy?'

I answer him laughing. 'Yes, I promise.'

'You can go tomorrow. If you behave.' I know he's joking to relax me, but I really want to leave.

'Wait, where am I?'

'You're still in Thailand.'

'Oh.'

'Don't worry. This is a really good hospital.' That's not what I was worried about. I've been here for two weeks. Who was visiting me? Mark and Frank for sure, but who else?

Night starts to fall, and I'm struggling to stay awake. I'm scared of falling into an eternal sleep, but my exhaustion is winning. Dr Marshal comes in, and that awakens me a bit.

'How's my favourite patient doing?'

'How small is this hospital?' He's looking at me, confused. 'If this is a small hospital, that's not that big of a compliment. If it's big ...' I trail off when I catch his expression.

'What happened to 'thank you'?'

'Sorry. Thank you.' He's smiling and shaking his head while he checks my vitals.

'I thought you would be sleeping. You look tired. If you can't sleep, I can give you—'

'No!' I don't let him finish, and he winces at my scream.

'What's wrong? Violet, talk to me. I can't help you if you don't tell me what's wrong. Are you in a lot of pain?'

How do I tell the doctor that I'm afraid of falling asleep? It's silly. I just shake my head. Man, I feel like a child.

'Okay.' He's quiet for a while before he speaks to me again.

'You can't fall asleep?' I look at him, and I really want to tell him that I can – I'm just afraid.

'You're scared.' It's not a question. 'I might have a solution for that.' He doesn't say anything else before he leaves the room. I hope he doesn't bring me pills.

I keep fighting with my weariness, trying hard not to fall asleep, looking at the stars, hoping their bright light will keep me awake until the door opens again.

Have I fallen asleep again? Am I dreaming? I jerk up at the sight, and the pain reassures me that I'm still awake.

'Calm down, girl, or you'll have to stay here longer than tomorrow.' The doctor teases me as he comes to check my shoulder. I can't take my eyes off Tom, and his are on mine, but he doesn't say anything. He just keeps his hands in his pockets and watches me.

'I want you to know that this is a one-time thing. It will not happen again if she has to stay longer.'

Tom nods at him, and I keep moving my head from one of them to the other. What's happening? The doctor finishes his checks, says goodnight, and leaves.

It's just me and him, and I can feel his anger. How do I start?

'Tom.'

'It's okay. You need to sleep. We'll talk tomorrow.' He sits on the bed and kisses my forehead.

'But …'

'Let's just sleep, hon, okay?' He kisses my lips this time, and I give in. I nod, and he lies next to me, wrapping me in his warm embrace.

It doesn't take long for me to drift off and have the best sleep I've had in weeks. It's still dark when my eyes open, and Tom is still wrapped around me. Instantly, I smile. It feels so comfortable to have him close to me, but right now, the toilet calls me, so very slowly and painfully, I get up, trying not to wake him up. In the middle of my business, someone bangs on the door and I am grateful the bathroom is so small that just the walls can steady me upright. Otherwise would have left quite a mess.

'Violet, are you in there?'

'Tom, keep your voice down, or you'll wake up the whole hospital.'

He doesn't answer. He just waits for me to get out.

'What?' I ask when I emerge from the toilet.

'What? Why didn't you wake me to help you? You're hurt. What if you fell?'

'I know I'm hurt. I can feel it. Sorry. I didn't want to wake you.'

'Hand.' He stretches a hand to me.

'What?'

'Give me your hand so I can help you to the bed.'

'You know I can walk on my own, right?'

'I don't care. Come.' He's sweet and thoughtful, and I keep feeling even guiltier, but why should I? It's not like I went looking for trouble. I was being careful and safe, or at least, I was trying.

We both sit awkwardly on the bed. A river of unspoken words between us I can't begin to know what's going through his mind, but this guilt has to stop. I done nothing wrong.

'How're you feeling?'

'I'm fine.'

'You're always fine.' He chuckles a little.

I don't say anything just give him a wry smile. I don't think there's much I could tell him right now that would make him listen or believe me.

'Back to sleep?'

No. I don't want to go to sleep. I want to talk. How do I tell him that? I don't. Just nod and lie down on the bed.

'We'll talk tomorrow. I promise. I keep my promises.' That feels like a knife I can't keep quiet anymore.

'And I don't?'

'I didn't say that.' He was about to put his arms around me but stopped halfway, clearly surprised that I said something.

'No, but you definitely implied it. How about we talk now and get things out of the way instead of stewing over it?'

He's silent and looking at me for a while, clearly fuming, but I don't give in. It seems like forever, and I think he won't talk, but he finally breaks the silence.

'You promised me you would be careful. Safe.'

'I didn't break that promise, Tom.'

'Really? How did you end up in that building?'

I start to sit up slowly. 'Didn't Frank tell you anything?'

'He said the story was yours to tell.'

Now I get why he's so upset – he doesn't know anything. I start smiling softly.

'What's so funny?'

'Nothing. What do you want to know?' Another moment of silence and I start shifting on the bed.

'I'm not sure what to ask exactly. There's a lot I want to know.'

'Why don't I start from the beginning, and if you have any questions just jump in, okay?'

He nods with a raised brow, and I sigh.

'Okay, so, from the beginning, after I hung up the phone from talking to you, I was so excited that I went for a walk.'

'You went for a walk in that town?'

'Yeah, I didn't think there would be a problem. I knew there was a temple nearby, and I wanted to go, but somewhere there I got lost, and I had left my phone with Mark so he could call Sam and Frank. So I couldn't find my way back. A lady was looking at me and smiling so ...'

'Smiling?'

'Yeah, she seemed nice and clearly saw I was lost, so I explained, and she said she would take me to the temple. Before I knew it, I was in front a big red door being whacked on the head. So, you see, I didn't go anywhere looking for trouble. Far from it.'

I see he's mulling over all the information, and the silence is killing me.

'So you didn't go in there on your own?' he asks.

'Of course not. I'm not stupid. The whole time we were surveying, we were always careful.'

'Okay, so what happened there then? How did you end up shot?'

'You might not like anything I have to say, but that doesn't mean I did anything wrong.'

Another sceptical nod and a sigh.

I don't hold back. I tell him of my dark, lonely days. I tell him about the desperate girls, the pieces of bread they threw at us and the stickers. He gasps and raises his brows but doesn't say anything so I carry on. I tell him about the fight when the cavalry arrived and how I went after the young girl, ending with me getting shot. He's quiet for some time, and I get restless.

'Would you do things differently?' I'm trying to get him to see things through my eyes, put himself in my shoes.

'No. I wouldn't be in that position to begin with.'

I can't believe he said that. My mouth hangs open, and I feel tears in my eyes. He brings a hand to caress my face, but I swat it away.

'I think you misunderstood. I wouldn't be in that position because I'm not as brave as you. I don't think I would have courage for any of that, and, no, you did nothing wrong.'

'So why are you still upset with me?'

'Because I'm selfish,' he says. I wasn't expecting such honesty. God, how I love him.

He continues. 'I want you all to myself, next to me always, and I know that, unfortunately, that's not going to happen. That upsets me.'

'Tom, we had this conversation a few weeks ago, and I told you that I wanted to go home. I just didn't know when.'

'Because you still want to do a lot of things.'

'Because I think I still can do something more.'

'When will it be enough? When the world is saved?' He pauses for a little before turning to me.

'That's not fair. I didn't say I wanted to save the world. I just wanted to help.'

'I'm sorry. I know I said I wanted to wait, but I'm feeling that I'll be waiting forever.' He doesn't meet my eyes. His head hangs low, and I slide my hand under his chin so I can look at him. His eyes aren't oceanic blue anymore. Instead, they're a dark grey, and I kiss him. Like I haven't ever or will again.

There's a lot going through my mind right now, but a solution for this problem isn't one of them.

Our foreheads are connected, and our breaths mingle.

'What do you want to do? Forget the waiting thing?'

'No. Is that what you want?' He snaps his eyes quickly to mine. He's scared of my answer, but I'm actually relieved he said no.

'No, it's not.'

'Thank God.' He lets a breath out and touches his forehead to mine again. 'I love you, V. I know I don't exactly have you, but I don't want to lose you.'

'I'm all yours, Tom.' My smile stretches across my face, and he kisses me to sleep.

Two weeks of sleep clearly wasn't enough because I slept the rest of the night in Toms cosy arms. No dreams, no ground opening up to swallow me whole just sleep all the way until the doctor wakes me.

'Good morning. How's my favourite patient.'

No more questioning. Just smile, V.

'Slept very good, thank you.'

'What is it?' He's checking my vitals again, and I'm trailing with my eyes again.

'So … can I go home?' Dr Marshall is smiling, but Tom doesn't seem happy for some reason.

'Are you sure she can go? Is she okay?'

'*She* is right here," I say, 'and I've been here for two weeks. I think that's enough.'

'Shhh. Let the doctor speak.' I get that he's concerned, but I don't think that's the only reason he wants me to stay here.

'She's fine. She needs to recover now, but she can do that at home. Lots of rest and no straining or heavy lifting, missy, okay?'

'Cool. I'll be careful. I promise.'

'I've heard that before.'

'Tom, I told you it wasn't my fault.' My tone is a warning. I'm tired of being told to be careful like I run around the streets arresting gangsters.

'I know. It just seems trouble always finds you.'

'Don't worry, Tom. She seems to be a tough one.'

'Thanks, Doc.' Finally, someone on my side. My eyes speak to Tom, and he sticks his tongue out at me. It's nice to relax and banter. We've had enough drama.

At midday, the doctor lets me go, and I thank him for helping me sleep. Half an hour later, I'm in Tom's hotel room, greed drapes shade us from the midday burning sun and the most hideous brown carpet I ever seen. I imagine he needed a place to shower and actually sleep, staying with me in the hospital for 2 weeks wouldn't be so comfortable. The air is full of questions of an unknown future. He's not going to like the answers.

'Do you want some water?'

'Nah, I'm good, thanks.'

'Do you want anything?' I just shake my head. He's probing. Afraid to ask, but we have to get this out.

'Tom, sit down.' I'm patting the space next to me on the couch and, at the same time, surprised that there's a couch in the room.

'I can tell this isn't going to be good.'

'Maybe not. I'm going back to Muie.'

'You're not serious.' He raises his voice a little, and I can't really blame him. 'You can't do anything. Who are you going to help like that?'

'I didn't say I was going to help. I just want to go and talk to Lauren.'

'You know that there are phones for that.'

I don't answer, and he shakes his head in defeat. 'Okay, I'll go with you and then—'

'No, Tom. I appreciate you coming here to take care of me, but I'm okay, and I'm going alone. There's a few things I want to check out.'

'You're doing it again.' He's pacing the room now. His arms crossed over his chest until he stops in front of me.

'What?'

'You're pushing me away again. For no reason.'

'I'm not really. I just need to take care of a few things right now.'

'Are you saying you're coming home?' He has a serious look on his face and sits back next to me. Very slowly.

'I'm not sure. Like I said, there's a few things I need to check and then maybe I was thinking—'

He doesn't let me finish. Instead, he wraps me in his warm and strong arms. I could stay like this forever.

'Tom, I'm not promising anything, okay?'

'Okay. I promise I'll try to be patient.'

I lean back a little to look at him and raise a brow.

'I said I'll try. I will.'

It doesn't take long for us to be in bed. He keeps saying that the doctor said I need to rest, but I know he just wants to keep me there longer, but I was not expecting what he said next.

'I'll buy the tickets today. I'll try to get a flight for tomorrow, okay?' I'm so surprised that the words get stuck on my throat. 'Don't be so surprised I might not like it, but I understand.'

'Thanks, Tom.' That's all I can say. He kisses my temple, and I fall asleep.

Every time I have to say goodbye to him, it just gets harder. There were no tears, but the crushing feeling in my heart gets worse. After hours of flight and stopping in India again, I'm finally landing in Lumbala. Can't wait to see everyone. To my surprise, Lauren, Frank, and Mark are waiting for me outside the little airport, and I have a feeling Tom had something to do with it.

'Why on earth did you come back here?'

'Hello to you too.'

Lauren is teasing and hugging me.

They drive me back to Muie. The mountains I walked on with Tom whizz by, and it seems like it has been forever.

'How are you feeling?'

'I'm okay, just a little pain. How are things here?'

'It seems you trained the guys well. There are no more mines.'

'You don't need to sound so surprised, Frank. You did teach me or more like bullied me to learn.' We're all laughing, and this doesn't seem like the world I've known for the last few months. Lauren and I go back to her office – girl time.

'So tell me why are you back here.'

'I wanted to say goodbye. It doesn't seem there's much more I can do here.' I smile at Lauren. She's very perceptive.

'It doesn't seem like you can do anything at all.' She points at my arm. 'Why don't you go home, at least for a while, and have some rest?'

'I am.'

She leans forward on her chair. 'You're serious?'

'I'm sure that Tom asked you to convince me, but I've made up my mind. I've seen a lot of things, and there's never much we can do.'

'Why am I not liking this speech? Are you going home or not?'

'I am, but then I'm going to the UN.'

'To do what? Get permission to travel the world?'

'No. But we need to do something more to help, and I'm sure we can.'

She starts leaning back on her chair slowly and shaking her head. 'Nothing is enough for you. Why?'

'Because we can still do more. I just came here because I wanted to say goodbye to you guys. I don't know if I'll have a chance to come back.'

At that moment, there's a knock at the door, and Mark asks.

'Did you finish your girly talk?' Mark is poking his head through the office door and as my eyes dance between them both Lauren blushes in her cotton blue dress while Mark goes to stand next to her, It's the first time I see Mark so comfortable around Lauren. Frank follows and comes to softly nudge my shoulder.

'Yeah. Talk all done. I just need to grab my things. I booked another flight for tomorrow.'

'You're leaving?'

'Frank, there's not much for me to do here.'

'So you're going somewhere else looking for trouble?'

'Maybe. I'm going home, and then we'll see.' I laugh a little. I'm going to miss them.

'You'll keep in touch, doll?'

'Of course.'

Three more goodbyes. Three more pains in my heart. It's good to know that there are still decent people willing to help in the world.

Chapter 11

I didn't tell anyone that I was coming, so there's a chance no one will be home. Nat might be working, and Tom is back in New York, so it'll be a waiting game.

As soon as I land in Birmingham, I feel like it's a whole new world, foreign to me. Do people have any idea what's happening out there? Do they care? We busy bees are so invested and involved in our own difficult lives that we can't find space for anything else. How can I change that?

Luckily, Nat is home, and my pretext to get in the building is a delivery of course.

She must think I'm a mirage or that she might be dreaming because she stands in front of me hanging on to the door as if she was hanging to dear life. It hasn't been that long since we last saw each other but she changed so much with the pregnancy, she looks beautiful and oddly enough shorter, somehow.

'You're here.' We both start crying for a while, standing in the doorway hugging and crying until we part and she gestures me inside. We're trying to wipe our faces from the tears, but they keep coming as we half cry, half laugh.

'Before I ask you how are you here and how's it been, can you please explain what happened to your damn arm?'

'Nat, I'm fine. This was just an accident. You look great, by the way. How far along are you?'

'Ah. Don't you try and change the subject. I want to know. You never tell me anything, and I get worried. Even worse since you got together with Tom because all he says is, "She's doing her own thing." I need more information than that, V.'

I lower and shake my head. 'Trust me – you don't. I'm fine really. Now tell me about you and the girls.'

'Do you think I don't care?'

'No, it's not that.' I shrug as I talk and put my bag down. 'It's just … I'm afraid if I told you exactly what was going on you would flip out and maybe would really get on all those planes you said and come get me.'

'Was it that bad?'

'Sometimes, but not just physically.'

'Coffee?'

'Please.' Always coffee with a talk. We always did that, and I start feeling comfortable.

'Where's Tom?'

'Oh, he's back in New York.'

'Why?' She raises an eyebrow, and I chuckle a little.

'He has to work. Plus, he doesn't know I'm here. He thinks I'm still in Muie. I actually didn't tell anyone I was coming.'

'In case you would change your mind and go back?' My eyes quickly find hers, and my coffee cup halts on its way to my lips. This woman really knows me, because deep down, I think that's one of the reasons I didn't tell anyone. So I take a deep breath and put my cup back down.

'Maybe, yeah. I might have thought that, but I also wanted to see you. I miss you.'

'I miss you too, darling. And the girls also.'

We're silent for a little while.

'So how long are you going to stay?'

I lower my head, avoiding her look. 'I'll be honest with you. I'm going to London. To the UN, and after that, I'm not sure, but, no, I'm not staying here for a long time, Nat.'

Another long awkward silence. I don't want to keep evading her questions. Might as well be honest.

'How about work?'

'I'm taking care of that now. Tomorrow, actually.'

'What are you going to do for money?'

I chuckle. 'I'm not sure, but I'll be fine. Nat, I want to do this. I finally found what I was looking for. I can't stop. Now's the time to do, not just try. I can't just try anymore.'

'I understand, but I'll miss you, and you're just going to stop your life to live for others.'

'I'm not going to stop my life. Nat, this is what I want to do now.'

'How about Tom? How does he fit in this new life of yours? What does he think?'

'I haven't talked to him about it yet.'

'I see. But you love him?'

'I do.'

She shakes her head. 'Only you to waste something like that.'

'Can we change the subject? How're the girls?'

She's still shaking her head and laughing. 'They're good. Chloe is still very wild, but Charlotte got really serious with Charlie. They're like official now.'

'Wow. Charlotte settling down. Can't believe it.'

'Yeah, but they're very cute together. They seem very happy.'

'Well, I'm happy for them. I was thinking you could arrange a lunch with them or something? But don't tell them I'm here.'

'Sure. I'll talk to them and try to make it this weekend.' I wasn't really intending to stay for so long. It's Wednesday today. What am I going to do till then?

'Hon, we all work. We can't just pick up and go.'

'I know. I know. It's fine. Just let me know what they say.'

'I will. What are you going to do now?'

'Hum, shower, clean my clothes, and I'll probably drop by the store instead of tomorrow and take care of things.'

'So you're really going to quit?'

'I can't work there anymore. Wouldn't be able to live with myself. I finally know what I want to do. It might not be easy, but that's what I want.'

'All right, okay.' She raises both hands.' I won't pester you about that anymore, but I'm still going to nag you about Tom.'

'Babe, I don't know what the future holds, but I'll be honest. I want to do all this changes in the world, but … I also want to be with Tom. Unfortunately, I don't know how to do that.'

'Haven't you guys talked about it?'

'We did when he was in Angola, but that was when we thought I was going to stay there.'

'So where are you going to go now?'

'I'm not sure. That will depend how things go at the UN on Friday. I have a friend there. Actually, he's Tom's friend. He helped us out in Thailand. We'll have a meeting, and we'll see.'

'Wait. Didn't you say you were in Angola?'

'Yeah, a lot happened. We end up going to Thailand to … help a friend.' Boy, my mouth. I have to start thinking before talking. She gives me a side eye.

'Explain please.'

'Nat, do you really want to know?'

'I do.'

'And you promise you won't flip out.'

'I promise to keep my judgement to a minimum.'

Another story time, but with Nat, I hide a few things. Just little white lies. So I tell her how beautiful Africa is. Tell her about all the magnificent animals that live there and the spectacular views. She asks me what happened in Somalia, and I tell her that was just corruption, no guns involved. I explain about the tobacco fields and how they were trafficking people and distributing landmines.

'That's how I end up in Muie,' I tell her.

'Landmines? Really?'

I keep repeating myself because she has trouble believing it. At some point, I lose track of what I was hiding and tell her why we ended up in Thailand.

'So that's how you hurt your shoulder?'

I nod. 'Yes, I was shot.'

Her brows shoot up, and her eyes bulge. 'Shot? You said you were fine. It was an accident.'

'I'm fine. Now. Nat, seriously, I can take care of myself.'

'Clearly.' She gestures to my injured shoulder, and I sigh. 'You always told me you were being careful and safe. You lied.'

'I didn't lie. I just didn't tell you everything. I was careful and had people looking out for me.'

'Okay, fine. What else?'

'What else what?'

'What else have you been hiding? What happened after that?'

'You sure you want to hear?'

'Tell me.'

So I carry on my story and tell her exactly what we went to do in Thailand and what happened there. I tell her that I was sleeping for two weeks before Tom came for me. She gasps and sighs as I talk, and when I finish, we're both silent.

'I need a tea.' Nat gets off the couch with an exasperated tone.

'Sure, a cup of tea solves anything.'

I'm laughing, but the look on her face is serious.

'I just need to calm down, smartass. I can't believe you did all of that. No wonder Tom kept saying you were doing amazing things.'

She puts the kettle down and hugs me tight and long. We sniffle for a while and she gets back to the tea.

We sit back on the couch like old times and talk for hours. She tells me what's like to be pregnant, and I explain her what I did with the mines. It seems such an insane conversation that if I hadn't lived it, I wouldn't believe it. After a few hours of talk, I go to the store to sort things out. They actually thought that, after all that time, I was going back to work. My boss and I were good friends, so I tell him a bit of what I did and why I want to quit. It won't be a big severance, but I still had a few hours and holidays banked, so I'll get a little. It'll help for a while.

Walking around town is squeezing my heart, so many people running in and out of shops, carrying bags full of useless gifts. The town looks beautifully decorated, ready for Christmas. The air smells cool. I'm sure it's going to snow soon, and I actually miss that. I miss the days of walking around town, not a care in the world. But that's just not my life anymore. I'm not that person anymore.

'So how did it go?'

I am barely through the flat door yet and Nat is asking already, I wonder if she is hoping I would back out and not actually quit.

'Okay. Josh is very understanding.'

'Hum. Hum.'

'What?'

'He always had a thing for you.'

'Oh, come on. He's married. Can you stop trying to set me up with everyone?'

She doesn't answer, just wiggles her eyebrows at me.

'I spoke with the girls, by the way. Everyone is free on Saturday. Scarlett is coming too.'

'That's cool. It'll be good to see everybody. Do you think we could do it in London?'

'London. Why?'

'My meeting is on Friday. Having to come back after that might be a bit tiresome.'

'Hum, I'm not sure I'll talk to them.'

'Thanks.'

For the next day, I pace around the flat, trying to get my backpack ready for when I have to leave. It feels strange having nothing to do. It makes me even more restless.

'So we'll see you tomorrow then. Where are you going to sleep?'

'There's always cheap places. I'll find something.'

She nods and kisses me goodbye. I know she doesn't approve of this carefree living style of mine, but having seen and lived so much, sleeping on the floor, I don't really worry about things like that anymore.

I've been talking to Kyle for a while. This meeting was his idea. I was just going in there and desperately asking for help. He thinks it's a good idea that the executives hear this from a person that actually lived it. Even though I don't have many pictures, having to always hide my camera. But I managed to take some with my phone as well.

We meet for coffee before we have to go to the meeting. Thought it would be a good idea, seeing we haven't actually met yet.

I'm here, I text him, hoping that will jolt some movement so I can recognize him. A young man gets up with his phone in his hand and waves me over. He must be around thirty, and he's very pretty, a ruffed hair and a bit of a rough beard kind of reminds me of Mike. I offer a hand to shake. He laughs in his beige sweater, swatting it away, and pulls me into a hug. It's weird. I feel like I've known him for a long time. We've talked so much, but now I'm looking into a stranger's caramel eyes. It feels weird.

'The famous Violet. Sit. Sit.'

'I'm famous?'

'You have no idea. You'll see. Coffee?' He laughs a little and smiles.

'Yes. Please.'

'You feeling better?'

I follow his gaze to my shoulder. 'Yeah. Getting there.'

'So. I really think the board is going to go for this, but I don't know if they will be willing to involve another office.'

I nod. 'Yeah, I can imagine, but—'

He cuts me off. 'We have to try.'

The smile broadens on my face. 'Yes. We have to try.' I continue to smile. Don't know what else to say. Talking to him on the phone is one thing, but looking at his handsome face is another.

'I still can't believe what you did in Thailand.'

'Look, everyone keeps calling me crazy, but I didn't go in there. I was taken. I'm not that crazy.' My voice raises a little. I'm getting really tired of assumptions and accusations.

'Whoa. Okay. I see I struck a chord. Sorry.'

'No, I'm sorry. It's just everyone has been judging me without knowing what actually happened. Like I said, I'm not that crazy.'

He sighs and raises his hands. 'Sorry. I should've known better. Let's forget that, okay? How are things in Muie?' That's a nice segue.

'They're better. All the mines are gone, and we're getting in prosthetics little by little.'

'That's good. But?'

'But what?'

'I felt a but there in all that positivity.'

I chuckle. 'Well, things are better, and I'm happy, but it could be so much more. There's so much that still needs to be done. People can't just fall into contentment and resign to the notion that that's the best we can get.'

He's looking at me and shaking his head. I've seen that look before. I want too much.

'I guess then we try,' he says.

A wave of gratefulness hits me, and my heart races. It's the first time someone doesn't judge me for wanting so much change. We finish our coffee and make way to the office. The building he brings me to is just behind Tower Bridge. It's shiny and sparkling, and it oozes money. We go through rolling doors and into a pristine elevator, and I find myself starting to stew over all the extravagant things I'm seeing. He guides me to an office, and we wait. It looks like a conference room. There's a long table and prearranged individual placemats, a bottle of water and a cup, a pen and dossiers. We don't have to wait long until the room is invaded by a series of bodies cutting the view I had from the Shard. Everyone sits before looking at me. At the top of the table, a red-headed woman, shorter than me, is standing.

'Finally, we meet brave Violet. Come, sit next to me.' She stretches out an arm to me, and I look at Kyle. It seems like I have trust issues now, but he nods and smiles at me, so I comply.

'I'm Rose, head of the department here.'

'Hi. Hum, thank you so much for your help.'

'Of course, if we can, we should help.'

I can't keep my eyes from rolling. Never liked bureaucracy.

'You don't agree?' We're both sitting as she asks.

'No, I do. It's just that a lot of people can help but don't. Can't really blame anyone. I myself was too absorbed in my own life to pay attention to the agony of the world.'

She's quiet for a while, mulling over my words, and I have a feeling she doesn't really like my attitude.

'Well, let's try and change that, shall we?'

I'm surprised by her answer. I actually thought she would come up with excuses or justifications. But for the next two and a half hours, we plan as I tell them my story and show them pictures. When we come up to the subject of Thailand, she starts to ask specific questions.

'Shouldn't you be asking this of Frank or Sam? They worked on the inside. I was a captive, deprived from my senses, food, and water. There's not many specifics that I could tell you.'

'Well, then maybe we need to contact them.'

'I can tell you one thing though.' All eyes quiz me. 'I was deceived by a woman. When I was trying to find my way back to the hotel, she offered to help. She took me to that place. Having a woman aiding these guys doesn't make the job any easier.'

They are silent for a long time, clearly waiting for Rose to speak.

'You're right. That definitely doesn't help, but we can't go to Thailand with the premise that all women are traitors. We need to study and do research before—'

'While you guys do all that in the cosiness of your offices, children, women, and men are suffering. Not just dying. They're suffering.'

I'm letting my temper get the best of me, and Kyle looks at me sympathetically. Rose might not like it, and I might get out of here without nothing, but it's the truth. I was expecting she would send me out of the room, but instead, she sighs and puts a hand on my shoulder.

'I can't begin to imagine the things you have seen, and I understand. Trust me. But I can't send someone out there without being prepared. I can't sacrifice a life even if I'm not sure if that would happen or not.'

I lean back on my chair. She's right. It would be crazy and irresponsible to do something like that even if we're trying to help.

So we start to plan again. Rose decides that Thailand needs time and better planning, and I can't really argue with that, so I bring up Mutimutema, and she gets quickly invested in sorting out the town. Although Kyle was right when he said they don't like to involve other offices, Rose agreed that united we'll make a bigger change. So I make my final pitch. I tell her how it all started with the party that the charity threw for people to meet celebrities and get donations and tell her that we should do that once a year. Then I suggest what my heart wants the most.

'But why you? There's better people to explain our case, no offence, Violet.'

'I know Rose and you're right. I'm not saying to send me alone, but I do think it's a good idea they hear these things from me.' She's still thinking about it, and I can tell that she knows I'm hiding something.

'I'll have to run all of thins through upstairs, but here's my proposal. I like the idea of having a charity ball or party. Meet a celeb for the charity is a great idea. So Christmas is coming; we'll do one then. People are more generous around the holidays, especially celebrities. You'll go to New York, but you have to be back by then. I want you at that party. Don't let New York steal you. I want you working for us.'

My heart is racing. I can't believe I'm getting what I want. I just keep nodding, not trusting any words that may come out.

'After that, we'll probably tackle Mutimutema. Anyone has anything else to add?' She speaks to the room, and I start getting nervous as I see

VIVIANA SANTOS

eyes going through all the notes that were taken throughout the meeting. But as they all nod, I let out a breath I didn't know I was holding.

'Okay, then let's make this official. I'll take you to human resources.'

'Now?'

She laughs. 'Of course. Let the investors pay for your ticket to New York.' When she sees my raised brow, she corrects. 'We have assigned budgets. You're not taking money from anyone.' It seems like I'm really easy to read.

Before she takes me to HR, I'm introduced to everyone in the room. I'm patted on the back and congratulated, and I can't understand why.

'So are you going to tell me what's in New York?'

I stop abruptly, looking at her. I thought I had gotten away with it. Suddenly, she starts laughing.

'There's no need to panic, Violet. I actually do agree with you. I just wanted to know.'

I don't know what it is, but I feel at ease with her now. 'Tom's there,' I blurt out before I change my mind.

'Ah yes. Tom.' Those three words tell me that she knows a lot more than what I thought, but there's no time for explanations because she ushers me in to the HR office to get all paperwork and ID done, which to my surprise doesn't take long.

After that, she brings me back to the main lobby where Kyle is waiting for me.

'So dinner anyone?' Rose offers

'I could eat.' Actually I am starving but thought would be best to be humble.

I look at Kyle, and he smiles, nods, and shrugs.

'Dinner sounds great.' I have to get her to tell me about Tom.

While she goes back upstairs to get her things, we wait.

'That went much better than I thought.' Kyle is genuinely surprised.

'You thought she wouldn't go for it?'

He nods. 'Not only that, I thought you would lose your temper and start cursing at everyone. That's where I would bet my money.' He's laughing and teasing me, and I find myself finally relaxing and playing with him, swatting his arm at his playful accusation.

'Shall we go?' Rose is eyeing both of us, certainly judging, and we both

174

stand without a word. It feels like we're children caught by their mother when doing something mischievous. We end up at a pub by the Thames, and I quickly realize that is the same one where I went with the girls and where I first saw Tom. I can't help but smile at the memory.

'You seem nostalgic.'

'You're such a good people reader.'

She chuckles. 'I actually am. It's not the first time someone has told me that, and I can tell you that it got me to where I'm today.'

'I don't doubt it. Being able to read someone easily is very useful.' I think back to the scum of people that I met and my failed relationships. It would have been useful then.

'Trust me: I understand. Now tell me about Tom.' She changes the subject so quickly that I have difficulty in keeping up and forming words, but she waits for me to regain composure.

'What would you like to know?'

She quirks a smile, knowing that she got me flustered. 'How did you guys meet?'

I smile at another memory and I tell her about the party.

'Is that why you want to do it once a year?'

'I think it's a good idea and easy way to get donations, plus if we get one or two people involved into helping like me, that's a plus no?'

'That's definitely a plus,' Kyle interjects. I had forgotten he was there.

'Yes. Kyle's right. If we can get people to donate and help, it's always a plus. So you guys stayed friends after that?'

My cheeks heat up, and I know I'm blushing.

'Or maybe more than that,' Rose says.

'Maybe,' I respond.

She smiles at me and opens a menu. We keep the conversation going through dinner. Kyle explains how, after Tom called him and he read the email, he burst into Rose's office.

'Yeah. He had a wild look on his face. It was scary. All he said was, "You have to read this." I didn't question it.'

Kyle looks embarrassed, and his cheeks pink a little, and I offer him a smile.

'Well, I can't thank you both enough for acting so fast. We would probably have lost the buyers.'

Rose lets a hand settle on top of mine. 'Darling, you don't have to thank us. That's the whole purpose of the UN, protecting all nations.'

'I know. The UN has loads of different departments and sub-companies, but the headquarters are in New York ...' I trail off a little, expecting her reaction, and she clearly looks bothered.

'Is there a question in there?'

'I don't want to pry, but why don't you want me working for them?'

She sighs and exchanges a look with Kyle. 'New York will always be headquarters, but other offices will still have to meet quotas and budgets, or we can't get enough finance to stay afloat. It's silly and bureaucratic when you think of the terrors of the world, but it's the reality.'

'So instead of working together and sharing resources, you guys are competitors?'

'You don't get it. It's not like I want it, but I have no choice. If I didn't fight it, we would have lost the office long time ago.' I don't push anymore, just nod. I do know what is like to feel powerless, but things can't be like that. If we fight each other instead of coming together against the evils in the world, we already lost the war.

So I quickly change subject. No point duelling on it right now. We finish dinner, and then Rose asks where I'm staying, and only then do I remember I forgot to look for a place, which must show on my face because she laughs and offers me her couch. Someone I've known for a few hours offers me a bed, and again her gesture causes a grateful wave to course through me.

'That would be great actually. Saves me trying to find a cheap hotel now. Thank you.'

She nods and steps away so I can say goodbye to Kyle. 'It really was a pleasure to finally match the voice with the face,' I say.

'Violet, it's not like we're never going to see each other again. We'll be working together soon.'

He winks at me and grabs my hand, and I start to feel so awkward I can't find my words.

'You really are an incredible woman you know?'

I blush all over, but I still have to let him know that I'm his friend, but how do I do that without being presumptuous or hurting him? 'Thank you, Kyle. I couldn't have done it without you and Rose or Tom for that matter. Maybe he'll come back with me, and you guys can get together sometime.' Simple and subtle.

'Yes, of course. That would be great.' It kills me to see that look on his face, but I can't give him hope. My heart belongs to Tom.

After saying goodbye to Kyle, Rose and I make our way to her house in Marylebone. More luxury to aggravate my nerves. We talk for a while. I tell her that I'm meeting my friends tomorrow. Talking over tea, I find out why she's so understanding of my situation, why she does this job.

With her eyes on the tea cup, she tells me she had a fourteen-year-old daughter, that just like me she disappeared in a second, and at the time, she was lost and had no idea what to do or who to turn for help. That's how she decided to join the UN and save as many as she could, for her daughter.

Then I share my pain, how my daughter was born, but just for a few minutes just enough for me to get to know her. We both have tears in our eyes, and I hug her, like a daughter would her mother.

'Thank you.' She caresses my cheek but I can't help to feel confused
'For what?'
We're both sniffling.
'For listening. For helping. For caring.'
'Anytime, Rose.'
'Well, I've talked to Tom quite a bit. About you.' She gets up to take the cups to the kitchen with a big breath.
'Me? Why?'
'Because you're important to him. He can't keep you out of a conversation, but he also told me how much of a troublemaker you are. I have a feeling I'm going to lose sleep every time I send you to the field.'
'I don't look for trouble. I just want to help, but I promise I'll always be careful.'
'You better.' She slides a soft palm down my cheek as she says this, and instantly, I miss my mother.

Thankfully, I have a dreamless sleep. I feel rested like I haven't been in a long time. After having breakfast with Rose, she tells me that my flight is on Sunday and I can pick up my ticket at the counter. I had no idea we could do that. I thank her before saying goodbye, and she reminds me that I need to be back for the Christmas party. At least, that will give me a week with Tom. It's better than nothing. Just as I was about to leave she calls me out.

'Violet. You're welcome to stay with me until you get settled.' What do I say to this kind woman?

'Thank you, Rose.' That's all I can say.

I wander around the city before I have to meet the girls for lunch. I take a stroll around Regent's Park before I make my way to Waterloo, the closest station to the pub. The last time I was walking by the river was when I first pushed Tom away. It broke my heart to do it and see him walk away, but at the time, I thought it was the only way. Now I know better. Maybe Nat is right. Maybe I can have both.

When I enter the pub, they're luckily all distracted looking at the menus, so I make my entrance.

'At least, you could wait for me to order.' All four heads turn quickly to me, and it takes them a few seconds to react.

'Violet.' Chloe is the first one up and running to me. She hits me so hard I drop my backpack. In a second, they're all engulfing me in hugs, mixed with tears and questions of how I am and what I'm doing there. All the while, Nat remains seated.

'You knew.' Scarlett is pointing a finger at her, and she smiles and nods.

'Take it easy, Scarlett. I asked her not to say anything.' They keep their eyes on me while I sit. Like I'm not real.

'So are you finally coming home?' The girls gasp and widen their eyes at her. But she seems unfazed by that.

'Are you crazy? She's a flight risk. You can't ask that.' While Charlotte is having a go at her, she just shrugs and pushes her hair back, looking at me, waiting for my answer.

'In a way.'

This time, Nat intervenes. She kept texting me to find out how the meeting went, but all I told her was good. 'What does that mean? You're either here, or you're not.'

'And what about Tom? Does he know you're here? What happened with you guys in Angola?' Chloe is spiting questions at me, leaving me dizzy

Before I can answer, Scarlett questions me too. 'Did you really get shot?'

They're all bombarding me with questions, and I stop listening for a while and start rubbing my temples. After a few seconds, they all quiet down.

'Sorry, hon. We're just excited to see you.' Chloes apologetic look helps me take a deep breath

'Yeah, and worried.' Charlotte's voice is genuinely concerned, so I take a breather.

'It's okay, but one at a time, please,' I beg and laugh, 'before anything else. No, Scarlett, Tom doesn't know, and I would appreciate if no one told him please.'

They're nodding when Nat hits the table with her glass.

'Don't you think that you done enough pushing away? When are you going to realize that you two belong together? When are you going to give him a chance and live your life?' She's really upset, but I'm a little amused by my hidden agenda and start smiling.

'This is funny to you?'

'Tomorrow.'

'Tomorrow what?'

'I'll start living tomorrow. I'll see to it as soon as I land in New York.' They all display blank stares, and I smile harder.

Nat puts a hand on my shoulder, and I wince.

'Sorry, I forgot. What do you mean?'

'I'm going to New York tomorrow. I have a meeting in UN headquarters on Monday and …' I can't stop smiling. I actually feel a sort of glee inside me, but Nat cuts me off.

'So you're going just for work?'

'If you let me finish, you'll find out.' She sticks her tongue out at me but doesn't interrupt anymore, and I proceed to share my news.

'So you'll be working in London then?'

I nod at Nat.

'But Tom is in New York.'

'Yeah, I'm aware of that Scarlett.'

'How're you going to be together with an ocean between you? How are these good news?'

'Nat, we've been in different parts of the world, and we were still trying.'

'Enough of trying – you have to do,' Charlotte interjects.

'Nat, chill babe.'

'No. You weren't trying anything. You were out there doing your own thing while he was pining around for you. You don't know what it was like …'

'I know exactly what it was like.' I can't take her accusations anymore. Even if they're true. 'Do you think I was sightseeing the world's wonders completely oblivious of Tom or my feelings for him?'

'No. But I know you. I know that you drown yourself in work or anything else to forget.' Her voice is low and soft, and I let out the breath I was holding in. She has known me for a long time. Sometimes I think she knows me better then myself.

'Hon, I found this opportunity. I can't work in an office all the time. You know that. I told you I finally know what I want to do with my life and that I also want Tom in it, but like I said, I'm not sure how to do that. I'm going there, and we'll talk. After that, I don't know, but I'll try.'

She rolls her eyes at the magic word, and I laugh. When we a quiet down, I look around the table and notice that everyone ordered burgers, and I can't catch the tear that escapes my eyes.

'You all ordered burgers.'

Chloe smiles at me from across the table. 'It seemed only fitting.'

'I missed you guys.' I can't say anything else without crying like a little girl.

We spend the rest of lunch sharing our news from the past eight months. Keeping the gory details to myself, I answer their questions about my 'adventure', as they call it, although that's not what it is for me. I feel like I finally found my purpose in life. After we leave the pub we decide to walk by the river, it's not always we have such a nice day in London.

'I actually need your help.' I turn to Scarlett in hopes that she can help

'Sure, hon. Anything.'

'I'm not sure where Tom is. I don't know who else to ask.'

'You ask me of course. I'll get you to him don't worry.'

I'm smiling and leaning on her shoulder already dreaming of tomorrow.

Chapter 12

I have butterflies in my stomach, and this time isn't because of the flight. I'm so nervous that my palms are sweaty, and I start to think that someone at the airport will notice and suspect I'm hiding something. That's how nervous I am. Scarlett gave me all the information I need to find him. She even told me to get in cabs. Otherwise, I would get lost fast, and I had my share of being lost. But I have to land at JFK; the taxi bill will be astronomical. The theatre he's performing at is close to Central Park, so there's no better reference than that. I won't get lost. I hope.

The air isn't as stuffed hot as in Thailand, but it still feels like we shouldn't be breathing it. This city really looks like it doesn't sleep. It's so busy and full of life. For a little while, all I see are blurry shapes. It takes time to get used to this bustle. I don't think I could ever live in a place like this.

It takes me a while to get to Broadway. I ask everyone how to get to Central Park, but I still managed to get in a wrong subway going down to Brooklyn instead of going to Harlem. I'm surprised when that doesn't bother me that much. I guess my carefree living style has settle in for good. The ticket Scarlett bought me is for 3:00 p.m. I still have a couple of hours, so I go to Central Park and have one of the famous hot dogs from a cart. I knew the park was big and I've seen many, many big parks. But being here after seeing it in movies so many times feels just like when I moved to London, an enormous glamorous place, just dreamy.

I had no idea it would be so cold. I knew it would be snowing, but this isn't like London. It's freezing. Still can't deny how beautiful the park looks covered in snow. It's magical. I get a coffee from another cart, hoping it will keep my hands warm until I arrive at the theatre. I'm definitely not dressed for this. Everyone is in a three-piece suit and gala dresses I wonder if they'll let me in. But I got to try, right?

I wait until almost everyone is in. If they don't let me in, I don't want to cause a scene. I can always wait for him outside. He might find a popsicle, but I'll be there. The usher looks at me up and down several times, as if I would be struck by fairy godmother and change into a princess gown, but I follow his gaze and smile.

'Miss, look—'

I raise a hand. 'I know. I know, but please, I need to be in there.'

'Can you change?' He gives me another sweep. I can tell that he's trying to be nice and help, so I do the only thing I can think of. I tell him the truth – why I'm there, what I've done, and where I've been. I even show him pictures and texts. This man now knows probably more than he should, but I really don't care right now. After a few seconds of looking at me, he finally speaks.

'Do you know how lucky you are that I'm working today? It's supposed to be my day off.' He's smiling at me and taking my ticket to punch it.

'I guess it's my lucky day then.'

'Tom, is a really nice guy, and since he's been here, we became good friends. He talks about you all the time.'

What are the odds of this happening? The one person I needed to be at that door today.

'Thank you so much. I'll sit in the back.'

'Nonsense. You have a ticket. I'll take you to your seat. I just hope he doesn't see you during the play.' I look at him, surprised. 'Don't get me wrong he'll be over the moon when he sees you, but he won't be able to concentrate, I'm sure.' He's still smiling at me, but I sense concern in his voice.

'That's why I chose a seat in the middle of the room. I thought I would blend well that way.'

'Yeah, you're right. He can't see your clothes there.' He's teasing me, and I can tell that his friendship with Tom is genuine. I don't answer. I just make a face at him while he shows me my seat. I can tell that the people around me are judging, but I don't care. I'm not here for them. The lights dim, and the room instantly mutes. It's been more than a decade since I've been to a live theatre show, and I had forgotten the feeling of wonder when you see someone telling a story, uniting audience with performer. It really is an art.

For the next hour and a half, I'm completely taken by him. One thing is seeing him in a movie, but live, he's mesmerizing. Nothing else exists. No one else is here except for us two. I'm still in my seat when half the theatre has emptied and the usher from before comes to find me again.

'Enjoyed the show?'

'Very much.' I'm still swimming in wonder.

He smiles and offers me his hand. 'It'll be my pleasure to take you there.'

The lady still sitting next to me looks at me sideways, a look of disgust on her face. Let them judge.

He takes me backstage, and I come face to face with his name on a door. I'm so nervous that I look at the usher as to ask what I do now. He knocks for me.

'Come in,' comes from inside the room, and the usher gestures for me to go in and mouths, *Good luck*. I'm nervous. I nod and smile at him before I close the door behind me.

There he sits across the room. Reading something on a brown leather chair. It's been about six days since I last saw him, but it feels like forever. He still hasn't looked up, and it's taking me everything not to speak. I wait.

'Who is it?' He's so immersed and distracted by what he's reading. He looks cute and annoying at the same time, but I remain strong, waiting for him to look up. What the hell is he reading?

Finally, he tears his eyes from the paper and locks on mine. The important piece of literature ends up on the floor, and he stands from the chair, walking very slowly to me, tears filling both our eyes. He grabs both my arms, as if to make sure that I'm real and in front of him.

'Violet …' His voice is charged with emotion, and he hugs me tight. He speaks on top of my head. 'I had seen you so many times in that audience that I thought you were another mirage.'

I try to push away, so I can look at him, but he doesn't let go.

'You saw me?'

'Almost every time I'm on that stage.' He nods and loosens his grip, and I look at him. Two seconds looking into my eyes and our lips crash.

We kiss for so long that when we stop, I'm breathless. He grabs my hand and guides me to a couch.

'Come.' We sit face to face. He keeps playing with my hair with one hand, and the other grabs mine.

'I still can't believe you're here. How did you know where to find me?'

I smile. 'Scarlett.'

'Ah, you called her.'

I shake my head and he furrows his brows.

'I got together with the girls for lunch, and Scarlett, of course. That's when I asked her for help.'

'Wait, you went to London?'

I'm trying to be cryptic. Make my news more elated, but I can't stop smiling.

'What's going on, V? Just tell me.' He's prepared for bad news, and they might not be great or perfect, but it's better than being anywhere in the world the whole time. So I take a deep breath and a big gulp. Let's hope he shares my opinion.

He stops playing with my hair, and his face grows hard and serious. 'Stop the suspense. Just put me out of my misery.'

'I arrived in Birmingham on Wednesday.'

He swallows hard but doesn't say anything.

'I got together with Nat, who scolded me like crazy, by the way. And then I went to my old job to take care of things.'

'Your old job? So you ended your sabbatical to quit?' He shakes his head.

'I did. I finally know what I want to do with my life, and working in retail isn't it.'

'Right. Going around the world and getting yourself into trouble is the dream.' He's up and pacing in front of me, but I'm calm and watching him.

'Sometimes it will be. It comes with the job.'

He stops abruptly. 'What the hell are you talking about?'

'Tom, please sit.' I pat the couch, and he blows a breath out as he sits. 'Now can you just listen to what I have to say?' He nods. 'Where was I?'

'Around the world.' He's mocking, but I laugh and proceed to tell him about my meeting with UN. The more I talk and explain, the closer he gets to me, and his eyes grow softer. Before I tell him about New York, he's smiling and breathing hard. Damn, he looks so sexy. He tackles me, interrupting my speech with a hot and desperate kiss. I can't breathe. I speak between kisses and mashes lips.

'Tom...' He doesn't stop or slow down. Not until he presses on my shoulder, and I cringe.

'Sorry. Are you okay?'

'Yeah, I'm fine.' We're fixing our clothes and going back to a sitting position.

'So what exactly does this mean? What are you doing in New York?'

Here goes nothing. 'Like I said, I'll be working with the UN in the field.' He crinkles his nose at the word. 'But it won't be always. Rose doesn't want me to, and for me to work there. That was one of the points I had to agree on.'

He smiles, a sexy, smug smile, and I purse my lips and shake my head. Have to keep strong.

'I have a meeting with New York office tomorrow. The offices don't get along, and we have to change that. They need to see that, to make a bigger impact in the world, they have to work together and share resources.'

'That's what your meeting will be about?'

'That's my first mission. Yes.'

'And Rose wants you working for them?' I nod. 'So ... you'll be working in London ... always?' He's trying to figure out the future. The possibilities, but I have to tell him the truth. Have to be honest.

'Yes. She said, "Don't let New York steal you," before I left.' I chuckle a little, remembering her serious face. 'But Tom?'

'Hum?'

'I'll still be working in the field sometimes. I can't be in an office all day. I'm still not sure how all is going to work. It's still very new, but this is what I want, Tom.' I stop talking for a little while. Waiting for him to digest everything I told him. He looks at me very seriously.

'So you came to New York to have a meeting at the UN. But what are you doing here then?' I can tell he's afraid. I guess now is my turn to fight for him.

'I think it was about time I came for you.' I'm smiling and searching his eyes. But he doesn't move, doesn't say anything, no reaction at all.

Maybe I missed my chance with him, pushed him away one too many times.

'So there's no chance for you to work in NY?' I shake my head as I sink back in the couch. 'I wish I could, but this is my opportunity to make some actual change. I can't throw that away.'

'And no more going around the world aimlessly?'

I shake my head again. Don't know what else to say. He gets up and offers me a hand.

'Okay. Let's go.'

'What? Where?'

'Just come.' He doesn't say anything else. Just grabs his things and we leave. I feel like I'm back at the party in the hotel, being dragged by him through hallways to that beautiful balcony.

We get on a subway and take a few minutes ride. The whole time, his arms are around me, but he still doesn't speak. We resurface again and continue to walk. I have no idea where we're going or where I am, but right now, I don't care. I don't want to ruin the moment by asking questions, so I follow him until he stops and grabs both my hands.

'Will you come up with me?' Again, I feel like we're back in London.

When I take a look around, I smile at the view, and just like when we were in front of London Eye, I squeeze his hands and ask, 'How are we getting a ticket now?'

We share a smile and a kiss.

'Don't worry. I got it.'

I giggle like a little girl while he pulls me into the Empire State Building. It's already quite late. I don't even know if it's still open, but Tom can make anything happen that much I know, so I watch, the same as in London. Some low conversation, a few smiles, and a shake of hands before he comes back to me with a megawatt smile on his face.

'Shall we?' Once in the elevator, I turn to him.

'You have to tell me how you do that. Do you just bribe everyone to impress a girl?'

He shakes his head and chuckles. Man, he's gorgeous. We're on opposite sides of the elevator when he moves to me, bracing his arms on the rail behind me.

'I have never bribed anyone.' And he kisses my neck.

'How do you get people to do what you want? After hours or without tickets.' He moves to the other side of my neck, and it's taking me everything not to put my arms around him and kiss him senseless. He keeps kissing me all over and talking.

'With my charm of course.' I laugh and feel all tingly. 'My wonderful personality.' A kiss on one cheek. 'My great looks.' Another smooch and I'm hanging by a thread. 'My generosity.' This time he stops his face inches from mine, my arms still crossed over my chest and our eyes linked. He kisses me softly, slowly, and his hands are still on the rail and mine under my armpits, itching to pull him to me.

Even though it's dark already, the view is still incredible all around – East River at one side and the Hudson at the other reflecting the moonlight. Snow in the air makes everything more magical. I can't see much of Central Park because it's dark, but from here I can see how vast it is. We keep wandering all around, taking in the views, stopping here and there, but not touching each other. We wander together and alone, sharing looks and smiles, but still not touching.

'Do you know how many times I imagined myself here?'

He stops to look back at me. My eyes on the view, and I carry on.

'I always said if I ever came to New York, this would be the first place I would come to.'

He starts to move closer to me, and I turn to face him. 'Thank you for bringing me here.'

He smiles and licks his lips. This man kills me.

'You're welcome darling.' And my body crashes with his. Our mouths mash together and our breaths mingle.

Never would I have thought a few months back that I would be here, with him, trying to sort out our life together or the possibility of it. We spend most of the time quiet, enjoying the view and the company. Occasionally, he points out a few important buildings and tries really hard to point out the exact place of Broadway. I can tell by the look on his face as he talks about all the different shows he's done that he loves it. He loves it more than being in a movie. I've found my calling, and by the looks of it, he has found his, and I remember what Nat said: *How are you going to be together with an ocean between you?* How exactly are we going to do that?

I was so excited to see him and to be here that I forgot how cold I was until a breeze blows through and I shiver all over. Tom stands behind me and wraps his arms around me. It feels like home.

'Your hands are frozen. We should go.'

I want to argue, say that I want to stay here longer with him in this bubble and enjoy the view, but I'm so cold.

'Okay. Maybe we can come back another day. With more clothes.'

'Yeah, another day.' He laughs and grabs my hand. We haven't talked about everything yet, so he doesn't know that I'm staying for a week. Hopefully, he'll be happy with the news.

He brings me back to the Upper East Side to a tall, red-brick building. His apartment is almost on the top floor and has a great uninterrupted view of the river. It's not majorly decorated. It actually is mostly grey.

'Welcome to my humble abode.' He stretches his long arms and disappears into a door. I stand by the wall-size window, contemplating the view and getting ready for what's to come.

'Are you hungry? I can cook us something.'

I shake my head, and he lowers his.'

'I'm hungry, but I think we have to talk first.'

'Do we have to?'

How I wish my answer would be no, but I can't live with uncertainty anymore. I need to know if we're going to try or give up. He sits on the couch and gestures for me to join him.

'Sorry. I know we have to. I'm just scared, I guess.' I cuddle his face between my hands, and he closes his eyes, touching his forehead to mine.

'I'm scared too.' He opens his eyes. 'But we need to talk. Can't keep going pretending everything is okay and that somehow things will sort themselves out. Life doesn't work like that, unfortunately.'

'I know. I know all that, but I'm tired of walking away from you, tired of never being in the same place as you at the same time.'

'I get it. Nat said the same. How can we be together with an ocean between us? Those were her words.'

'What did you tell her?'

I look at him. Afraid of his reaction to the fact that I have no idea. 'I told her that I wanted you in my life.'

His eyes soften, and he smiles.

'That I finally found what I was looking for to do with my life and that I wanted to try.'

'Try what?'

'Try to fight for you. To be with you.' I'm so nervous and scared that I can't meet his gaze anymore.

'And what did you come up with?' The golden question. How the hell do we do that? Do I give up Rose's trust and try to get NY's office to take me, or does he quit what he loves to do now and go back to London. What do we do? He's watching me having this internal discussion with myself. Until he starts to shake his head but smiles.

'I'm not sure either.' My eyes well up, and I hug him. Can't keep crying in front of him. I think we had enough of that, but this time he's the first one to break. He collapses against me and holds me tight in his arms. We stay like this for a long time, sobbing softly in each other's arms. I can't help but feel like we're saying goodbye.

'I love you, Tom. I do, but I'm not sure what to do. I want so many things. I don't know what to do.' He's wiping my face now.

'I love you too.' And with that he pulls me to him. One leg on each side of his lap, no more talking. We had enough of that. His kisses start slow, sweet, and we start removing pieces of clothing one by one in between kisses until we're just in our underwear. He stops to look at me, and I blush. He smiles.

'So beautiful.' Our lips unite again, and he lifts me up, my legs wrapped around his waist while he carries me to his bedroom.

'I hope you're prepared this time.'

'I had imagined sometimes that you would come here to stay, and I actually remembered, so …' He stops just by the edge of the bed, still holding me. He sits me on the bed and opens his second drawer on his nightstand, and I blush again.

'I don't think we'll need that many.' He looks at me. Such a savage and hungry look on his face that I have to squeeze me thighs. God, I need him. He doesn't close the drawer. Moves to me. Kisses me softly, pushing me back on the bed. I'm all his. We spend the whole night making love. Now I know the difference between that and having sex.

At some point in the night, we find ourselves on the couch. We were in desperate need of a snack break. We talk a little about Rose and Kyle,

VIVIANA SANTOS

and then we go back to bed where the sinful drawer is still open. I sit on the bed and move my hand to close it, but he stops me and shakes his index finger at me.

'Uh-uh. I'm not done.' And he pounces again.

It was a tiresome and blissful night. Our first time. Well, lots of firsts. But I sure hope it won't be the last.

Chapter 13

'Good morning, sleepyhead.' He kisses me awake. I've never felt happier in my life. Time could stop now.

'What's this?'

'Breakfast in bed, love.' I kiss him, and he sits next to me. Such a mundane routine. A common couple.

'What time is your meeting?' Reality calls.

'At ten. What time is it?'

'Seven.'

'Really? I think we should go back to sleep.'

'Yeah, we could …' He's looking at me over his coffee mug and wiggles his eyebrows.

'Seriously? You're insatiable, man.'

'For you, I am.' We finish our breakfast, and he takes me to the bathroom for a communal shower.

'So what's your schedule like?'

'I'm free today.'

'And the rest of the week?'

'What do you mean?' His eyes quickly find mine on the bathroom mirror.

'You know. Your schedule, or more like, your availability, for the rest of the week?' I'm smiling, but he still doesn't believe what I'm saying.

'You're saying you're going to be here for the whole week?'

'I didn't say it yet, but yeah. I have to be back in London on Sunday, though. Rose went with my idea, or more like, your charity's idea, to host a party.'

'You're going back for a party?'

'Hum. Hum. Meet a celebrity, donate to charity,' I sing it out, and he starts laughing.

'It's a good idea. So what are you going to do the whole week?' He's taunting me.

'Depending on your schedule and how this went I was hoping I could spend it with you.'

'You were. Were you?' He turns to me and grabs me by my hips, plants kisses all over my face. 'Maybe I should have held off from taking you to the Empire State Building yesterday.'

'No. Yesterday was perfect.' He touches his forehead to mine before stepping away.

'I have plays Tuesday, Wednesday, and Saturday. Always in the afternoon or at night. We rehearse some mornings. Other than that' – he pauses to look at me – 'I'm all yours.'

We both go to NY UN, and even here, people seem to know Tom from his work with the charity. We're all in a conference room, similar to the one in London. Everyone is chatting and shaking hands, and I'm waiting to be heard. Once seated at the top of the table, Richard turns to me. He has that same powerful look that Rose holds but on a much sterner face. A silk black shirt held in place by suspenders makes him look more overweight than he actually is. Judging by his grey hairs and heavy wrinkles I would say he is over fifty, but never know.

'I've been in contact with Rose, and she says we should listen to what you have to say.'

'I appreciate that—'

'But' – he interrupts – 'if you're already bound to work for her, why should we? Don't get me wrong. We all know your story, but lots of people go through that. What makes you so special?'

I'm silent for a while, trying to find the best and least offensive words.

'I'm not special, and this isn't about me. It's about all those people you speak of, about the millions lost in the world. It's about you, as an entity, prioritizing budgets and quotas, maintaining rivalry with all your offices instead of working together, instead of sharing resources. Can't you see that together we can change the world? So no. This isn't about my story – it's about theirs.'

I was expecting him to protest. To call me naive or, like everyone else, crazy. But those words don't come he just sits there not quite looking at me with a ghost of a smile. I feel like I'm losing this battle.

'Rose was right. You definitely are an asset. I'm pissed she got to you first.' Is that his main concern? 'Don't look at me like that. It's just how the world works.'

'It doesn't have to be.'

'Do you think it's easy?'

'If it were, it would have changed by now. We have to stop seeing each other as separate individuals. We have to work and think as one. Alone, we can't do any real change. I didn't do anything by myself. I had lots of help, and that's the whole point—working together.'

Richard still doesn't look at me. He rises from his lavish black leather chair and stands by the window. He exudes the same type of power as Rose. Everyone in the room waits for him to talk, and I exchange looks with Tom. Is that how it should be? Aren't people entitled to have an opinion without the threat of losing their jobs? His expression is the same when he comes back to his seat.

'Rose said after the party and the new year, she wants to tackle Mutimutema. I guess that's a good place to start, and we'll both keep planning to get back to Thailand.'

I keep moving my eyes to Tom, but his look tells me he understood as much as I did from that speech.

'I'm sorry what does that mean?' I ask.

'It means if we're working together and sharing resources, we're sharing everything.' He sighs as he smiles slowly at me and gives me a pointed look on that last word.

'I don't know if Rose will like that, but I'm in. If that's what it'll take for everyone to work together.'

'Don't worry about Rose. I'm sure we'll get to an understanding. Now let's set the dots where they're needed before you leave.'

At those words, every single person stands and exits leaving behind the three of us.

'When did you talk to Rose?' I narrow my eyes in suspicion

'Yesterday.'

'What did she tell you?' He leans back in his chair.

'She said you always find trouble wherever you go.'

Tom laughs and snorts. 'You have no idea.'

'Hey. Like I told her, I don't look for trouble. All I want to do is help. I might have been misguided before, but having help and sharing resources, working together, I'm sure that will help keep me safe.'

They both laugh, and I'm feeling like a petulant child.

'Okay. Okay, trouble finds you somehow. But, Violet, you really have to be careful. Always.'

'I will I promise.'

'You'll have to.' What does he mean? 'We need you. Hell, we need a lot more people like you, but I can't have you out there in the field being reckless again. Like I said, the world needs more people like you. It needs you.'

'You're being very flattering, and I appreciate all of that, but what the world needs is more people like me, people who care. But what exactly are you saying?'

He's exchanging amused looks with Tom. It seems they both know something I don't.

'It means, Violet, you will be working for the UN based in a UK office, but as we're now sharing resources, you're also go from time to time to other offices.'

My eyes fly to Tom. A spark of hope grows.

'But if you're ever careless or reckless out there, I'll seat your ass in an office faster than you can get in an airplane. I don't care what Rose says.'

As silly as it seems at that moment, seeing the stern look on his face and his authoritarian voice, I start to wonder what it would be like to have both him and Rose in the same room.

'So ... um ... okay ...' I'm not exactly sure of what to say. I'm scared I might say something wrong and mess up my opportunity.

'We'll be in contact. Don't worry. For now, I understand you have the week off,' he says with a wink, and I instantly feel at ease with him as I felt with Rose. 'I'll see you Sunday then.'

'You're coming to the party?' I sound a bit more surprised than I probably should, but I can't help it.

'Of course. Wouldn't miss it for the world.' Okay, that's not weird. He laughs, and we leave.

This whole time, apart from a few interjections. Tom hasn't said much.

I actually thought he would have said a little more. I was sure he was as interested as I that this meeting go well, but he doesn't talk until we're outside the lavish building.

'So, I guess that went well?' It's a question. It sounds like a question, but I'm not sure if it is.'

'Yeah, I guess so.'

'How quickly can you get into trouble?'

I stand there on the sidewalk staring at him. My brain too slow to understand what he's saying. He doesn't say anything else. He's patient, sweet, and kind. He waits for me. He has been for a long time, so I break into a wide smile and throw my arms around his neck.

'All right, enough schmoozing. Coffee?' I smile and nod. And then, just like in London, he grabs my hand, and we walk down the streets of New York hand in hand.

'Oh my God, I can't believe it.'

'I thought you would like it.' He kisses my temple sweetly, but I can't tear my eyes from Central Perk. I can't believe I'm walking through these doors. The big orange is taken. Of course. But we got a seat by the window.

'So this is like a date too?'

'Absolutely not. I told you I'll do it right, starting with picking you up, not coming from a meeting.'

We sip coffee in silence for a little while. I'm trying to figure out what these changes in my job mean for us, and he opens his mouth just when my phone starts to ring.

'Sorry, it's Rose. I have to answer.'

He gestures for me to go ahead.

'Hi, Rose.'

'Hey, my little star. How're you doing?' *Star?*

'I'm good. A little wiser now.'

'What is it, your birthday?' Tom's eyes quickly move to give me an inquisitive look, and I shake my head at him.

'When did you make all these plans with Richard?'

'How did you know I did?'

'Oh, come on. I might not know you very well, but I could clearly hear your voice in Richards's speech.'

'Well, somebody's clever. I hope you're happy with it.' She has no idea.

'I'm very happy.' Tom steals his eyes from the window again to look at me, a beautiful smile on his face.

'Good. It's actually good news for both of us. But that's not why I'm calling I need you to come back on Saturday. I'll send you the tickets.'

'Wait. Saturday? But the party is on Sunday'

'Yeah, I know, but I need you to try the down to make sure it fits, in case alterations are needed.'

'Gown? What are you talking about? I don't need a gown. I have a dress.'

'What's going on?' Tom looks so confused, but I have to take care of my curiosity first.

'Ah. I'm sure your dress is very cute, but you represent the company now so you'll have to look more than cute.'

'That's ridiculous, Rose. It doesn't matter what I look like as long as people donate.'

'Violet, I've been doing this for years. You have to trust me, please. Now I'll see you Saturday.'

'Okay. See you then.' What else can I say? I have to go.

'So you're leaving Saturday then?' Tom asks.

'Yeah, I'm sorry.' He shrugs. 'It's ridiculous. I have to be there to make sure the gown fits.' I make air quotes signs.

'Well, appearances make a difference in these things.' I can tell he's not happy about it. I'm not too thrilled of losing a day either.

'Tom, I'm sorry.' I try to grab his hand, but he reaches for his coffee.

'It's fine. I have a play that day anyway.' I feel my heart crack a little. It's so tricky, this situation between us, that I'm afraid the littlest thing we say the little we have will fall apart.

'You finished. Shall we go?

'Sure.' Why can't things be easy and simple?

'So I was thinking we take a stroll around Central Park and then have some lunch. We can go to the zoo if you want to, and after that, I was thinking we can hit a few museums or anywhere else if you have something in mind.'

'Hum, the zoo sounds good. Maybe if we have time we can check a few bridges.'

'You came to New York to check out bridges?' He quirks an inquisitive brow, and I laugh.

'No. I came here to be with you. Wherever that is.' We were just about to go down to catch a subway when he stops one step below me. Our eyes are on the same level, but mine are darting to his lips. He looks like he's going to say something, but he doesn't. Instead, he snakes a hand around my waist, pulling me to him, and he slides the other behind my neck, fusing our lips together until I'm breathless.

'Can we leave the talking and thinking for later and just be together?' his eyes plead

Postpone the inevitable. I'm all in.

'Until Friday.'

He nods and grabs my hand again.

Like planed we spend part of the afternoon in the zoo and the other half we go and visit 9/11 Memorial Park. There are no words that haven't been said before, so we pace together. I remember exactly where I was and what I was doing at that moment. I couldn't believe what I was seeing on the news. I actually thought at first that it was a movie or a prank of some kind. I'm sure that everyone else remembers exactly where they were and what they were doing.

'Shall we go back?' his hand catches mine

'To your apartment?'

He chuckles. 'Yes.'

'It's still early. We can visit a few more places.'

'We can, or instead, we can go home, take a shower, put on that dress that you like to pack and let me take you out.' *Did he just say 'home'?*

'Are you saying you don't like my dress?'

'I do. I like the dress, but I looove what's underneath.' He pulls me to him and kisses down my neck. How can you say no to him?

'Hum, that sounds good. Where are we going?'

'You'll see.'

We stumble out of the elevator and into the apartment, tangled in each other. He's fumbling with the keys but doesn't get his hands off me.

'You know you need to let go of me to actually get the key into the door.'

'I can't get my hands off you. Damn the door.'

'I'm not up to a public display. Give it.' He doesn't think twice. Plants the keys in my hand and grabs my ass.

'Hey. I can't concentrate on the door like that.'

'Yeah, I know.' He starts kissing my neck as I'm opening the door and pieces of clothes start to fly off. He quickly picks me up bridal style and kicks the door shut before taking me to the bedroom.

It's a good thing that we don't have reservations this time. We would definitely not make it.

'Um, excuse me. What it that?' Tom is looking at me as I walk out of the bathroom, mouth half parted and his eyes running all over my body. I smile innocently as if I have no idea what he's talking about.

'What?'

'You …' He trails off for a second, licking his lips and swallowing hard. 'That's new?'

'What my earrings?'

'No. That incredible, sexy, crazy dress.'

'Do you like it? I got it before I came.' I've never thought I would ever wear a dress like this, but in these past few months, I lost so much weight that I went shopping for a new dress, hoping I could seduce him if I needed. The dress is a dark shade of red and hugs me to just above my knee. It has a perfect V-neck line. Not too deep of a cut, but not too conservative either.

'I love it, and now I'm thinking to keep you here.'

'Oh, come on. It would be a waste to leave all of this here.' I slide my hand down the length of my body slowly, and he stares me with his hungry eyes.

'The first guy that lays eyes on you will get a punch, and we'll leave.'

I laugh and shake my head. This business of setting our messy issues aside is taking the pressure off, and I feel so much more comfortable with him now.

'Have you thought that maybe the guys can be admiring the dress?' I'm teasing him, and when I see his eyes glisten with a ray of jealousy, I gloat. He walks slowly to me, slides his hand around my waist, and pulls me to him hard.

'They better.'

The drive takes about half hour, and we make small conversation as I watch the city lights fly by on the car window.

'What are you doing?'

'Getting out of the car.'

'No. No. No. You don't get out of the car alone. I'm a gentleman. You'll wait for me to open the door and help you out.' I just freeze there, one leg out of the car.

'Tom, I'm not a damsel in distress.'

'I know, but this is a date so just indulge me, okay?' The amount of smiling I do around this man is going to give me premature wrinkles.

'Did we get out of one apartment to get into another?' We go from the car into a building, a beautiful, dark grey-stone building. I'm actually surprised how tall this building is. It looks so old like it could be at least a century old, but it still looks great, sturdy.

'Just wait.' I'm usually very patient with surprises. I always thought if I'm going to eventually find out why should I fret? But he makes me so excited and giddy that all I want to do is ask questions about it.

The elevator doors open, and I'm so speechless that I don't even get out. He has to pull me out before the doors close again. We are unloaded on the most beautiful terrace. There are fairy lights hanging on the night sky and a candle on each table, beautiful flowers all around, the New York skyline gracing us. All of this under a sparkling, dark blue night sky. It feels like a dream.

The hostess takes us to a reserved table by the edge of the terrace. I almost don't want to sit I would rather just lean over the ledge and take in all the views. This whole side of the terrace overlooks the piers that adorn the Hudson. I can even see the forms of the faraway glowing bridges.

'It's beautiful here.' This whole time I was so absorbed by the view that I hadn't notice Tom's beautiful smile. Now that was a view.

'Do you come here often?' I'm usually the quiet one, so either he wants to go back to talk about our issues, or he's just thinking about them. He tears his eyes from the view to look at me.

'Once.' A single word answer and I'm wondering if he came alone.

'You know, usually, I'm the one who does the thinking.'

He chuckles a little, nodding his head, eyes on his empty plate. 'I came here a few months ago with the cast.'

He's still not meeting my eyes, like there's something he wants to tell me, but he's not sure if he should. So I just nod my head, hoping he'll continue.

'We had a really good night. Full house. There were even some critics in the audience.'

'That's a good thing, right?'

He nods, and for some reason he still hasn't looked at me since we sat down. He looked at the waiter as he took our order and brought our drinks. He looked at a passing guy as the guy roamed his eyes over me. But he still hasn't looked at me.

'It was a fun night, and I couldn't stop thinking about you. I still didn't know what you were doing. I thought you were back home. We drank so much that I think I actually forgot my name for a while. But I couldn't forget yours, so I did something stupid.'

Now I see where this is going. Why is he telling me this?

'Tom, I don't really ne—'

'I need to tell you. I need you to forgive me.' He raises a hand to land on mine, finally looking at me.

'I don't have to forgive you, Tom. You don't owe me an explanation.'

He fixes his eyes on mine for a few seconds, and I know what he's thinking so I correct.

'At that time, you didn't owe me an explanation.'

He sighs and tightens the grip on my hand. 'What if I want to?'

'Do I have to as well?'

He's surprised by my question. I know we already talked about this, and I don't want to get into it again.

'You already did.'

'No, I didn't. I only told you that I had slept with him. Not why. But do we really have to talk about this?'

'We don't have to, but I wanted to.'

'Why? Do you really think I want to know what it was like for you to sleep with another woman?'

He doesn't get to answer as we're interrupted by the waiter with our food. I sure hope he didn't hear what I said.

We eat in an uncomfortable silence for a while. This was supposed to be a good night. A romantic night. We were supposed to forget our differences and just enjoy each other, but instead, we have fallen into a foul mood. I need a little distance.

'You okay?'

'Yeah, just going to the loo.'

I needed a little perspective, a little alone time to do what I shouldn't. Think. Why does it have to be so complicated between us? I admire myself in the bathroom mirror. I do look good. I wish Chloe could see me now. I don't know if it's a good idea or not, but if he wants to talk maybe I should hear him. I was about to exit my cubicle when a familiar voice sounded.

'You've been here a while. Please tell me you're not crying.' I smile behind the door and remember the first time I heard his voice, so I re-enact.

'Am I in the men's?'

'No.'

'So you're in the ladies. Lost?' This time I'm smiling as I talk, and I can see the tip of his shoes just outside the door.

'Not really.' His voice is so low and smooth that I'm already melting before I even open the door.

'Are you okay?' I purse my lips and nod. Even without looking at him, this man does something to my body. Can't really trust my words right now. As I move past him to wash my hands, two leggy blonds come in and stop abruptly, looking at him. I think only then he remembered where he was because he blushed a little and went outside.

When I leave the bathroom, the blondes are still whispering and giggling. I can imagine what they are thinking. I would usually be mortified, but right now I don't care. Can you blame me? He's gorgeously delicious.

I thought he would be waiting for me outside, but I find him back at the table, gazing at the river. The silence drags until I draw out a breath and let it out slowly.

'So. You wanted to forget my name. What happened next?'

'Do you really want to know?' His eyes flash to me quickly.

'Well, I don't expect you to tell me what it was like with her. That's for sure.'

'I wouldn't do that.'

I know that, but I still wanted him to know how uncomfortable it was to hear it. So I nod at him to continue.

'Like I said, we were drunk. Very drunk. I wasn't planning for it to happen. Neither of us were, but I was still pissed that you rejected me. I guess I wanted revenge …' He trails off for a little while. Shame covers his face, and I know exactly how he feels.

'I was so pissed that I shouted your name when I was with her. I don't think she noticed. She was drunker than me. I'm not trying to hurt you or anything. I just want you to know that it happened because I was drunk and upset I …'

His words falter again, and a light ignites my brain. He's trying to tell me he would never betray me like that, not if we were together. I put on the sweetest smile I can muster and grab his hand.

'You're forgiven.'

His eyes glisten, and he bites his lower lip before it curls into a smile. I hope he doesn't ask about me. I don't want to talk about it. Not now. Our linked eyes are broken by the waiter asking if we want any desert, but we both just want to leave, so while he takes care of the bill and goes to the loo, I go to the far end of the terrace.

This side looks towards the end of the bay, and I can see the erect lady holding her perpetual torch, illuminating a path for those to come. I still can't believe I'm in New York. How many times have I dreamt to be here, visiting all the landmarks, absorbing the fast pace of life? It would still fell like a dream if it wasn't for him, if his hands weren't wrapping around my waist and his face nuzzling my neck.

'I thought you left me.' He starts to kiss my neck, and I turn around in his arms.'

'I never want to leave you, Tom.' I speak slowly and steady. My eyes never leaving his. I wanted him to know it broke me every time I left him. He kissed my lips softly and hugged me.

'Let's go home.' There it is again: *home*. We're on a pause, V, no getting depressed. After we're in his home and had each other for desert, I fall asleep in his arms. I feel warm and comforted.

We spend next morning in bed, having breakfast in between kisses. We talk about nothing and the places he wants to take me.

'Do you want to come and watch the rehearsal?'

I start hesitating and fidgeting.

'What's wrong?' he asks.

Why can't I hide my feelings?

'I'll see you tonight after the play. I think I'm going back to Central Park and visit the zoo,' I say.

'Why?' Only one word and I'm back to hiding from him, but he doesn't let go. He was buttoning his shirt when he stops halfway and moves to me, grabs my chin, and tilts my head. 'Please. Tell me.' His eyes are stormy blue now.

It's not a big deal, right?

'I don't want to go.' His eyes dilate, and his frown grows. God, how I want to kiss it away.

'Why not?' He still hasn't released my chin.

'Because I have a feeling that your stupid drunk is going to be there, and I would like to see as little of her as possible.' That's me being utter honest.

His hand doesn't drop. His gaze doesn't falter, but his frown disappears.

'I'll tell the usher to let you in a sit at the front, okay?'

That's it? I can't form words, so I nod.

'Good. This time, I won't be imagining. You will really be there.' He kisses me softly and sweetly, and I forget everything.

We have lunch together before he goes, and I spend most of the afternoon roaming Central Park and going to the zoo. I went back to his apartment to change into my little purple dress before going to the play. Soon as I get out of the taxi in front of the theatre and the same usher from the other day sees me he says right away.

'Now that's what you should have been wearing the other day. You look great.'

I can't hide the blush that creeps up my face, and he smiles.

'Thank you.'

'I'm John, by the way.'

'Pleasure.' He starts to walk me in.

'Tom said you would come by tonight. I take things went well the other day.' we talk as he walks me down the stairs to my seat.

'Yeah, something like that.'

'He looked different today when he came in.'

'Different how?'

'He had this bounce in his walk.' He has a faraway look like he's remembering and chuckles.

'A bounce?'

'Yeah. He has always kept to himself most of the time. We went out for a couple of drinks from time to time and that's how we became friends. He started to talk about you and how he missed you.' He pauses as he gestures me to my front seat and settles beside me.

'I missed him too.'

'When he came back last week, he seemed pissed off.'

'Really? Why?'

'I don't know if I should be telling you this or not, but you guys definitely need a push.' I smile at his words. We probably do. 'When I asked him about it all he was saying was that he was going to lose you and there was nothing he could do about it.' I bow my head. I don't want that to be true, but I can't control everything around me.

'A couple of days ago we went out again, and he told me what happened. Only then I understood what he really meant by "losing" you. I could see it in him. He was feeling broken and lost. He didn't know what to do.'

'Neither did I.'

'That's not really true.' My head snaps to him. 'I think the problem is that now you know exactly what to do, but what scares him most is that what you want isn't him.'

'But I do, John. I do want to be by his side, but I also want to do this. I just don't know how to do both.'

'He's not your first priority, and I think that's what scares him. I think he's always expecting you to leave. Why don't you try for a while? Be with him. Maybe you'll be happy.' My sigh is a soft smile.

'You don't think I haven't thought about it? Just be together and forget the world, but I couldn't live with myself if I did that, and I'm pretty sure I would end up resenting him. I don't want that. He doesn't deserve it.'

He's nodding his head slowly with a cocked smile on his lips. 'But that all changed yesterday apparently.'

'He told you?'

'I had to ask. He was smiling to himself. He never done that before.'

I start smiling, looking at the red velvet curtain in front of me. 'He said that maybe there was a way.' My heart quickens, and I breathe heavily, but our conversation is cut off by the blinking lights.

'Enjoy the show.'

'Thanks, John.'

It's strange that we talked more about our issues and concerns with friends than with each other, but at least, now I know, and I certainly hope he doesn't change his mind.

None of that matters. For the next ninety minutes, the world disappears. There's no one else in the audience, just me and his brilliant performance. It really is a whole other world, and I can tell he's in his element, where he belongs. No wonder he calls this home. How could I ever ask him to give this up?

Everyone is on their feet, applauding. When the cast comes up front to bow, he winks at me, and I feel like I'm his groupie. The curtain closes, and I sit back down on my fluffy chair. The room is completely lit now. The walls are adorned with velvet drapes like the stage curtain, and beautiful wall lamps radiate light every two steps. It's a gorgeous room. This time, John didn't come back for me, and I'm not sure if I can go backstage, but I'm too restless waiting, so I start wandering around the room.

There are seats on top and what seems to be private viewing balconies. I walk up the stairs slowly. My hand runs against the velvet wall. When I get halfway up, I turn around and do the same on my way down. I'm always looking around the room, the dressed walls and the beautiful sculpted ceiling. Only when my foot sets on the last step do I notice a shadow.

There he stands in the middle of the stage in an immaculate suit, hands in his pockets. He looks so handsome that I can't help a smile spreading on my face. He raises a hand to me, and I don't even wait a beat before I'm on the move. He keeps his hand up while I make it to him and place mine on his. He takes my hand to his chest. With the other, he grabs my free hand and places it on his shoulder, and then he sets his own hand on my hip and starts swaying.

'What are you doing?'

A smile crosses his face but is quickly replaced by a serious expression. 'I'm dancing. Obviously.'

Again, I'm smiling and shaking my head.

'Do you need to stand on my feet again?' He's talking to my ear, and I feel my body shiver as his breath caresses my skin.

'I think I'm good this time.' Our eyes connect.

'Yeah, I think you need to practice.'

'I told you I'm not a dancer. I don't do dancing like this.'

He raises an eyebrow. 'You'll have to.' Seeing the confused look on my face, he continues. 'For Sunday.'

'I'm going to have to dance?'

He smiles and nods. I'm so scared to ask, but I have to. I want to.

'Can you come?' My heart is hammering in my chest, and my eyes are pleading. He's looking into my soul door, really looking in silence for what it seems like forever.

'Did you know that your eyes have a little bit of green in them?'

No one ever noticed that. Wait. Was that a no?

'I don't think anyone ever saw that.'

'Neither have I. Until now.'

I shrug. 'It must be the light.'

'Yeah, it might be.' He kisses me softly, and the whole time, we keep dancing on the empty silent stage. He sighs.

'Sunday is a special day ...' He doesn't finish, but I understand. I wanted him and the girls there, but I guess that won't happen.

'It's okay, Tom. I understand.'

'You're beautiful, Violet. You look really nice tonight.'

'Thanks.' I'm blushing. He still makes me blush.

'You look very handsome too.'

I smirk. 'You like?'

'I loooove.' He laughs, throwing his head back, and my chest swells at the beautiful sound.

'I love you.' The words fly off my mouth as a whisper, but I know he heard it. He stops laughing and finds my eyes. The hand that was clutching mine to his chest moves to my face to caress it.

'I love you too, V. I didn't know I could love someone as much as I love you, and that's scary.' He kisses me again, and we keep dancing.

'I don't want to leave.' He takes me in his arms, lifting me of the ground, and I laugh a little. He twirls me around, causing me to break into a full-on laughter. I've never done that before.

'I love to hear you laugh.' He sets me down, but we keep dancing. 'What did you think of the play?'

'Oh, I loved it.' I'm actually excited now. 'You were amazing. Incredible, really.'

'Wow. That's high praise.'

'I'm serious. Your presence on this stage is commanding. I totally lost myself in the play from beginning to end. It's really great.'

'Thank you.' He touches his forehead to mine, and we dance until the lights go out, and he raises his head to the exit.

'John.'

'Sorry, I didn't know you guys were still here. You want me to turn them back on?'

They're shouting to each other from end to end of the room. It's funny, but I don't really believe John's excuse.

'Maybe we should go,' I say. 'They might want to go home.'

He smiles and shakes his head at me.

'What?' I ask.

'Always thinking of others.'

I tilt my head to the side and purse my lips.

'Sorry. Let's go then.'

We say goodbye to a very chipper John and get on a subway. I notice we don't get off at the station by his apartment, so I look up at him.

'I wanted to take you somewhere, but it's too late now, so we'll go tomorrow, okay?'

'Where did you wanted to go?'

He kisses my temple. 'You'll see tomorrow.'

'So where are we going now then?'

'You'll see.'

I chuckle. 'You could work for the CIA. You give no information.'

'Maybe you should torture me.' When I look at him, I can see his eyes filled with lust, and all I want to do is take him home.

'You're right.' He looks surprised, but I don't let my expression falter. 'I guess we still need to find out each other's weaknesses.' I wink at him, and he kisses me hard.

He brings me to the East River. We walk down the sidewalk in silence. The smell of the river here is different from London. The air isn't so cool even though is winter, and the smell of algae isn't as strong. There are no piers on this side. At least, none that I can see.

'Is that an island?'

He follows my gaze. 'Yeah. It's Roosevelt Island.'

'I didn't know there was one here. It's so small. Anything special there?'

He shrugs. 'Hum, there's parks and schools, I think.'

'You think? You haven't visited yet?'

He chuckles. 'Do you think I have all this free time to do sightseeing? And I haven't been here that long.' He went from funny to serious and flustered very quickly.

'I'm sorry. I was just joking.' I'm searching his eyes, but he doesn't look at me. We just keep walking in silence until he turns me to him and squeezes me between the ledge that separates us from the river, and then he kisses me soft and long, and I find myself wishing I could stay here.

'I'm sorry.' He lets out the hair he been holding in his chest

'You have nothing to be sorry about.'

We both sigh in each other's arms.

'Why can't things just be simple between us?' I feel him shaking his head, as if the solution is right in front of him but he cannot see it

'Because that's not how life works.'

I smile into his chest and hug him tighter.

'We should get going. Have to wake up early tomorrow.'

'How early?'

'Early.' Damn his secret service face.

I wake up on his bare chest. His smell musky and spicy. I love it. I start kissing up his chest to his mouth until he wakes up.

'You can't wake me up like that.'

'And why not?' I continue kissing him all over.

'Do you not hear the alarm? We have to go.'

'Oh, come on. We have time.'

He rolls me off him and jumps out of the bed.

'Hey.'

'We don't have that much time. Rehearsals start earlier today, and we have two places to visit.' At that moment, my phone buzzes on the nightstand, and I turn on the bed to read the message. I'm stomach down on the mattress as I'm unlocking my phone when I hear him groan behind me. I turn my head.

'What?'

'You're killing me, woman. I'm serious we have to go.' He's leaning against the door of the en suite, both his hands behind his back. He's so tense.

'I'm just reading a text. What's up with you?'

'You don't know?' Both his brows shoot up.

'Know what?'

He walks slowly to the bed and bends down on my body. I thought he was going to help me up, but instead, he bites my ass. I just gasp. I can't find words.

'You're even more cute because you don't know how sexy you are.'

My head is still turned back to him, and he's still grabbing my ass, and I feel myself blush. I feel so hot I'm sure I'm all the shades of the sun.

'But like I said, we have to go so cover that fine ass and stop tempting me.' He slaps my butt as he gets up, and I gasp again. I might be red as a tomato, but I've never felt so at ease with anyone else.

'It's Scarlett. Well, actually, it's all of them, we have this group chat, it's nice'

I'm getting out of the bed to get some clothes from my bag and reading the text when he exits the bathroom.

'What did I just say?'

'I'm getting my clothes relax. I can multitask, Tom.'

'I know that, but I can't and seeing you parade around the room in your underwear isn't really helping.'

'I think it's better if you wait in the living room.' He doesn't answer. Instead, he sweeps his eyes over my body before he leaves, as if he wanted to memorize it. I continue to get dressed while reading the text.

Hey, darling. So how did it go? You never said anything, and we're all anxious to know. Please tell me he didn't shut the door on you. I'll kill him if he did. Just let us know if you're okay. Take care.

I smile to myself. If only she knew I was standing in his room nearly naked. I decide to send a collective message.

Hello, darlings. I hope you guys are okay. Sorry I didn't say anything earlier I've been … busy. I've been staying with Tom, but there's still a lot we have to figure out. The meeting went really good I'll tell you all about it at the end of the week. Xoxo.

They'll definitely not like the lack of information there, but not even I know much more than that.

'Are you ready?' The knock on the door wakes me from my perpetual dilemma.

'Almost.'

'Hurry up.'

'Jeez, you're so stressed today.'

'Just hurry.'

Since we woke up, he's been agitated and stressed and sometimes giddy. I actually saw him giggling to his phone. Where is he taking me that is making him so anxious?

It doesn't take long for us to be in a subway tunnelling towards Brooklyn Bridge. I'm smiling inside. Finally, he's bringing me to see a bridge. It seems silly I know, but growing up, I saw so many movies, so many heart-touching and romantic scenes on this bridge, that at some point I started to wish and dream that it was happening to me.

We all know I like to do research wherever I go, but this time, I only studied the map of New York. I just wanted to be with him. But when we miss my wished exit, I know that's not where we're going. We get off a couple of minutes later. Today it's really cold. It's not snowing yet, but it shouldn't be long. I'm clutching my jacket close to me.

'You should go shopping. You'll freeze in the clothes you brought.' He's rounding his arms around my shoulders pulling me to him.

'I'm okay. I just need a few more layers.'

'Or a blanket.' We start laughing, and I start wondering if this is what it would be like to spend my life with him. I start to wander in my mind, thinking of what could be, and I mute everything around.

'Hey. Are you listening to me?'

'Sorry. Sorry.' Only then I notice we're at the edge of the land.

'I wanted to come here yesterday. This is Battery Park. It's not very big, but it's pretty.'

'That's nice, but why are we getting on a boat then?'

'It's not a boat. Well, it is. It's a ferry. We're going there.' I follow his finger. He's pointing at the perpetual lady, and I smile. That's better than the bridge.

I still don't say anything. I just hug him and give him a peck on the cheek. He holds me during the whole ride. It's very, very cold I might actually have to buy some clothes.

It's an incredible experience to be here. There's so much history. So many pictures of memories that tell the story of friendship and workmanship between France and the United States.

'We're usually allowed on the crown, but they're doing some maintenance today sorry.'

'It's okay. I'm sure I'll have other opportunities to go in the future.' His eyes are glued to mine. Filled with unspoken promises and wishes. Oh, I wish we could actually say it. We spend the next two hours absorbing the mounds of history with him reading to me. Every plaque. Every piece that describes a picture and he also tells me facts that he has learned since he came here. He tells me how Alexandre Eiffel designed the framework, which I already knew, but he also takes me to the museum where the original torch sits.

'I had no idea that they had changed it.'

'Yeah. They changed due to some damages and poor maintenance. Now this is its new home.'

I nod. I'm really not liking that word: *home*. I'm driving myself crazy thinking if he's trying to tell me something or if it's just my imagination. Why can't my brain stop thinking?

We take the ferry back to Battery Park, already swallowed by snow. I think I'm dormant. I don't feel cold anymore. We walk around the park hand in hand. He tells me about peculiar people he met since he moved to New York.

'You find all kinds of people here, but it's not what people think.'

'What do you mean?'

211

'Most people are nice and friendly. Yeah, they keep to themselves and don't take shit from anyone but think most people are like that anyway.' We fall back into silence. The words are itching my throat, but I can't ruin this. I can't.

It doesn't take long for us to be back on Broadway.

'The play starts at six today. I'll see you then?'

'I'll be on the front seat.' We're standing by a side entrance, hugging and kissing. Even if it's just for a little while it's always hard to say goodbye.

'I really have to go, babe.'

'Okay, just one more. It's cold.' He holds my face with both hands, and just before our lips graze, he steps away.

'Hey. Not fair. How am I going to keep warm now?'

'With clothes.' He winks at me, and I stick my tongue out.

It feels so good to banter with him like this. There's no worries or issues. Just him and me. No bullshit.

I find myself walking down a street laced with stores, covered in snow. There are lights and Christmas decorations everywhere. People swarm in and out of shops, hurrying to have all Christmas shopping done on time. I stop looking at a window of a charity shop. There's a sparkling gold dress, and I really want to try it on. If only Nat would see me now trying on dresses. I should really be buying some gloves and a scarf, but I can't help it. I want to surprise him. I end up buying the dress and a warm jacket. No more freezing. I go back to roam the little paths of Central Park before going back to the apartment. I could really spend hours here. It soothes me.

I was watching the sea lions when an older woman stood next to me. I did a double-take at her head. Her hair was so white it looked like it was covered in snow. Her lips were so red that I couldn't help the laugh that escaped me. She was snow white. With white hair, that is.

'Are you all right, dear?'

'Oh yes, I'm fine, thank you.'

'I'm Mary.' She smiles and looks back at the proud animals. They seem to like visitors they're always showing off. Her eyes are still looking forward.

'I'm Violet. Nice to meet you.'

'I saw you yesterday.' My head snaps to her immediately, but I'm speechless. I would remember if had met her before. She chuckles at the expression in my face. Man, am I dramatic.

'I was at the play yesterday. I was just behind you.'

'Oh.' What am I supposed to say? 'That's nice. Did you enjoy it?'

'I did. Since I was little I loved plays. They make me dream.'

I agree with a smile, and she carries on.

'I saw you stayed behind. I'm sorry. I didn't mean to pry.'

'What do you mean?'

I can see her cheeks blush, but she still doesn't turn to me.

'I was curious so I stayed there by the entrance watching you.'

'Why?'

She shrugs.

'Because of the way you were looking at him during the play. I used to look at him like that too.' I'm not sure how to react. I can't speak all I know is that my mouth is hanging.

'Oh no dear. I didn't mean him, no. You see, I lost my Chris two years this Christmas.'

'Oh, I'm so sorry.' I can't help my hand flying to her shoulder. She truly looks desolate, like half of her is missing.

'It's okay, dear. You know, one time he got us a ferry at night. I still don't know how he did that.'

'Did he tell he used his charm and good looks too?' She starts laughing.

'Yes, he did.' We laugh together. 'That night we danced under the stars. For hours.' Her eyes are dreaming, and she's swaying a little.

'When I saw you two dancing there I kept remembering that night. I couldn't tear my eyes away.'

I don't know this woman, and yet I can't help the affection I feel for her. There's not much you can say to someone in her situation apart from 'Sorry', so I do what I think it's best. I take her into my arms and hug her tight. We part after a long while, and she's wiping tears away. Tears I didn't hear her shed.

'You hold on to what you have, dear. You're both so in love you have to really live it and enjoy it. You never know when it will end.'

'It's a little more complicated than that, Mary.' Now I'm the one with tears.

'It's not. Either you love each other, or you don't.'

'Even if we live in different continents?' She's quiet for a few seconds.

'Well, then one of you will move.' Wow, I hadn't really thought of that.

'Mary, his work is here, and he really loves it. I could never ask him to leave it. And as for me, well, I'm in London and sometimes out there.'

'I don't understand.'

Neither do I sometimes.

For some reason, I tell this woman everything as we walk around the zoo. She occasionally asks some questions but mostly keeps to herself. We are walking by the pond when she stops.

'I still think the solution is simple.'

'Did you hear everything I just said?'

'Yes. I did.' She speaks slowly and calmly as she sits on a bench. 'You have to choose – either him or the world.'

I let a breath out. 'Mary, it's not that simple. I want to do this. I've compromised too much to please others. I've been through enough. I think it's time I live my life as I want.'

'You're still compromising. You're trading your happiness for others. Can't you see that he's scared? He thinks you'll never choose him first. Even with you living in separate countries, I think, if he thought you would put him first, he would chase you anywhere.'

I can't find any words. I just sit there processing everything she said and it seems very similar to what John said, and I cover my face with both my hands. She doesn't need to see me cry. I feel her hand caressing my back.

'It's okay, dear. When you love someone that much, everything seems overwhelming.'

'It is. It really is. I'm scared, Mary. I don't want to lose myself in another man again and forget about what I want. I can't do that again.'

We're quiet for a very long time, watching ducks, children, and snow. I want it all – live to help the world, live for him. I want the children and even the ducks. Maybe Mary is right. Maybe it's one or the other. I can't have both.

'Are you going tonight?'

'Yeah. Actually, what time is it?'

'Um, four.'

'Oh I have to go. I need to get ready. Mary …'

'I'm going too. How about we get a cab together, dear?'

I smile. 'He sends a car for me. I can pick you up.'

Her smile matches mine. 'I would love to, and, Violet?'

'Hum?'

'I'm sorry if I was nosy or too forward with you, but I lost what you have. I really don't think you should waste it.'

I opened my mouth to say something, but she raised a hand.

'I do understand your situation. Maybe not entirely, but I do, and I won't say anything else about it don't worry.'

I smile again, looking at her, take a deep breath, and shake my head while I hug her.

'Thank you, Mary, for everything you said.'

We part ways after exchanging contacts. Tom was right. There are nice people in New York.

It doesn't take long for me to get ready. I was never one to fuss about how I look, but for Tom, I want to look good. I was about to open the door when I noticed something white on the table. My curiosity got the best of me. There was a square black velvet box with a folded note on top:

'Hey, Gorgeous, I saw this the other day and thought of you. I hope you like it. See you tonight. Love you.'

How am I going to leave this man behind in three days? Inside the box was a necklace, a small purple heart hanging from a silver chain. It's beautiful. I want to text him to tell him that I love it, but I'd rather see the look on his face when he sees me wearing it.

'Wow, you look beautiful.' Mary gives me a quick hug as she enters the car.

'You look really nice too.'

We chat lightly throughout the ride. She tells me about Chris and all the surprises he did for her, how they met in school and how she made him chase her even though she was already in love with him. She also tells me that they couldn't have children, so they decided to adopt. They have a beautiful story. Every bad thing that happened to them, they turned into something good. Every wrong, they wrote it into a right. Can I do that?

Can Tom and I do that? When we arrive at Broadway, the sidewalk is filled with people and photographers. It's crazy.

'There must be someone important coming to see the play today.' I shrug it off

'Or maybe it's because of the famous ones already inside.'

I laugh as we make our way to the entrance. But something stops me on my tracks.

'Miss Violet, who are you wearing?'

'How long have you been seeing each other?'

'Do you like his plays?'

I can't say anything. I can hardly see with so many flashes in my face.

'Come, dear. Let's get you inside.' I follow Mary, leaving behind the inquisitive paparazzi.

'How'd they know who I am?'

'Well, like I said, he is famous. Maybe some of them followed him and saw you together.' She shrugs, but her arm is still around my shoulder trying to soothe me. I wasn't expecting that. It was really overwhelming how does he deal with it all the time?

The lights started to blink, announcing the imminent start of the show. Mary says she'll find me later and goes to her seat. As soon as the curtains spread and I see his face, I smile and forget what just happened.

Another incredible performance by the whole cast graces the audience. I even caught him looking at me and smiled, a beautiful small spread of his lips. When the play ends and the drapes close, I look for Mary. She's again behind me.

'It was lovely.' Her eyes are sparkling.

'It really was. Come.' She gives me an odd look, and I nod for her to come. I'm taking her backstage. I think she'll be happy to meet them.

'Are you sure we can be here?'

'Let's find out.' I shrug as I knock on Tom's door.

'Just a second, please.'

'He's polite.' I can't help but laugh.

The door opens, and I don't think he even saw Mary standing next to me. His eyes ravish me until they set on the necklace.

'It looks good on you. Almost as good as that dress. Come here.' He pulls me into a warm embrace and kisses me.

'You look beautiful.' He whispers against my lips, and then we hear a noise behind us.

'Hum, hum.'

'Oh, sorry. Tom, this is Mary. She's a big fan.'

'It's a pleasure to meet you, Mary.' They both shake hands, and I see Mary blushing. It's such a foreign look on her.

They exchange pleasantries. She gushes about how many times she has seen the play, and then I tell him I have to take her home.

'Nonsense, dear. I'll take a cab.'

I was about to argue, but Tom beat me to it. 'We can drop you off on our way. It's no problem.'

'But I—'

Tom doesn't let her continue. 'We need to make sure that you get home safe.'

She sighs in resignation. 'Thank you.'

'Just let me change, and I'll be right out.'

After we drop Mary, we go back to his apartment. For some reason, he's very quiet. We're in the elevator and I can't take the silence anymore.

'Are you okay?'

'Yeah. All good.' He keeps looking at his phone.

He goes straight to the kitchen when we enter the apartment and buries his head in the fridge.

'You hungry? I'm starving.'

What's up with him? I stand on the living room. Waiting for him to look at me. He's halfway through making a sandwich when he finally looks up.

'Want some?'

Two can play that game. 'Yeah, sure.'

His expression tells me he was expecting me to turn my back. 'Mustard?'

'No. Mayo, please.'

While he prepares the meal I slip off my shoes and put my legs up on the other stool bar with a sigh. The knife he was using to cut the bread stops mid-air, and he licks his lips.

'Water?'

'Do you have any wine?'

Now he's swallowing hard. I don't really like wine, but it was the only thing that came to my mind at the time. He hands me a cup and a plate with the sandwich and goes to sit on the couch.

'Okay. We don't have time for this. Did I miss something? Did I do something? What?' He has half the sandwich in his mouth when he looks at me. Dammit, he looks cute.

'Wa—?' His phone buzzes again, and I see him smiling at what he's reading. He puts the plate and cup in the sink and turns to me.

'I guess you weren't that hungry.' He gestures to my untouched plate, but I say nothing. 'So we have two days, right?'

'What?'

'We have two days left together. I think we should go somewhere.'

'Like where?'

'You'll see.'

'Tom, what's going on? Why are you acting so strange, and why are you always smiling at your phone?' The man dares to smile widely at my questions and then moves around the island to face me.

'Wait. Are you jealous?'

'Shut up.'

He lunges at me capturing my lips in his.

'Tom.'

'Hum?'

We talk between kisses.

'I need to breathe.' I feel him smile against me.

'I'm already giving you mouth to mouth. You'll be fine.' God, this man undoes me. What was I upset about again? Finally, he slows until he stops.

'You have two options. Either we leave now and drive for a few hours, or we get up really early tomorrow. You choose.'

'You shouldn't drive now. You had long day. Better have some rest and we can go early, yeah?'

'How about you drive?'

'Yeah, no. I haven't driven in years. You want me to do it in a different country? Nope.'

'Why haven't you driven in so long. Scared?' He's making fun of me, raising a single brow.

'No. I never needed to drive in London or even when I moved to the Midlands. I always took the bus.'

'Hum. Okay. I'm not tired actually. We can pack and go.'

'Tom, you had a long day. Come on have some rest. At least, take a nap.'

He caresses my face as he talks. 'It's very cute that you're worried. I love it, but I'll be fine trust me.'

I'm still not convinced. I know how dangerous it is to drive when you're tired.

'Tell you what. If you see me falling asleep or closing my eyes you can slap me.'

I think my whole face is a smile now. 'Really?'

'You don't have to be so happy about it.'

'I'm not happy. I'm just … thankful that I'll have a job to keep me awake.' Total crap and he knows it.

'Sure. Call it that.' He kisses my nose and disappears into the bedroom. 'Are you coming?' I was still on the stool, wondering where he's taking me and what secrets he's keeping from me.

'Make sure you take warm clothes. Your dresses are super cute, but it's very cold where we're going.'

'Okay, so no dresses.'

'No. No, take a dress.'

'But you just said it was going to be too cold for a dress.'

'If we go to a restaurant, do you want to go in your jeans?'

'I wouldn't really care if I was in jeans. But I like that you like me in a dress, so I'll take one.' I was talking and getting closer to him. By the time I finish, I wink and kiss him on the cheek before I grab my bag.

'You're a tease, you and your dresses. You look great in anything, babe. If you don't want to take a dress don't. As long as you're with me, I'm happy.'

I still have the bag in my hands while he's talking and rounding his hands on my waist, but I drop it when he ends his speech. I can't help my eyes tearing up. Like he said, we have two days left together. What comes after that? He kisses me tenderly, and we finish in silence.

'How long does it take to get there?'

'If I tell you, you're going to start the math to figure out where we're going?'

Damn, he knows me better than I thought.

'I thought so.'

I just stick my tongue out at him. There's no point in saying anything else because I would have done just as he said.

We're driving away from Manhattan. I'm still trying to figure out where we're going, of course, reading signs or at least trying. He drives fast. But I can't tell where I am.

'Can you stop whipping your head around? Just enjoy the ride. I'm not going to tell you, and you're not going to find out. Just relax, baby.'

He's right. I know he is, but I can't my stupid brain.

'Sorry. I'm just curious I guess.'

'Love you.' He grabs my hand and kisses its back before setting on the central console. His eyes are on the road and mine on our hands. In this moment, all I care about is him, being with him, making him happy. He waited long enough. He deserves it, but do I?

We drive along the coastline. Its night-time, maybe around ten thirty now, so all I see are lights floating on the dark sea. I can't see the moon or any stars, only darkness above and beneath. I'm not superstitious, but maybe the night is so sad to let me know that this might be our last chance, our last borrowed time. He stops the car on a driveway. It's too dark to see the whole house, but it's two storeys high, and from the smell that hits my nose, we're close to the sea.

'Be careful coming up the steps.' I was under the spell of the sea scent when his warning came. Of course, I had to be clumsy or distracted. I can't be just like a normal person. No. Not me. I trip on the first of four steps and instantly have a flash back to when I broke my jaw the same way. That time, it was stone steps, and I was a child, but these decked ones hurt too.

'Violet. Are you okay?' He flew to me, but I had already hit the hard steps. I can taste the blood in my mouth. Damn, it hurts. I so hope I haven't broken any teeth or jaw again. Now I miss the sling holding my shoulder. As soon as my elbow hit the ground, it was like a shock shot all the way up to my shoulder.

'Pleath tell me I didn't bake my jaw again.'

'Again? Woman, you're always breaking yourself. Come, let me help you up.'

I start whimpering when he grabs the wrong arm.

'Sorry. Sorry.'

I'm bleeding from my mouth and limping after hitting my knee. I think my whole weight fell on my elbow and knee. God, this hurts more than being shot.

'Fuck, it hurts.'

'Language, little lady.'

'Please don't make me laugh. It hurts more.'

He's chuckling and shaking his head. 'Okay, we'll never get in like this. It's freezing.'

I let a squeal out as he picks me up. 'Tom, you don't have to do that. I can walk.'

'Sure, you can, and by the time we get in, we'll be frozen.'

As he's carrying me inside I'm smiling and remembering Mary and Chris, how they turned every bad situation around for them. To me, this one is just like that, a very bad situation that end up with me in his arms laughing. Can't ask for better.

'All right, let's see the damage.' He's setting me on a fluffy orange couch. The room is beautiful and bright. There are so many colours, yellow-and-white pillows on chairs and couch, with matching curtains on softer tones. One of the walls is red. Which seems a bit too much for me, but it actually works for the room.

'Tom, stop looking at me like that. Just tell me how bad it is.'

'Hum, I don't know. Wait.' And he walks away.

'What? Tom.'

He comes back with an ice pack. 'Where did you hit?'

'My knee.' I'm whimpering again. Too much pressure.

'Sorry, but you need it.' He leaves me with the pack and disappears again. I really need to take my mind off the pain, but it is really not a good idea to let my brain wonder. We all know what happens when I do that.

'Okay, let's see those beautiful lips.'

'I don't think they're up for anything right now.' See? I can tease too. He has a first aid kit in one hand and mouthwash in the other.

'Is my breath that bad?'

'Don't be silly. I would kiss you right now if it wouldn't hurt. Now rinse and spit. I need to see what's broken and start cleaning.'

'Broken?' I move my hand and touch my bottom lip softly. Even that hurts and slaps my hand. 'Hey. I'm already in pain.'

'So stop touching and let me work.' He busies himself in front of my face. After I rinse, he starts cleaning the blood. His eyes are so focused on my mouth, like nothing else exists in the world. They are dark blue, like the ocean raging outside.

'What?'

'What. What?'

'You're smiling, V.'

'Am I? I hadn't noticed.'

Now he smiles, and my lips want to spread further.

'Stop that. You have a serious cut on your lip. If you keep spreading it, it will never heal.'

'So basically, you're telling me not smile. I don't know if I can be serious for that long and—'

'You'll have to try. And what?'

'How am I going to hide how happy I am?' I painfully smile again.

'I so want to kiss you right now.'

I smile harder now, and he starts kissing my face all over.

'God, why do I have to be so clumsy?'

'It's punishment for being so pretty.'

I know I'm not that pretty. I'm average at best, but, man, he makes me feel good and special.

'Come. We should go to bed, and we'll see how you're doing tomorrow.'

'At least, I didn't break anything this time.'

'Yeah, you did.'

'What? I certainly didn't break the floor.'

'No. You broke those beautiful lips, and now I can't kiss you.' Another smile. Another sting on my lip. At this rate, I'll never heal.

He helps me out of my clothes and into a nighty that I bought at the same charity shop as the golden dress.

'You're really going to sleep in this?'

'Yeah, why?' I'm pretending to look down at my little dress, looking for a problem.

'You can't ... I mean ... that's ...'

'Yes?'

'How can I sleep with you dressed like that?'

This time, I laugh, and instantly, my hand moves to my mouth. 'Ow.'

He's shaking his head and smiling too, and then he sits on the bed patting the space next to him. I'm there in two steps. We get under the covers, and he wraps his arms around me.

'Goodnight, love.'

'Goodnight.'

I want to be able to say goodnight to him like this every night. I want to feel like this always. Before I notice, I have tears escaping my eyes. Thank God there are no sobs. Is he expecting a forever goodbye after these two days or is he willing to make a plan. A commitment to try? Or is it I who doesn't want to commit? These are my last thoughts before I sleep take me.

'Good morning, gorgeous.' He wakes me with feather like kisses on my face.

'Morning. How bad do I look?'

'You look great. Your lip is a little swollen, but I'm sure it'll get better soon. It has to, or Rose will kill me.'

'What?'

He stutters a little and diverts his gaze. 'If you show up there for the party like that, I'm sure she'll come here to kick my ass.'

'Oh. I'm sure I'll be fine by then.'

He kisses my nose and leaves the room. For a second there. Just a second. I thought he was lying or hiding something, but that's usually my move. Shake it off, V.

This bedroom has the colours of a calm sea. Soft blues cover the bed and dress the floor to ceiling windows. I have to see that view. I can already hear the splash sound of the waves. The sea blends with the sky on the horizon. They're almost the same shade of pale blue. The waves are furious, aggravated by the wind. I know it's cold, but still I step out on the balcony. The salt in the air fills my nose.

'Now that's a beautiful view. Aren't you cold?' I just shrug and sigh before I turn back to gaze back the view.

'It's beautiful here. I forgot how much I miss the sea sometimes.' He was carrying a tray when I saw him. Breakfast in bed again. But he puts it down on the bed before he comes up behind me.

'It makes you appreciate it more, doesn't it?'

I nod, snuggling more into his arms.

He's kissing my neck and my ear and whispers, 'I love you so much.'

I close my eyes. Tears roll down my face. In my mind, it's already Friday. In my heart, it's always goodbye.

'Come on, baby. Don't think yet. Not yet.' He kisses my tears away like he always has done. 'Let's have breakfast, yeah?'

I give him a ghost of a smile. My eyes are definitely not smiling, and I know that he knows it, but like he said, it's not time yet.

'So what's the plan then?'

His lips instantly turn up in a sexy and mischievous smile.

'What are you plotting?'

He winks and kisses my cheek. 'You'll see.' I know nothing with this man. All I know is that I'm so wildly in love with him and want so desperately to be with him always.

We spend most of Thursday in the house. My knee still hurts a lot, and I don't want to strain too much. He tells me that this house belongs to a friend of his. How nice it is to have friends that will lend you their beach house. We take a few strolls on the soaked beach, and I'm so happy I bought a warm jacket. The cold here sometimes feels like daggers cutting through the skin. We play loads of board games, make love a lot. He cooks for me naked, and as I'm sitting on the kitchen island, I can't help to think that there's nothing sexier than that.

By Friday, I'm feeling a lot better, so we visit a few nearby museums. There's a candle museum/factory. I actually think there will be some scented candles but am disappointed when I find there is only regular wax. After that, we have lunch in a little restaurant by the sea. At least, it's not so windy today. We can eat out in the veranda.

The swelling on my lip has come down, and it's almost gone now, but the cut still hurts a lot, especially when we get carried away and devour each other's mouth. That afternoon, we visit a whale museum, and let me tell you, I'm not sure if going there after eating was a good idea. Did you know that people use every little bit of the whale to make many different things? Well, I didn't, and I certainly didn't need to know. I can't describe it or say it. We should not kill an animal like that for nothing. It's like when poachers kill an elephant for its ivory. No one needs ivory except an elephant. We don't finish the tour. He can tell how upset with that I got, and he's not too thrilled either.

'Sorry, I had no idea.'

'It's fine. Let's just go take a walk by the beach. I could use the fresh air.'

This time, we don't walk hand in hand. Sometimes I'm ahead of him. Sometimes I'm behind. We can feel our time coming to an end. We haven't talked about the future, about feelings or possibilities, and when we're having dinner, I finally think it's time.

'I think we should make a schedule.' I can tell by the way he looks at me that he wasn't expecting me to get into it, but I think we've delayed it long enough.

'What do you mean?'

'I mean synchronize our agendas. Like when you're off from the play, I can come, take the same days off.'

'My schedule is not always the same.' He's still very sceptical.

'Okay. We can coordinate and go from there.'

'And when you're out there in the world? How's that going to work? Do I fly to wherever you are, or we just don't see each other?'

That's the money question. How's that going to work? 'Tom, I won't be away as often now – you know that. I think we can make the sacrifice, or at least, we can try.'

He scoffs at the damned word. 'Violet, I've been trying for nearly seven months. I'm tired of trying. I want to do now.'

'So that's it then? We just part ways and give up?'

'What time do you leave tomorrow?'

'Tom, come on. We have to talk about this.'

'I don't want to talk anymore.' He gets up suddenly and starts doing the dishes. The last time I saw him so upset was when we found each other in Muie. God, that seems like it was a lifetime ago.

'You told me yourself that if I want to make a change, I have to be willing to do some sacrifices and—'

He turns to me abruptly. His eyes are dark and clouded with tears. 'Again with the sacrifices. Don't you think you sacrificed enough? You almost lost your life.' He's shouting at me now, letting out all he wanted to tell me at the hospital. I take a deep breath and remember what he told me when we walked the mountains in Lumbala. It's a cheap shot, but I need to take it.

'About a month ago, you told me that you were willing to wait. What changed?' I try to keep my voice calm and soft, but the look in his eyes tells me how hurt he is.

He comes close and hugs me. His mouth talks next to my ear. 'The realization that I could lose you when I saw you in that hospital bed changed that. The fact that you'll never choose me before any of those things that you have to do changed it did too. I love you, baby. I do, but I don't want to be a second choice forever. I don't want us to have to constantly book time on our schedule so I can have some time with you. If you're available, that is.'

My eyes are cloudy, filled to the brim, but I'm not letting the tears stream. I need to be rational and calm. We're finally talking. It might not be what I wanted to hear, but at least, we're talking to each other.

'For so long, I felt lost, like I didn't know what my purpose in life was. I was just drifting. Until that party.'

He sighs at the memory, and I keep talking into his ear.

'I found what I wanted to do, and even though I didn't know exactly how to do it, you helped me. You said, "You can try."'

He exhales again, and I feel him shaking his head. He's trying to pull away, but I don't let go. We have to finish this now.

'So I went out in the world and tried, and again with your help, I saw the impact I could do in the world. I was so sure of what I wanted to do with my life that I made myself forget about everything else. I have that ability, you know?'

He squeezes me a little, letting me know he's still listening.

'But all of that changed when I saw you in Muie.'

I feel his body freeze, and he stops breathing for a while, but I carry on. 'I couldn't forget anymore.'

'Is that why you were so pissed when I wanted to talk to you?'

'Yeah. I thought how can I do this to myself again. Change my whole life for a man? But after those days with you, I couldn't stop thinking.'

'About what?'

'The possibilities.' I feel him smile against my cheek. 'I went to

Thailand thinking of you. I left that room to visit the temple thinking about you. I was a prisoner in that house of horrors and in the middle of all that suffering I actually thought I might die. So I just kept wishing I could see you again. No save-myself-and-the-rest-of-the-lost-souls. Just you. In my arms.'

He holds me tighter and I can hear him cry.

'I've never loved anyone like I love you. I thought I did, but I had no idea … I …' I keep trailing off. The hard words are wanting to come out and my heart is fighting with my head for leadership. 'I want to help as many people as I can.'

I feel his body deflate in my arms as if he was becoming a shell of himself. 'Now I know what kind of change I can do and out there in the world is the minimum I can possibly do.'

He leans back to look into my eyes. He's been crying this whole time. I can tell by the path his tears left.

'I don't understand … what … um … what?' I chuckle a little at his confusion.

'It means that I know, without serious help, I can't do anything I want.' His eyes are still narrowing at me in confusion. I sigh for what it seems like forever. My heart wants to make the decision my head is struggling with, and I'm really thinking I should let it happen.

Letting go of him, I step out on the balcony. Contrary to two nights ago, the night sky is awake and sparkling. Maybe I'll see a shooting star and ask it to solve my problems for me. I inhale the sea air until I can't take it anymore and start coughing the excess out. I feel his hand patting my back, and my mouth resumes spilling out my thoughts.

'I need to think.'

'It's never a good thing when you think.' Both our eyes are on the dark ocean, and we start chuckling. 'We both need to think, babe, but for now, can we just go to sleep?' He has his arms around my waist and kisses my temple.

'Yeah, let's go.'

Before laying down I grab my phone and go to the bathroom. My heart is driving now.

'Hello, Rose. What do I have to do to stay in New York?'

I hit send on the text and lie next to Tom. We stay awake for a long time, studying each other's eyes in the darkness and then fall asleep, wrapped in peace and warmth. I want to stay here, with him. It might not be as bad as I think. It might not crush my soul.

I wake up when the sun is rising, so I watch it from the front porch. Don't want to wake him up. It's still very cold, but as the warm sunlight pushes the darkness away, I start to feel comforted, hopeful. When all the sky is a light blue, I go inside to make breakfast. It's my turn now.

'Good morning, sleepyhead.' I'm waking him with kisses, and he pulls me to him.

'No. I need more sleep, please.' He has me trapped in his arms. I'm laughing, and he's kissing my neck. Is there anything better than this?

'Breakfast is going to be cold.'

'You made breakfast?'

'Yeah, why?'

'No. Nothing …' He shrugs.

'I do know how to cook, Tom. It's just nicer when you do it.' I'm teasing, and he starts kissing again.

'What time is your flight?'

'At twelve.' My heart beats faster, but I can't let this kill the mood, so I kiss him and get of the bed to grab the tray.

'Oh, I forgot the orange juice. I'll be back.'

'We don't need it now. Sit.'

'I won't be long.' I'm chuckling at the desperation in his eyes. We both know the goodbye is coming.

'Hey, your phone is ringing,' I hear him shout.

'Who is it?'

'Rose.'

I run to the bedroom to pick up the call and answer it on the balcony.

'Hey Rose.'

'What did I tell you?'

'Rose …'

'No. I told you don't let New York steal you. I actually thought you knew what I was talking about.'

'You don't want me working for Richard.'

I hear her scoff and laugh.

'You're so innocent it hurts. I knew the risk of you going there and seeing Tom, but I thought after we made an agreement you would stick to it.'

'Rose, it hurts to say goodbye. I don't want to do it anymore.'

'I know it hurts. I feel it every day when I remember I couldn't say goodbye to my own daughter.'

'Rose, that's not fair.'

'Life isn't fair. You want to stay there? Fine, but don't call me ever again.' And she hangs up the phone. I was pacing the deck, but now I sit in defeat, tears in my eyes. I can't hurt her like that.

'What's wrong? Are you okay?'

'Yeah. Everything is fine.'

'Are you sure? Because you were arguing on the phone, and now you're crying.'

'I'm not crying.' I speak a little louder than I intended. 'It's fine. Let's just finish breakfast, so we can go.'

He doesn't follow me inside. I don't finish breakfast. Just start packing.

'You know you can talk to me, right?' I smile at those kind eyes.

'Yeah, Tom I know. I'm sorry, but I don't want to talk right now.'

He smiles and nods. After we cleaned and tidied the house, we're back on the road. Maybe in a worst situation than the one when we arrived.

I tried. I know that I did. I tried to fight for him, but it doesn't seem like it was enough, or I didn't fight enough. I can't betray Rose like this. I can't.

We arrive faster to his apartment than when we left. Maybe he's just wanting to get it over with. I pack the rest of my things, and he takes me to the airport. It's still very early so we sit on a booth drinking coffee. He's sitting next to me, and for a long time, we don't talk. We don't touch. We don't look at each other. My body is itching to throw itself in his arms. Ask him to loop me and never let go. Just never let me go. I want to tell him all of that, but what's the point now?

I was so lost in thought and pain that only when my body hits his do I realize his arms are around me.

'We'll figure something out.'

'Will we?' I don't really believe his words, and he knows it.

'Yes. We just need a little time to think.'

'I'm tired of thinking. My brain hurts.'

'Then don't. Just kiss me.'

I kissed him until we were out of breath. Until heads started to turn towards us. I kissed him until the tears stopped flowing on both our cheeks.

Somehow he managed to take me to the gate. Maybe it's the last time I'll see him use his charm to impress me and faster than I wanted I was once again inside a plane fastening my seat belt.

Deep down, I thought I could have solved all of this. I thought if I showed up there and he saw me everything would fall into place. I thought I wouldn't be going home alone. How arrogant and conceited am I?

We made no promises to keep in touch or wait. We agreed we both need to think after that we'll see. What I don't know. Judging by all the things he told me he had enough of being pushed away and forever hold the second place in my life and I can't really blame him for that. Maybe it's better this way. It'll hurt for a while, but love fades with time, so maybe one day I'll forget him and stop hurting. I found myself while I was searching for my purpose in life. I can't lose that.

Ingram Content Group UK Ltd.
Milton Keynes UK
UKHW041832280323
419329UK00002B/12